THE
VIOLET
HOUR

THE VIOLET HOUR

Whitney A. Miller

flux®
Woodbury, Minnesota

First Edition
First Printing, 2014

Book design by Bob Gaul
Cover design by Lisa Novak
Cover images © iStockphoto.com/21512431/sugar0607,
              iStockphoto.com/6056270/Huchen Lu

Flux, an imprint of Llewellyn Worldwide Ltd.

This is a work of fiction. Names, characters, places, and incidents are either the product of the author's imagination or are used fictitiously, and any resemblance to actual persons living or dead, business establishments, events, or locales is entirely coincidental. Cover model used for illustrative purposes only and may not endorse or represent the book's subject.

Library of Congress Cataloging-in-Publication Data
Miller, Whitney A.
  The Violet Hour/Whitney A. Miller.—First edition.
      pages cm
   Summary: "Seventeen-year-old Harlow Wintergreen, plagued by mental voices and visions while traveling through Asia, must confront the evil sources of them when the hallucinations start bleeding into reality"—Provided by publisher.
  ISBN 978-0-7387-3721-8
[1. Cults—Fiction. 2. Visions—Fiction. 3. Supernatural—Fiction. 4. Love—Fiction. 5. Fathers and daughters—Fiction. 6. Horror stories.] I. Title.
  PZ7.M63913Vio 2014
  [Fic]—dc23

                                                 2013038454

                                    Flux
                        Llewellyn Worldwide Ltd.
                          2143 Wooddale Drive
                        Woodbury, MN 55125-2989
                            www.fluxnow.com

                   Printed in the United States of America

Always for Reid.

Thanks for showing up to that party in Silverlake.

UNDERTOW

Purity. Death.

Our train neared Harajuku Station. A frisson of electric anticipation rolled through the Ministry kids. Pressed between the throngs of mid-day commuters, we trembled like grape clusters on the vine. All of us had reason to be nervous, but only I had reason to be afraid.

The voice had invaded my mind yesterday with a vengeance. It was my first episode in years, as if arriving in Tokyo had opened some kind of mental floodgate. I was stupid to think the meds had gotten rid of Her. First came the buzzing in my brain, as familiar to me as breathing. Then came the visions. The occupation. The harder I resisted, the more She writhed and bloomed.

Cleanse. Kill. Suffer.

I scrambled in my bag for Subdueral and surreptitiously swallowed two. The VisionCrest doctors had tried to suffocate my symptoms with prescriptions since I was knee-high, and finally the Subdueral worked. The official diagnosis was "it's nothing a little blue pill can't fix." Anything to appease my father. The Patriarch had no defects. Except his daughter.

But now the voice was back with a malevolence that all the Subdueral in the world couldn't stifle. She was stronger. Like She hadn't been stifled at all, just biding Her time.

She was part of me. I couldn't escape Her, but I wouldn't let Her have what She wanted. Not now and not ever.

The train car shuddered and Dora glanced at me, rolling her round-as-quarters eyes from behind her naughty schoolteacher glasses. "Watching how Mercy acts around him makes me want to poke my inner eyes out," she said.

Up ahead of us, I spotted them. Mercy Mayer tossed her hair, catching my eye. A studied indifference tugged at the corners of her mouth. Her hand slid along the curve of Adam's biceps with intent, her fingers slipping beneath the hem of his white T-shirt. A patchwork of angry new tattoos sleeved their way up his arm. His gaze followed Mercy's, and for just a second he saw me—really saw me. Then he looked right through me again. The indifference on his face was real. A fist of crushing disappointment lodged itself behind my sternum.

A man in a suit jostled me into the surly looking skate punk standing in front of me, who turned and glared from above his hospital mask. Instinctively I grabbed for Dora. Her father, Prelate Elber, had been promoted to the Ministry when we were ten, and she was my own personal miracle. I'd been clinging to her *screw this* sarcasm ever since.

"D, this crowd is making me manic," I whispered.

My muscles strained as the thing inside me reared Her head, feeding off my insecurity. I should have faked sick. Stayed locked in my hotel room. Instead, I'd indulged my curiosity and now it was too late. I was losing control and I had no idea what would happen if I couldn't keep Her caged. A bead of sweat rolled past my temple. I had to get out of this train car, out of this crowd, before She broke free.

The train slid to a stop at the station. I squeezed Dora's arm tighter.

"I need to bail, D. Just for a few minutes so I can catch my breath. Give me cover?"

Her pupils zeroed in. It wasn't the first time she'd seen me have a panic attack. I hid behind a ruse of social anxiety. I didn't dare tell anyone the truth of what was really happening inside my brain. Keeping that secret was tantamount to survival.

"Bail where? In case you haven't read the memo, we're in the middle of the Socialist Republic of Japan. There are for sure plainclothes VisionCrest Watchers with us," she said, cutting her eyes toward a particularly unlikely looking grandma. Normally easy to spot, the Ministry's elite force were rumored to sometimes go undercover.

"Yoyogi Park's just outside the station. I just need a few minutes to chill out. Let the goon squad catch up to me—it's not like I care," I said, feeling the walls closing in.

"Easy-peasy Japanesey, is that it?" Dora asked. "And miss all the Harajuku shenanigans?"

Before I went mental, this excursion to see the Hara-juku chicks rock their gothic Lolita had been my idea of heaven. Now the only thing I cared about was lulling Her back to sleep.

Obliterate.

"Exactly," I agreed, my palms sweating. "I need this, D."

Exsanguinate.

"It might really be dangerous. You're Harlow Wintergreen, as you might recall," she warned.

We both knew there had to be a reason we were on this trip, one other than our academic edification, but this was as close as we'd come to discussing it. In an unprecedented move, thirty of us had been sent out on a publicity tour for the Ministry, the elite inner circle that surrounded my father, the Patriarch of VisionCrest. As children of the chosen few, our faces had been shielded from public view all our lives, and suddenly we were being paraded around Asia for everyone to see. It was weird. Curious onlookers snapped pictures with their phones and shielded polite whispers behind their hands.

"It's a park, not a piranha pool," I said. "Besides, nobody knows my face. I could be any VisionCrest brat."

Dora scrutinized me for a moment, then smiled. I'd convinced her.

"I bet you a bubble tea that Brother Howard bursts a blood vessel when he realizes you're gone," she said.

The doors slid open and passengers surged around us in every direction. Brother Howard, our teacher and chaperone, waved his ridiculous flag. It featured the VisionCrest logo— the All Seeing Eye—and he'd been parading around with it all week, drawing extra attention to our already conspicuous group.

"See you in a few." I squeezed her hand, then darted into the throng.

"If this keeps us from visiting the sixty-foot Gundam statue, it's on your conscience," Dora yelled as she hopped off the train behind me. Seeing a five-story anime robot was Dora's idea of a life-altering moment.

I shoved my way through the people on the platform, determined to ditch any Watchers who might be tailing me, at least until I could get a grip.

Purity, the voice that was mine-but-not-mine whispered in my ear. *Death*.

I was a ticking time bomb. And I was about to explode right in the middle of the Tokyo rush hour.

HARAJUKU MADNESS

The tide of commuters carried me out of the station and up the stairs to the Yoyogi footbridge. As the rush of people thinned, bodies breaking away in every direction, the voice receded, momentarily muted by a dose of fresh air and sunshine. I took a deep breath, feeling the *dub-thrub* of my heartbeat against my rib cage.

I glanced over my shoulder. The VisionCrest crew snaked out of the station in the opposite direction, a tartan-uniformed centipede. I caught sight of Dora's rainbow-striped socks. She was laughing and joking with our classmates—classmates too afraid to talk to me. It made me jealous and sad all at the same time; it was so easy for her to be herself, yet still fit in. My heart tugged as they headed toward Takeshita Alley's zigzag of shop fronts and flashing rainbow signs without me.

I fell in behind a pack of vamped-out teens in black dusters and bouffant wigs. Their proudly displayed freak flags made mine feel a little more normal. The voice was a barely discernible whisper. The terror had subsided, at least for the moment.

Boys and girls littered the pathway into the park, playing their boom boxes and posing for one another. I wasn't all that out of place in my VisionCrest uniform and sunglasses—wacked-out Asian schoolgirl was a popular motif. I spotted a secluded bench under a stand of near-naked cherry trees; the last battered blossoms clung to branches thin as witches' fingers. An expanse of dishwater grass blanketed the ground. It was the perfect vantage from which to observe the absurdity of normal kids desperately straining to be anything but, while I wished for exactly the opposite.

I wasn't used to being outside the VisionCrest compound's gates, much less the United States. They'd told our group that we were coming here for a "cultural immersion," but I knew for a fact this was a lie. I'd overheard Prelate Mayer selling my father on the trip as a safety measure—she said that since the kidnappings had escalated, the only safe place for Ministry children was in the public eye.

Over the past year, VisionCrest devotees had been disappearing at an alarming rate. It started with our general population, but quickly escalated to the Ministry's inner circle. The Ministry was keeping it on the hush, but I knew these were not defections, as they claimed publicly. They were abductions. Why, and by whom, nobody seemed to know. I wanted to tell Dora what I knew, but something kept stopping me. Like saying it out loud would make it real.

I reached into my bag, my hand closing around the reassuring spine of a book. Solid, real.

A Khmer History. Not exactly light reading.

One of the few things my father (or the General, as Dora and I liked to call him behind closed doors) would say about my roots was that he'd found me in Cambodia, that sun-scorched land where the Khmer civilization—the most powerful in the history of the world—had flourished and perished. I was clearly of Asian descent, but with green eyes and freckles. Adults were always telling me how "exotic" I was. I didn't want to be exotic. I just wanted to be normal.

In pursuit of normalcy, I pored over any text that might help explain how I could make Her stop, how I might decode the evil inside me. Neurology, physiology, astrology. But none of them could explain Her voice or how to get rid of it. History was about the only stone I'd left unturned.

She was back, and I had nothing. I was out of time.

Purity. Death.

The me-but-not-me voice snuck up behind me. Tapped me on the shoulder.

Kill.

No. I snapped upright, as if someone else might hear the intruder raging in my head. My fingers itched against the splintered bench; I knew instantly what my hands wanted. To wrap themselves around the powder-white neck of a particularly beautiful Harajuku girl loitering only feet in front of me.

No, I insisted. *I won't let you have her.*

We both knew it wasn't up to me. The voice seized control of my mind.

I examined the delicate girl.

It wouldn't take much to crush her voice box. To squeeze

the life out of her. To dig my thumbs into her eyes until they snapped free from their optic nerves. To make her pay.

Inside, I screamed for the invader to stop. Even though I knew the evil wanted to see it through to the bloody finish.

I was an abomination.

The Harajuku girl was taunting me. A life-size doll. An enormous powder blue wig perched atop her head, and ringlet curls cascaded in elaborate piles around her porcelain face. She looked like a tiny Beethoven. Peek-a-boo hands fluttered to her pursed lips, shielding her giggle from a boy with skinny leather pants and red contacts in his eyes.

Hunger rumbled in my brain.

Kill. Kill. Kill.

The energy of my thoughts pinned the Harajuku princess down—she was a butterfly, and I was her shadowbox. She looked over.

The rest of the world fell away.

She walked toward me.

An aura struck. Squiggly worms began to cha-cha-cha across my cornea. It was the ten-second warning that the voice was going to strike me with a vision, soon to be followed by a migraine the size of a Texan's belt buckle.

Everything around us was an old film reel, catching fire and melting from black to white. A pyrotechnic array of glowing orbs.

It was only us.

Me, her, and the intruder rasping in my brain.

Purity. Death. Kill.

Frilly cupcake dress. White knee-highs. Satin top-hat

tucked under the crook of a skinny arm. Translucent worms corkscrewing their way across my visual cortex.

I bit down on the meaty part of my tongue, trying to draw myself back. The tinny taste of blood filled my mouth.

The Harajuku girl sat down beside me on the bench.

Was this really happening, or was it only in my head? Was I really going to do something this time, or was it just my imagination? I couldn't tell.

I was afraid.

My hand floated up to the soft curve of her throat; my fingertips curled around it, matching themselves to vertebrae. My thumb bounced against her beating pulse.

The high sheen of a fever glossed the Harajuku girl's skin. She clutched at her abdomen, slumping forward. As if my touch had transferred some horrible virus.

Flecks of raspberry froth crept over the edges of her lips. Scarlet boils bubbled beneath the surface of her skin, bursting from the pale expanse of her bare thighs.

Kill.

My free hand slid up her apple cheek, my fingers anchoring behind her ear. My thumb hovered over her terror-wide eye.

I didn't want my body to do that, but I was no longer its master.

The girl's fringed lashes skittered open-closed like frantic spider legs. Her chest heaved.

No. Please. Stop, I begged the thing inside me.

My thumb pressed against the sweet firmness of her eyeball, savoring the pop like an overripe cherry.

A bloom of blood vessels burst forth from the whites of her eye.

I could hear the tinny, faraway sound of squealing laughter, friends carrying on with an oblivious Sunday.

The girl and I were locked in a Kabuki embrace.

A storm of pain.

For a moment, I broke through. I wanted to help her, save her from the thing inside me. Tell her to run.

The urge was extinguished by the voice. *Kill.*

Pressure sprang free against the fleshy pad of my thumb, a rubber band breaking loose. Her milky eye dangled free from her skull. Nails raked down the tender skin of my forearms, my flesh tearing like tissue paper, blood seeping from the burning skin. I knew from experience that the marks would remain.

The girl dropped to her knees in front of me and vomited blood onto my lap. Tiny scarlet spots sprayed my shins. I could feel the warmth of each slippery dot shivering against my skin. I wanted to help her, but the voice wouldn't allow it.

Wounds opened on the girl's soft-curved skin, then putrefied; the stench of spoiled meat weighed the air.

Her top hat tumbled to the ground. She tumbled after it.

The Harajuku girl lay in a pool of her own blood, seizing like a fish robbed of water. One dislocated eye floated on the surface, the other met mine for a last look.

A fat red tear slipped from its corner.

The girl exhaled.

Everything was still except for a round trail of blood cutting its way down her cheek. I watched it fall.

Death.

My brain had been hijacked by terrible things before, visions of the unspeakable deeds I'd fought not to commit. But none so ripping real as this.

Years of Subdueral had dulled my ability to fight back. The invader had lurked patiently while I was numbed into submission. And then She pounced.

I was undefended. She was invincible.

The seams of my sanity split in two. Consciousness gave way to blackness.

While I was submerged, something else happened.

Strong arms scooped me up, cradling me, bringing me home. I buried my face in sun-warmed skin and soap: the smell of safety. The earth floated beneath me, and I was innocent again.

Later on, I would recognize the incident for what it was.

A keepsake. The beginning of the end, with love from Japan.

SLEEPING SICKNESS

Dora's voice sloshed around my abyss, swinging me layer by layer back into the kingdom of the conscious.

"Har-low ... Haaaaaar-looooooooow ... Wake up, little snoozy ... heaven can wait, but Tokyo on your seventeenth birthday is a limited-time offer ... "

A hand shook my shoulder so hard I thought my head might come loose.

"Hrmmph ... " I slurred my way one layer higher, my tongue an uncooperative slab of stone.

I squeezed one eye open and fixed it on the two-headed blurry Dora hovering over me in my modern Park Hyatt hotel room. Japan was one of the few countries where Vision-Crest didn't have its own compound, so we'd taken over the top floors of the fanciest hotel they had.

A quick body-check revealed I was still in one piece. The flesh of my inner arms burned. Even though I knew the whole Harajuku thing had been a hallucination, I also knew, without looking, that there would be bloody rake-marks across my skin. Mercifully there was no voice, no squiggly worms. Only the low static buzz. And my best friend and only lifeline. For now.

"Signs of life! Sleeping Beauty opens her eyes at long last! Quick! Somebody get some toothpicks and prop those emerald lovelies open!"

"Very funny," I managed, my voice hoarse. But it earned her a weak smile.

Dora was always Dora. She almost made me feel normal. I loved her.

"I just wanted to wake you up to say—wait for it— Brother Howard has a total crush on you."

Dora got her desired effect. Both my eyes popped open and I screwed my face up into a sour cherry.

"Disgusting! You have serious mental issues." I sat up, pushing her back onto the bed.

Brother Howard was most proud of the fact that he'd been teaching Chem since the year they invented the Bunsen burner. The only thing being crushed was his overexposed junk in the too-small blue polyester pants that he wore day after day.

"Did you see the way he handed you that beaker before the final and was all, *Here's your HCl, Harlow*? I mean, hell-oo."

"You're a psychopath."

Dora leaned in for a bear hug. She was the only one I would let get that close.

"Hold me closer, tiny dancer. You've been out for *days* and I've been *boooored*."

"Sorry," I muffled into her shoulder.

She leaned back and examined me like a specimen under a microscope. "Tell Nurse Dora where it hurts. How's our patient feeling?"

"Like I'm hoping you got the license plate of the truck that hit me. I need it to come back and run me over, so I can die of embarrassment."

"His license plate, no. But I did get a good look at his incredibly attractive—"

"He? He who?" I panicked, knowing exactly he who.

"He who do you think? Adam found you in the park and brought you back."

"Oh, god."

Dread closed in.

"He noticed you were gone right away. We went to find you—he was pissed at me for letting you go. I'm pissed at me, too, actually," she said.

"It's not your fault," I answered. "Leaving was my choice."

I wanted to crawl under the hotel bed and never come out. Just live in there with some crackers and my shame for all eternity. Adam had found me in the park and carried me home. Adam, who for some reason had barely spoken to me since his miraculous return. Holy hell, my life was so screwed.

Dora put a hand on my shoulder, gripping almost tight enough to hurt. "Seriously, what happened?" she asked.

"It was just a really bad panic attack, like when we were little," I lied.

Her mouth pressed into a thin line of concern. "It didn't make the media, so you have that going for you," she assured me.

I hadn't even considered that. The meltdown wasn't front-page news, but it was undoubtedly Ministry news. Mercy Mayer was probably dancing on my social grave. My eyes darted around the hotel room, taking in the Spartan lack of anything rehabilitative. No handcuffs, no straightjacket.

The Harajuku girl's face popped into my head; the way I dismembered her with my mind. Even though I clearly hadn't done any of the things I imagined, it felt absolutely real. I snuck a look at my scabbed-up arms. Nausea crashed over me.

I pushed Dora out of the way and dashed to the bathroom without a second to spare. I barely made it before the meager contents of my stomach splashed against the bowl.

"Hare Krishna, are you okay?" Dora's voice was strained. I ached to tell her what was really wrong, but I couldn't do it. Every secret exacts a price.

I came back to the bed and climbed in. "Never better. So what'd I miss?"

Dora gave me a pleading look, like she didn't want me to pretend. But she played along. "A trip to the Tokyo fish market and about thirty-six hours of diplomatic meet-and-greets that was a total chafe. Lucky for you, Brother Howard brought along a care package of heavy duty tranquilizers in case we ran into a black bear in downtown Tokyo. He put you down harder than Seabiscuit."

I groaned and she waggled her caterpillar brows at me. *Pound-pound-pound.*

The sound of a fist beating hard against the door made both of us jump. I looked at Dora with a sharp-edged question, but she shrugged her shoulders like she didn't know who it could be.

Pound-pound-pound.

"Hello Kitty, keep your pants on! I'm coming, I'm coming!" she yelled toward the door, winking at me.

It was probably Brother Howard and the sedative express, under strict orders from VisionCrest headquarters to keep a lid on Harlow the Liability. But when Dora opened the door, she startled upright like a soldier to battle.

"Patriarch." She dropped her knee to the floor and bowed her head as he entered. Dora was profoundly faithful to the Fellowship—her deviance, unlike mine, did not extend to disbelief. "May your Inner Eye bring Inner Peace."

Right—it was my birthday. One of the only days of the year my father gave me the time of day would now be tainted. I was guessing he didn't come bearing party hats and cake.

"You're dismissed, Sister Elber."

Dora scurried from the room without a backward glance. My stomach dropped.

My father lumbered into the room, slow and deliberate like a grizzly bear. His head swiveled on his massive neck and he all but sniffed the air. One of his eyes was covered by a black silk patch; the other slid up to my face and locked on. If ever there was a stare to turn flesh into salt, the General's was it.

"Harlow, we have a brand to protect."

"Yes, sir. I know, sir."

I clutched the duvet tighter to my chest, trying to shield

myself from the disappointment that rolled off my father in waves. Trying to hide the carnage on my arms.

The General wasn't a bad man. The philosophy he preached came from the heart. He believed that there was a wellspring of immortal peace inside every human being that could be accessed through meditation and devotion to the Fellowship. Ironically, he insisted on attributing Vision-Crest's development to me, someone who didn't believe a word of it. I wished it was true; the only wellspring within me was oily and dark, covered in slippery blackness. The General knew it; the way he looked at me said as much. His expectations weighed a heavy crown on my head. I wanted to live up to them, but I was something dark. Maybe I didn't deserve to be loved.

He dropped into a mahogany chair across the room with a leaden sigh. It was the sound of exhaustion, from his non-stop trips around the world promoting VisionCrest while pretending everything was okay. And of exasperation. Bringing peace to mankind was difficult enough without your natural disaster of a daughter having conniptions in a public park.

The hard look in his eye softened to resignation. For a moment, I caught a glimpse of the father I used to have— the one who read me bedtime stories and told me I was his treasure. That father had been gone a long time.

"What happened?" he asked.

My eyes shifted to the swirly pattern on the comforter. I could feel his heavy stare even though I refused to meet it.

"I don't—I got a migraine. A bad one. And I passed out, I guess."

"And why is it, exactly, that you were off by yourself?"

"I was disoriented. There was a crowd." It wasn't exactly a lie.

"Harlow. Millions of people look to us for guidance, for strength. We cannot afford to show any weakness."

I nodded. It didn't escape my notice that he hadn't asked if I was okay.

"I know, sir."

He ran his hand through his hair and I noticed for the first time that I could see light shining through it in places. The wrinkles on his face seemed suddenly deeper, pressure chiseling pieces of him away right in front of me.

My heart twisted. He was my only family and I was his. That used to be enough. I looked up and met his eye. The hardness was back again. And behind it, a familiar fear—like he was afraid of me. Well, that made two of us.

"Harlow, you're not stupid. There have been disappearances and you're a high-value target."

"A high-value target?" I repeated.

"Your need to assert independence is endangering the Fellowship," he said.

His callous words cut deep, as if my life were nothing but a petty series of antics aimed at annoying him. Never mind that I might be putting myself at risk; my actions were bad for the Fellowship.

"I won't do it again," I lied.

"That sounds familiar. Brother Fitz convinced me to let you come with the rest of the Ministry kids. I knew it was a bad idea."

"Adam convinced you? Why?" I asked.

"Because he's worried about you, just like I am."

I thought for a moment he was going to come sit on the edge of my bed. Hug me. Tell me that I wasn't a bad person and everything was going to be okay. Instead, he rubbed his hand across his forehead and sighed. Then he stood up and walked to the end of my bed, fixing me with an authoritarian glare.

"I'm assigning a member of the Watch to keep a personal eye on you, make sure you stay in here until we leave."

So I was going to be a prisoner in my own life—even more than I already was. I couldn't stifle my protest. "You're locking me in my room?"

Tears stung my eyes. I didn't add what was weighing heaviest on my mind: that he hadn't even bothered to acknowledge it was my birthday. Guess he didn't consider it much cause for celebration.

He thrust his fist toward me. There was an orange prescription bottle in it.

"I ran your situation by my personal physician. He bumped up your Subdueral dosage. It's for your protection. In case you have any other . . . emergencies."

I took the bottle from his hand. It was packed so tight with the tiny tablets that it didn't even rattle.

"Take two every six hours," he said. "You'll stay in your room until you're well."

I fell back on my pillow and let the tears flow free. What would happen, now that the medicine wasn't working anymore? I could be stuck in isolation forever. The static buzz of Her presence began its low keening in my ears.

The General moved to leave the room, then looked back. He sighed. Then he continued out the door and let it slam behind him.

Screw him and his stupid Fellowship. I deserved love and I shouldn't have to pop pills to get it. I threw the bottle of Subdueral across the room, and the robins-egg-blue pills spilled onto the floor.

There was one other person who'd loved me once. Adam. I needed to know why he'd convinced my father to bring me to Asia. Why he came looking for me in the park. Maybe he wanted to repair whatever was wrong between us. Deep inside, I'd always thought it was the power of Adam's friendship, not the Subdueral, that had helped me conquer Her the first time. Maybe if I could regain it, I could fight Her again. At this point I had nothing to lose.

I slipped out of my room, and a minute later I was knocking on Dora's door, two floors below. There was no time to waste. Even though I looked like I'd been six feet under, wrestling the hot mess fairy for the last thirty-six hours, I had to get out of my room before the Watcher showed up. And if I was going to see Adam, I needed the kind of resuscitation only Dora could provide. She was a fashion magician.

Dora's eyebrows shot up when she opened the door and saw me. "My, my. Look at this special package."

I moved past her, glancing over my shoulder. "Let me in. The General's sicking a Watcher on me. I had to split before they barricaded me in."

Dora practically choked. "You are clinically incapable of following the rules. We're both going to end up in a VisionCrest Sequestery scrubbing tile with toothbrushes for the rest of our lives."

I flopped down on her bed. "Nah. That would mean our fathers admitting to their own imperfection. Their children running amok. Never happen."

"Alrighty, Aphrodite. Now what?"

"Now I'm going to Adam's room to thank him for saving me from public humiliation. And to invite him out. We need to go to Koenji tonight—it might be my only chance."

"It's about time you make your move! Like the famous king of punk, that Sid's cruisin' for a Nancy, and you"—Dora stabbed one black-chipped nail in my direction—"are just the Sex Pistol for the job."

"You do realize that Sid knifed Nancy and then overdosed on heroin, right?"

"Exactly. Just like Romeo and Juliet." Dora didn't even blink.

"So, what are we waiting for? Make me punk rock." I grinned.

She flicked the sole of my foot with her finger. "It's on like Donkey Kong, sister."

THE BLUE HOUSE

Fifteen minutes later I was standing in front of Adam's door, in charcoal eyeliner and fishnet tights, nervously bouncing from one Converse to the other. Dora was hiding around the corner, hissing at me to just freaking knock already.

I was torn between fear of being discovered by the Watcher, who I could only hope was innocently stationed outside my room and not already scouring the hotel to find me, and being humiliated for a second time this week in front of the boy who made my heart do tilt-a-whirls in my chest.

I knocked.

Behind the door, Adam cleared his throat and a thousand-volt heat wave radiated through my body. He cracked the door and peered out.

"Harlow?" His voice was raspy, his hair messy like I'd woken him from a nap.

He wasn't wearing a shirt. My eyes traced his tattoos as they swirled down the side of his chest: a patchwork of blood red, moss green, and sea blue symbols carefully etched into his body. I followed the line of his hipbone under the waistband of his briefs.

"What is it?" He ran a hand over the back of his neck and squinted at me.

The gesture sent a thrill through me that started in the pit of my stomach and raced out to my fingertips. I couldn't believe I was standing there with him—alone for the first time since he'd come back. It was my chance to settle whatever invisible awkwardness had come between us while he was away.

"I need to talk to you," I said.

His hand fell to his side and his body tensed with wariness. "Why?" His eyes flickered over my shoulder.

There it was again. That distrust I didn't understand.

"I just wanted to thank you for helping me."

He was stone still. Silent.

"And I was hoping there was something I could do to repay you." I tried not to let him hear the hope straining my voice.

His face darkened. "You don't owe me anything, Harlow."

It was now or never. I went kamikaze and just blurted it out.

"There's this punk club in Koenji I want to check out, and I was hoping you'd come with me. I mean, not just you, not alone, not like a date or anything. Dora's coming, too. And also, it's my birthday."

Shut up, Harlow. Just shut up.

Adam closed his eyes for a second. Dark lashes against

tanned skin. For a fleeting moment I was transported back to the carriage house behind my father's megamansion. Adam and I listened to endless hours of contraband punk rock there; precious vinyl he'd stolen from the storage bunker beneath my house. VisionCrest's home base was full of buried treasure.

Those secret hours were the most exquisite and excruciating of my life. Longing looks exchanged over spinning records—friends with benefits just waiting to be cashed in. Before he and his parents were taken.

It seemed like another lifetime.

"I thought you might like to see the birthplace of Tokyo punk. For old times' sake. Just … please." My voice melted to a whisper.

He opened his eyes and surprised me with a look that, just like in the train car, made it seem as if he were seeing me—really *seeing* me—for the first time since he'd been back. One side of his mouth turned up in a hint of appreciation. It was like my words fractured his shell, and a sliver of the real Adam escaped.

"Does the Patriarch know?"

I looked over my shoulder—the General's minions might come barreling down the corridor at any moment. I shook my head no.

He looked at the floor and laughed quietly to himself, shaking his head a bit. Then he tilted his gaze up to me, fixing me with a stare that made the soles of my feet burn.

"There's a service elevator that lets you off in the back of the lobby, by the bathrooms," he offered. "I found a little side door there that the Watch doesn't seem to be aware of. I've been using it to do a little sneaking out of my own."

I was rooted to the spot by disbelief, unable to move for fear I'd shatter the moment.

"That sounds like fun." A voice sliced through the intimacy of the moment, smashing it to pieces.

Mercy. Inside Adam's room. While he was half-dressed and looking like he'd just rolled out of bed. It was like a roundhouse kick to the stomach. Her face appeared behind him, her chin settling itself into the curve of his shoulder in a way that made me want to smack her teeth crooked. Adam's expression was unreadable.

"Oh." The word escaped me and hung over my head like a cartoon thought bubble of humiliation.

Adam closed his eyes again and leaned against the door-frame like he was Atlas shouldering the world. Then he opened them and looked at me.

"Meet us downstairs, by the service elevator. And try to stay out of sight."

Us. Like he and Mercy were a club and I was not a member.

"Oh. Okay."

Mercy reached out and swung the door shut in my face. Her singsong voice called out as it clicked shut, "Bye-bye, Harlow."

It almost made me miss Her voice. Almost. I turned on my heel and staggered around the corner to where Dora was hiding. She was oblivious, doing the funky chicken down the hall toward me.

"Oh, yeah. Uh-huh. Downstairs, by the service elevator, Adam wants you."

I clamped my hand over her mouth.

"Shhh. Did you not catch the fact that *Mercy* was in his room and totally invited herself along?"

Dora froze mid-poultry-strut and her face got serious. I could see her doing the math.

"Mercy's been psycho-stalking him since he got back. She probably conned her way in there two seconds before you arrived."

It was possible, I supposed.

"He was acting all weird and intense."

"Adam? Intense? Wow, what a surprise. Um, hi... have you met him before?"

"He only said yes because he feels sorry for me."

Dora groaned. "Let's just nail you to the cross right now, Moan of Arc. Are you gonna be this big of a drag the whole trip or just for your super-sweet seventeen? He agreed to go, didn't he?"

She had a point. I was sneaking out. In Japan. To a kick-ass punk club. With Adam. On my birthday. Even if Mercy was going to be there, she didn't know anything about punk rock. At least I had that on her.

"Everything is Swizzle Stick." Dora had adopted the name of her favorite candy to mean anything that was good and pure and full of light. Swizzle Sticks were colored sugar inside a preservative paper tube—disgusting, I thought.

"Say it," Dora commanded.

"Everything is Swizzle Stick."

I should have been ecstatic. But the seismic rift that had developed between Adam and me was niggling at me, and Mercy's constant presence at his side was the uncrossable moat that kept us from reconnecting. It had all started when he came back, and I didn't know why or how to stop it.

———————

Of all people to deliver the news, Mercy Mayer was the one who'd told me Adam was back. It happened three months prior to our trip, as I was leaving the All Knowing, the school we attended at our main compound in Twin Falls, Idaho. The All Knowing was shaped like an immense winged bird in flight, the smooth white wings of the roof capping massive, three-story black-glass walls. The sons and daughters of the Ministry were educated in the Bird's Eye, sequestered from everyone else. Mercy had caught up with me as I took the winding staircase from the Bird's Eye to our dedicated exit, lording the revelation over me like a trophy and savoring the moment my elation turned to hurt.

"He's been back for a week. It's my birthday next week— he's going to be my second at my initiation into the first Rite. You didn't know?" The smile that crept across her face told me the question was rhetorical.

"I don't keep particularly close tabs on your social schedule," I said, trying to conceal my shock.

Mercy sniffed. "I wouldn't classify being inducted into the mysteries of the Inner Eye as a social event. That would apply more to the dates Adam and I have been on the past few weeks. Not that you care." She snapped her gum.

Adam was back, and he hadn't bothered to let me know. Of course, the only thing that mattered was that he was okay. I could nurse my petty disappointment in private, later. Not to mention how I felt about him taking an intimate role in my rival's initiation into the Fellowship, which meant he had been initiated himself. Right then I just needed to see him, touch him, know that he was really there. It was like he'd come back from the dead.

Adam and his parents were the first Ministry members to disappear. Other members of the Fellowship had preceded them, but this was different. Adam's father was the Eparch, the second in command. He was with the General when my father discovered me. Since there's no religious allegory more classic than the abandoned baby, it was no shocker the General claimed to have found me as an infant, squalling on the steps of a forgotten temple. He said the structure appeared to him out of nowhere, deep in the Cambodian jungle. Somewhere in the exchange he lost his left eye, but no one ever spoke about it. I knew there was more to the story, but my father clammed up like an oyster whenever I asked. All he would say was, *You came to me in the Violet Hour, when stars succumb to fate and the world hangs suspended in between. Let us pray.*

The Violet Hour, just before dawn, was therefore our religion's most sacred time. It had an entire meditative devotion ascribed to it, and it was said to be the time we were most attuned to the power of our Inner Eye. Prophets are prone to hyperbole, and I concluded that my father was one for the record books; because of his talent, VisionCrest had gone from a cult to a multinational corporate religion in seventeen short years. It comprised high-ranking government officials from every country in the world and claimed a full quarter of the world's population as its followers. What took most religions centuries to amass, my father accomplished practically overnight—almost as if some unseen force was driving his success. And I was at the heart of its symbolic center. Yippee.

The way the story went, my father had disappeared without a trace. The Eparch searched frantically around the temple all night, until the General re-emerged through the mists of dawn with me in his arms, missing an eye. The Eparch was my father's first believer, though certainly not his last.

Given all this, the absence of the Eparch and his family was impossible for the Ministry to hide, especially as the abductions were growing bigger and bolder. The official claim was that they were on a mission in Africa. The tension in my father's shoulders told me he was lying, and I'd heard enough of his whispered conversations to know the truth. Besides, Adam would never leave without telling me. At least I didn't think he would.

The Fitzes were gone for nine months. I was like a coiled spring ready to snap the entire time. No VisionCrest follower had ever come back or been found, dead or alive, after a disappearance. It felt like my life was on pause—like I hadn't slept, eaten, or even breathed since it happened. So Adam's return was a miracle. There was no other way to put it.

"Where is he?" I demanded.

Mercy shrugged. "Probably at the Blue House. That's usually where I see him."

"*You* were at the Blue House?"

The Blue House was a beat-up squatter house that wept baby blue flakes of paint every time the wind blew. It housed the near-constant rotation of skate punks and castoffs that the town of Twin Falls collected like Cracker Jack prizes—most of them the severed children of VisionCrest believers. Severing was the process of being officially cast out of the Fellowship; it was like being sent to live on another planet. The house was infamous among VisionCrest kids—a real-life cautionary tale that most had never seen with their own eyes.

Adam and I used to make a habit of sneaking off the compound to hang out there, fully committed to the idea of anything that gave the middle finger to VisionCrest. But Mercy's mother, Prelate Mayer, was one of the twenty Prelates around the world who comprised the Ministry layer below Eparch Fitz, and Mercy was a model follower. I couldn't believe Adam would hang out with her at all, much less at the Blue House.

Mercy was looking at me with narrowed eyes. "There's lots of things about me you don't know, Harlow. In fact, there's lots of things about lots of people you don't know. Take Adam for instance. He's a True Believer now."

I pushed past her. There was no way that was true, and I was going to find out for myself. Adam and I had sworn to one another that we wouldn't take the Rite when we turned seventeen. We wanted to be black sheep—different, difficult, out of step, and out of line. Just like our favorite punk rock songs preached. There must have been some other reason for him taking the Rite, or maybe Mercy was lying about it all.

"If he wanted to see you, he would have called!" Mercy yelled after me.

I headed toward the narrow gap in the perimeter posts of the VisionCrest compound; my secret escape hatch. An hour later, I was standing in front of the Blue House, desperate to see Adam but paralyzed by a gut-clenching fear that he didn't want to see me. The citizens of Twin Falls ogled me as they drove by, too intimidated by the Fellowship to intervene. It was as if they were seeing a tiger who escaped from the zoo walking down the middle of the street—look but don't touch.

Smooth clacking sounds, of wheels rolling over wooden seams, bounced off the river-rock lawn of the Blue House. This told me exactly where I could find Adam: the skate ramp around back. I stuck a leg through the gap-toothed fence, the weather-beaten slat scraping my bare skin. I turned sideways and squeezed my way through, then dusted off my skirt and squinted up at the skate ramp.

I spotted Adam among the rag-tag collection of grommets. He was taller and more filled-out than before. His shirt was off in the afternoon sun and my eyes lingered, transfixed. I followed the line of his shoulder and the ink that wound across it. The tattoos were like a billboard announcing that he had changed. They were strange and beautiful—and completely at odds with Mercy's claim that he was now a buttoned-up believer. I felt a rush of relief. He was different, but he was still my Adam.

I thought about the last time I'd seen him. How he'd leaned me up against the side of the carriage house and pressed his body into mine. My face tilted up to the warmth of the sun. His breath against my lips. Before the gardener happened along and interrupted what most certainly would have been the single greatest moment of my life.

Adam.

Little glints of gold in his dark hair caught the sun; it was like seeing a mirage in the desert. He held his hand up to shield his eyes, and they flicked up and down over me. No smile of recognition lit up his face, no dimple appeared on his right cheek. The skin around his left eye was bruised, ringed in fading purple. I wondered if it was a souvenir of his kidnapping, or if he'd been fighting one of the lost boys. Either way, I knew he wasn't as tough as he pretended to be.

"Harlow," he said. His dark blue eyes skewered me.

Not the friendly greeting I was hoping for.

I only had two friends. My heart couldn't bear losing one of them for a second time. I shifted uncomfortably, suddenly feeling every inch the awkward little girl I once was.

Adam hopped on his board and rode it down the curve, flipping it at the bottom and jumping off. He stalked toward me. Even the way he moved was somehow different. I toed the dirt with my Converse, unsure what to say or do.

"I'm so happy you're back." I instinctively reached to hug him.

He flinched, backing away. My heart dropped. I waited for the smooth line of his jaw to pull up into a smirk, a smile, an anything that said he was only joking—but he was expressionless.

"Yeah. I am."

Why was he looking at me like I'd just killed his dog? Everything about him screamed *stay away*.

"You're not living here, are you?"

"Look, Harlow, I don't really feel like talking about this. Not to you. Why don't you just ask Mercy if you want all the juicy details."

All traces of the Adam I'd known had been swept away, vacuumed up, and scrubbed out with bleach. I stood there awkwardly while a menagerie of eavesdroppers smoked cigarettes and whispered from the periphery. Everyone was enjoying the show—Harlow Wintergreen, daughter of the Patriarch. Making a fool of herself.

"Where are your parents?" I finally asked.

"Probably dead. Happy?"

"What?" I stuttered.

"Go back to the compound, Harlow."

He turned and walked toward the sagging porch. I practically fell over. His parents were probably dead? Why would that make me happy? I wanted to run after him, throw my arms around him, make the hurt written all over his body disappear. But he'd rejected me. In a weird way, it almost felt like he *blamed* me. I turned and ran, before I'd give them the satisfaction of seeing me cry.

Two weeks later, Adam was back on the compound, glued to the General's side just like his own father had once been. It looked like Mercy had been right about his one-eighty after all—since if there was anyone Adam should hold responsible for his parents' abduction, it would be the man who'd started the Fellowship in the first place. Yet Adam was now more devoted to my father than ever, and it was me he held at arm's length.

Three months had gone by since his return, and still he barely looked at me. For reasons I couldn't fathom, he preferred Mercy's company. Mercy, who he once dismissed as "supermodel-marshmallow: flash where it doesn't count, fluff where it does." Then he gave me a feline grin and leaned toward my ear. "I don't really go for that."

In reality, there was more to Mercy than met the eye. She wasn't at all the ditz she pretended to be, something I'd known since we were playmates as little girls. Maybe Adam had finally discovered it too.

Still, he'd agreed to come out with me to Koenji. And there was only one way to find out if there were still any feelings for me behind those tortured eyes. It was time to bring the counterattack. No mercy.

TOKYO PUNK

Forty minutes later, Dora and I were skulking in the lobby by the service elevators, hiding behind an arrangement of calla lilies so massive it looked like it had been FTD'd straight down the beanstalk. The hotel seemed to be made entirely of reflective surfaces, all smooth black marble and mirrored walls.

There was a zero percent chance the Ministry would look favorably on four members of the VisionCrest royal family melting into the Tokyo night unchaperoned, but the penalty for being caught couldn't be too bad. I was already sentenced to isolation, and they couldn't keep us all hidden away. It was worth the risk if I could get even one minute alone with Adam.

Dora and I stayed shifty-eyed, looking for Watchers. True to Adam's word, there were none lurking. Even though I wasn't taking any chances on ruining my big night, I hated cowering in the calla lilies like a fugitive. Adam and Mercy were late, and my mind ran wild with all the reasons they could be lagging.

I started second-guessing my outfit, the thought of Mercy's pearl necklace and sweater-set look making me pull at my fishnets. I might as well wear a flashing neon sign that said *desperate for attention!* Maybe Adam was going for something more … normal, these days.

"Stop doing that or you're going to rip them right off your legs. You look tough." Dora eyed me approvingly. For her, that was high praise.

I parted the sharp-edged leaves of the arrangement with my fingertips, just in time to hear the elevator ding and see Adam amble into sight. Mercy was right behind him, rocking a miniskirt and platform heels. So much for the pearls—maybe she was the one who'd changed. If it were possible, Adam looked even more delicious than ever in a tight black Sex Pistols shirt and gray-wash skinny jeans. He looked casual-amazing, like he might go skateboarding or make out with a fashion model … he just couldn't decide.

Dora elbowed me in the ribs when she saw his shirt, like it was some kind of sign from the universe.

"Ow!"

Adam caught me peeking out from behind the fronds. He bent over a bit and squinted as I let them snap back into place.

"Harlow? Are you hiding in the flower arrangement?"

Dora tugged at my hand and we did our best to step out casually from our hiding place, as if we'd just been getting a closer look at the shrubbery. She looked at me and said, "And *that* is how photosynthesis occurs."

Mercy's face was a mixture of amusement and horror. Her pity was infinitely worse than her scorn. Adam was unreadable, as usual.

"You ready to hear some awesome music?" I asked.

"If it's not awesome, we're totally switching and going to a dance club," Mercy said.

Adam and I exchanged a look, and for a split second it was like old times—Mercy wouldn't know good music if it bit her in the ass. As I looked away, I swore I saw the corners of his mouth turn up for a second. That tiny gesture gave me a boost of hope. Was it possible he was coming back around?

"Um, guys … hang on just a minute longer, if you don't mind." Dora glanced down at her phone and then looked past Adam and Mercy like she was expecting someone.

As if on cue, Stubin Mansfield materialized from behind the black granite column closest to us and walked right up like he owned the place. He pushed the sleeves of his pea-green cardigan up to his elbows and shook one knee and then the other, like he was limbering up for the 100-yard dash.

Stubin was the son of a low-level Sacristan and a total know-it-all. That was pretty much all I knew about him, other than the odd fact that my best friend had apparently invited him along. The kids of the Sacristans, who made up the majority of our Ministry group, usually kept their distance from the kids of the higher echelons. It was just how it was.

"Hey cats and kittens, what sort of Meow Mix are we

getting into tonight?" Stubin asked, as if it was the most natural thing in the world to be hanging out with us.

"We're going to a punk club. That sweater looks awesome—is it vintage?" Dora was fawning. She never fawned.

"Yeah, I bought it cuz it matches my eyes. And aren't you just a chick biscuit tonight," Stubin responded. There was so much Velveeta on that comment, I could barely hold back the gag reflex. Dora was looking at him like he was some kind of celebrity.

I forced a smile.

Stubin looked pointedly at Adam. "Surprised you're willing to risk the Patriarch's wrath by sneaking out on the town with his daughter. Though I guess I shouldn't be."

Adam looked at him with confusion for a second, likely recognizing his face but not knowing his name. He wasn't used to being challenged, even by the people who knew him well. He blinked, and then he smiled wider than I'd seen since he returned.

"I guess we have that in common, sweater guy. I don't believe we've been formally introduced. I'm Adam Fitz."

He held his hand out to Stubin, who was so flummoxed he visibly wavered between charmed and irritated. He offered up a wary handshake.

"Stubin Mansfield. I know who you are."

Adam shrugged and looked at the rest of us. "We're all acquainted then. Let's rock."

We hustled after Adam through an unmarked door that led into some sort of service hallway. He pushed through another door into a dark alley, the nearby smell of exhaust and the whir of traffic beckoning to us. Mercy picked her way gingerly behind Adam, trying and failing to catch his arm as she dodged little pools of street sludge. I watched her like a hawk and secretly wished for her to bite it, even though I knew I shouldn't. Dora was giggling behind me as Stubin whispered something she couldn't possibly find funny. It felt lonely.

A moment of doubt tugged at me. Willed me back to the safety of my hotel room. There were a million ways this mostly innocent outing could go horribly wrong. I was risking disaster going out when the voice was running loose. It could sneak up on me at any moment, and there was no telling what might happen. But I forced myself to keep moving forward.

There was a minivan cab waiting at the end of the alleyway. Adam must have called for it. He looked over his shoulder and caught my eye. There was something there: an entreaty, a dare, or a warning. I couldn't tell which.

The cab door swung open automatically as we approached. Only in Japan. Adam took the front and the rest of us piled in back.

"So, where are we going, exactly?" Adam asked.

"Koenji. MegaWatts," I said.

Adam turned to the driver. "*Nippon no panku no genten ni tachite kudasai*. MegaWatts."

He was speaking Japanese. It was impossible not to crush on him when he busted out unexpected intellect like that.

"I didn't know you spoke Japanese!" Mercy gushed, tipping forward. She wasn't going to fade into the background like a wallflower. "What did you say?"

Adam looked over his shoulder and smirked. "Take us to the origin of Japanese punk."

"The origin of Japanese punk?" She looked confused.

"MegaWatts—it's a club where the punk movement started in Japan," he told her.

"It's a livehouse," I corrected.

"Ahh," she said, like she had any clue what that meant.

"In Japan, they call a show a *live*, and so a venue is called a *livehouse*," Adam explained. His eyes met mine, an almost-smile playing at his lips. My heart beat a little faster.

"Personally, I prefer classical." Mercy sniffed.

"MegaWatts is like the CBGB of Japanese punk," Stubin chimed in enthusiastically from the way back.

"You know about CBGB?" Adam asked him, incredulous.

Adam and I had learned all about the epicenter of the old-school New York punk scene by digging through the confiscated scrapbooks of some once-famous Fellowship member. We'd found the scrapbooks molding alongside the punk rock vinyl—there was all kinds of interesting stuff in the bunker beneath my house. Most of the high-ranking Ministry members were once celebrities, academics, or politicians.

"Yeah, my dad used to be, like...in a famous punk band or something. He had a stage name but refuses to tell me what it was. Sometimes he talks about the old days." Then Stubin seemed to think better of it and added, "Mostly just to say how glad he is to be reformed by the Fellowship."

Adam and I exchanged a look of disbelief. Dorky Stubin Mansfield's dad was probably the original owner of our stolen records and the frontman of one of our favorite bands. The silent connection between Adam and me was back, and stronger than ever.

"Harlow's the punk rock princess. You'll have to tell her some of your dad's stories." Dora nudged Stubin playfully. "My girl's got mad taste."

"She certainly does," Adam agreed, turning to face forward in his seat.

This time I was sure. I didn't know what had changed, but he was definitely smiling when he said that.

———————

MegaWatts was decidedly off the beaten path. We got out of the cab on a street that looked like its overhead wires were supporting the telecom infrastructure of Southeast Asia. There was a small chalkboard A-frame sign perched on the street, right outside a 7-11 knockoff and a porn shop. It said "MegaWatts" in English, and a list of other things in Kanji characters—bands, presumably.

There was a collection of gutter punks hanging outside— disaffected Tokyo teenagers who I instantly identified with on some misfit level. Adam opened our door and Mercy climbed out in front of me. He held her hand as she climbed out; jealously sawed at me like a dull blade. She slipped her hand into the crook of his arm.

Dora looked at me pointedly. What could I do but act oblivious?

"I can't believe we're actually here," I said.

"Me either." Stubin nodded vigorously. "Super cool."

I examined the grungy half-lit entrance, the thick crowd spilling out of the club. It was do-or-die time. I knew I shouldn't be out on the town in my tenuous mental state, but my common sense was drowning in the thumping bass of the club—and in the idea that maybe, *just maybe*, my Adam might return to me.

"So are we just gonna stand here? Let's go in," Mercy said.

"Hell yeah. Let's do it," Adam said.

Dora grabbed Stubin's arm and they plunged into the crowd together. Mercy, Adam, and I followed after.

We forced our way down the sticky stairs and, within seconds, were entombed in a low-ceilinged black box that smelled like steamed gym socks and stale beer wrapped in a million decibels of skull-pounding grindcore. Beat-up leather jackets and peroxide mohawks were everywhere. The walls were covered with crudely painted anarchy symbols and it smelled like cigarette smoke. It was so loud I could barely hear myself think.

I stayed right on Adam's heels, immediately losing sight of Dora and Stubin. Panic rose in my throat, but I resisted the urge to pinch the back of Adam's T-shirt. I wasn't sure if our tenuous reconciliation extended to physical contact, and Mercy had staked a claim on his arm. The three of us traced the curves of the crowd, weaving our way through clumps of Japanese teenagers.

The air curved in on me like a sinusoidal sound wave. I knew that feeling—that trapped feeling. The one that often preceded something worse.

I actively ignored it. Maybe if I didn't acknowledge it, nothing would happen. Club-goers bounced off my shoulders, causing electric explosions of sight and sound in my head. Another bad sign. Why had I set this in motion when I knew what could happen? Now I was stuck—either back down and be an even bigger freak than I already was, or stick it out and hope for the best. Unfortunately, my best wasn't very good.

Adam halted before the thickest part of the crowd, on the fringes at the back of the room. At the front of the room there was a teeny-tiny stage where a shirtless Japanese rocker, with chicken legs in skinny jeans and row upon row of studded belts, was screaming into a scratchy microphone. The spikes of his glo-hawk grazed the ceiling as the band's drummer energetically pounded the sticks behind him like the cymbal might go out of style at any moment. I stood at Adam's side, my knees knocking as I surveyed the rolling knot of tangled bodies bouncing to the music. For a second I thought he was going to plunge right in, but he looked at me and hesitated.

"This is probably far enough for now," he said.

I nodded. "Yeah, let's start here."

"I'm going to the bar," Mercy announced, like she went clubbing all the time. "What do you want, babe?"

Babe? Adam turned to her with a quizzical look, like even he couldn't believe she said it.

"I don't drink," he said.

That was a lie. I drank with him twice in the carriage house. Once, playing Truth or Dare, he dared me to kiss him and I chickened out. I wished he would dare me now.

Unfazed and completely fearless, Mercy walked away. Oh, to have her confidence.

Adam turned his attention to me, searching my face like he was looking for something he'd lost. He looked away. Then back to me. Like he didn't know how to talk to me anymore. The feeling was mutual.

"Is it what you expected?" he finally asked.

I was keenly aware of his hand, inches from mine. He might have been asking about the club, but it almost felt like he was asking about us.

"It may be just the teeniest bit more intense than I imagined," I admitted.

He started laughing, and for the first time since he'd disappeared, his smile was genuinely for me.

"No joke. This is insane," he said.

"Right?" I laughed as kids bounced by like pogo sticks right in front of us. It felt good to let go a little.

Suddenly the entire room seemed more vibrant, more alive than it had been only moments before. My anxiety and fear were replaced with the slamming bass of possibility, which vibrated through my bones.

Adam's eyes scanned the crowd. He was taller than pretty much everyone in here.

"So, Japanese guys have an art form that's, like, based on using cheesy pickup lines to snag cute girls," he commented.

As usual, it felt like we were talking about something more than what we were talking about.

"It's called *nampa*." He looked down at me, waiting for my reaction. There was a playful tilt to his shoulders.

"Maybe you're *nampa*-ing *me* right now," I teased.

Out of nowhere, it was like old Adam and old Harlow were back.

"Using *nampa* to pull a *nampa*." He paused, as if considering it. "That would be so meta of me."

There was an exhilarating undercurrent to this exchange. Talking to him had always been like sticking my finger into a light socket, but this was different—more intense. My world was being rocked right now, and it wasn't the roiling beat of the music that was doing it. I tried my best to keep my voice even. We were in uncharted territory in the best possible way.

"You are the master of meta," I said.

He moved closer, his bare arm pressing into me ever so slightly but with absolute intention. He bobbed his head to the slamming music. He looked over at me and I did a double take, looking away and then looking back again. He held my gaze and raised an eyebrow, then leaned closer to speak into my ear.

"You have really smoky eyes," he said.

"Oh, the eyeliner? I told Dora it was too much."

"No, your eyes." He pointed to his own eyes. "The color. It's like seafoam with clouds of smoke blowing through it. Mysterious. Your mystery's always been one of my favorite things about you."

His words made me feel special in a way that had nothing to do with whose daughter I was. Adam had always made me feel that way. I looked at the tattoos swirling over his skin and the strange runes embedded there like a code.

"So what's the story with the tattoos?" I asked. I was

afraid of fracturing the fragile shell he'd built around himself, but I wanted to understand this new version of him.

Adam shifted back to the stage, his shoulders stiffening. "It's just ink."

"It doesn't look like just ink," I said. I wanted him to feel me reaching out for him. I wanted him to reach back.

Instead, he kept his stare steadily on the band. This was a risky subject. It wasn't like he'd been banished, like Romeo gone to Mantua; his family had been abducted. But I wanted to understand who this new person was. And I didn't see any way around it. Only through it.

"This band is awesomely terrible." He tried to change the subject, his voice strained.

I examined his face, searching for some clue as to what was going on with him. He turned and met my stare—the vulnerability in his eyes like an open wound for a split second, and gone just as fast.

"Maybe it sounds better up front," I joked.

"Want to go closer?" he asked, completely serious.

I glanced in the direction Mercy had gone. There were certain benefits to changing coordinates, namely her inability to find us in the crowd. But the air was feeling tight again and I could almost hear the beat of the voice building in my head. Not now. Not here. I'd been so in control a moment ago.

"Absolutely," I lied.

I didn't want to be swallowed by a crowd. What I wanted was to feed the current of whatever was happening between me and Adam. I was walking a tightrope; one misplaced step could send me hurtling toward the abyss.

The moment we immersed ourselves in the knot of bodies, I realized what a huge mistake I'd made.

Purity.

Her voice was following me. The walls of the room started to close in.

Penance.

I kept moving, as if by some miracle I would be able to outmaneuver Her. The universe would be my friend tonight. This wasn't happening. I wouldn't let it.

Adam showed no sign of pausing as we passed the halfway mark to the stage. I reached out to tug on his shirt. I couldn't go any farther. I needed to pause and get myself together. Adam turned to me with a question in his eyes, and I pointed down to the nice little island of space I was rooted to.

Onstage, the singer bent his legs, arched his back, screamed full-throttle into the mic, and then threw it to the ground. Looking out over the crowd, his eyes fixed on the space near me. He leaped headfirst into the crowd. Right toward me.

Obliterate.

I turned my shoulder against the impending blow.

Decimate.

At the last second, Adam snatched me out from under the incoming missile. I didn't register the crowd filling in behind me and body-surfing the singer over their heads, the song exploding to its raging climax. I was too busy with an explosion of my own.

Exsanguinate.

My eyes met Adam's. His arms tightened around me,

and a feeling like the closing of an electric circuit between us coursed through me.

Exsanguinate.

Adam's head jerked up at the sound of the voice. Like he'd heard Her, too.

Exsanguinate.

The vision overtook me.

The kid standing next to us turned to look at me, clotted blood streaming from his empty eye sockets.

"Exsanguinate," he said, his voice like a howl of rushing wind through some faraway tunnel. A petite girl at his side convulsed as red bubbles formed at the corner of her mouth. She clutched at Adam, then vomited a river of red down the front of her artfully tattered white shirt.

The entire room erupted in chaos. Geysers of blood sprayed across the room. Through the haze of my vision, I watched as Adam's eyes followed their arcs in disbelief. Now I was sure. I was like a livewire of horror in Adam's arms, channeling my visions into him. He was seeing what I was seeing.

His eyes locked onto mine. The sensation that he was seeing me for the first time washed over me again. Only this time, it wasn't pleasant nostalgia I saw reflected there.

It was fear.

All around us, clubbers fell to the floor in convulsions. Pustules erupted across their skin. Meanwhile, people continued dancing on the edges of the vision like marionettes dangling from strings. It was the only thing that let me know this wasn't really happening—the normalcy at the edge of my nightmare. Our nightmare. As if Adam and I were the only

49

two people left in the world. Maybe we could pull each other out of it.

I looked at him. Tried to tell him to run.

Obliterate. Obliterate. Obliterate.

I couldn't tell, but it almost sounded like the words were coming not from Her voice in my head, but from me. Adam's grip on me went slack. He gaped at me, stumbling back. I reached a hand out for him, pinwheeling blindly in the pitch blackness, searching for a lifeline. I wanted to bring him back. To explain that She wasn't me. She was something I fought against. My balance failed me, and I fell to the floor.

The lights blinked out in MegaWatts.

AFTERSHOCK

A shiver of panic rocked the crowd. The blackout was real, not part of my vision.

The lights flickered on again for a second, then pitched us back into darkness. Shrieks. Feet tripping. Panic. I anchored my palms to the floor and pushed myself to sitting. Adam. Where was he? A strobe came on, mixing with the pulses in my brain to create a full-force migraine.

I looked up and there he was, staring down at me. His face was lit up in bursts of light. The haunted look I saw there told me I was right—he'd seen my vision, heard Her voice. There was an accusation in his eyes. Like I was responsible. Maybe I was. The possibility of us was slipping through my fingers like sand, and every part of me screamed to make it stop.

Sprinklers went off. Manufactured rain drenched us, raindrops bouncing off the floor. I couldn't distinguish it from the tears I felt slipping down my chin. The feedback from the abandoned microphone onstage squealed an ear-piercing alarm. It combined with the fading footfalls of the fleeing live-goers like some kind of portent of the world's end. I stood up and reached out to Adam.

He flinched, shaking his head like he was emerging from a trance. His face registered disgust. He saw me now for what I truly was: a freak, a menace, someone to stay as far away from as possible. He turned to follow the crowd, running from something more terrifying than whatever had set the alarms howling. Me.

An overweight boy with his hair dyed in pink checkers grabbed my arm and pulled me toward the exit, yelling at me urgently in Japanese. He didn't know I couldn't be saved.

The boy's fingers pressed into my arm, forming little inden-tations there. As he tugged me along behind him, I watched the flesh fall away from his arm in blackened chunks. He turned to me, tears of blood running down his face. The last threads of the vision invading my psyche.

I wrenched my arm away. The visions were bleeding over into my reality at an alarming rate. It was getting hard to tell what was real and what was not. As the tide of bodies finally swept me onto the street, the cool black air slammed me in the face. Clusters of confused hipsters were pointing and ogling just outside the club.

I fell to my knees at the curb and heaved into the gutter. When the retching finally subsided, I wiped the wet tendrils of hair from my face and searched the crowd. I had to find Dora.

Finally, I saw her glasses through the crowd at the same moment she saw me. Relief flooded me as she elbowed her way over, Stubin in tow. There was no sign of Adam or Mercy.

I hoped they were safe, or I would never forgive myself. I didn't know how it had happened, but this disaster was my fault.

Dora took my hand and pulled me to my feet.

"Adam?" I wheezed. "Mercy?"

"Holy Hera in a handbasket! Where the hell have you been? I tried to go back, but the bouncer thugs wouldn't let me in!" Dora wrestler-hugged me. Stubin shoved his hands in his pockets.

"I'm happy to see you, too. Now we have to find Adam and Mercy," I said.

As if on cue, Mercy Mayer hobbled like a wounded glamazon out of a thicket of punks, ravaged platform heels in hand. She was sobbing and shivering uncontrollably.

"It was so awful! People were stepping all over my shoes and then the sprinklers turned on and they got all wet and Harlow left me and—" A hiccup interrupted her rant long enough for her to notice we were missing someone. "Where's Adam?"

She flung the question at me like an accusation, as if I was keeping him hidden in my pocket only to increase the cruelty of her evening. I looked down at my feet, shame washing over me.

"He left," I answered.

A wounded look flashed across her face. I almost felt sorry for her.

"Is he okay? Was he hurt?" Her eyes darted around the crowd, looking for him.

"I'm not sure," I whispered.

"Everything you touch is a disaster," she hissed, her voice scalding.

She was right. I'd known what this foray could mean and I did it anyway. I was selfish.

"We're getting out of here." Dora stepped between us, defending me. "All of us. Taxi. Pronto."

She took my hand and tugged at Stubin's sleeve. He leapt into action.

"I'm on it. Taxi! Taxi!" Stubin started waving like a madman and charged down the street. We followed him, melting away from the crowd, as sirens approached, like dandelion seeds scattered on the wind.

As we tottered down the street, I looked back. A broken little piece of me hoped to see Adam combing through the wreckage for me, desperately wanting to tell me it was all a big mistake

But all I saw were anarchy signs, and in my heart and mind the reckless unnamed anarchy of *Her.* The one I couldn't stop, closing in around me. Blotting me out until I ceased to exist.

———

As usual, the ride to the top was lonely.

Tonight, it was just me and my warped reflection in the stainless steel elevator, watching the number creep up, up, up while Muzak assaulted my gray matter. We'd tried the service elevator and it was out of order. Which probably meant the Watch was on to our disappearing act.

I considered whether to go camp outside Adam's door

until he returned. Demand that he speak to me. Try to explain the unexplainable. Make him see that I was still the girl he spent those endless summer nights with in the carriage house.

Until Mercy's phone lit up with a text.

"It's from him—it's from Adam!" she screamed. She thumbed her way through the words, biting her lip in concentration.

"He wants me to meet him in his room," she said, aiming the words at me like a gun.

I felt nauseated. After what had passed between us tonight, how could he run to her? But the more I thought about it, how could he not?

The bell dinged. Everyone but me was getting off. I wasn't going to fight Mercy for Adam's attention. He didn't deserve to have me barging in on his life and destroying it. Still, my fingers itched at my side and my cheeks burned.

Dora looked at me reluctantly as she and Stubin stepped off the elevator after Mercy, who practically sprinted away to meet Adam. "Are you sure you don't want us to go up with you?" she asked. "Make sure you get there okay?"

I looked at her hand firmly ensconced in Stubin's. It had taken me all night to realize it, wrapped up in my own self-involved world as I'd been, but I was really excited for Dora. She had an actual boyfriend. A boyfriend with a rock-star pedigree. Someone to care about her and love her.

I shrugged. "What's the worst that could happen to me on an elevator ride?"

Her beetle-brows drew together in a frown as the doors slid shut. She knew I was taking the fall for the rest of us, and she also knew I wasn't going to let it happen any other way. I'd instigated this mess, and there wasn't any point in taking the rest of them down with me. Besides, there was always the off-chance I'd be able to sneak past a sleeping sentinel and get away with the whole fiasco scot-free.

I noticed my reflection in the metal doors of the elevator—something was off. The image smirked back at me. Then she winked.

Ting.

I jumped backward as my reflection split in two and the doors slid open. *I'm seriously losing it*, I thought as I stepped onto the dimly lit hallway. Silence. The stress was playing tricks on my mind…or something.

A thread of light crept out from beneath the mahogany doors of the master suite where the General was sure to be slaving away at his desk, answering pleas from devoted followers or revising his next speech. Maybe nighttime would soften him into something more closely resembling the father I used to know, the man who was little more than a memory these days. The father who had me ever-present at his side, who used to hug me and tell me I was the most important thing in the world. Even parental disapproval held a certain appeal right now. At least it was acknowledgment. I needed someone to see me.

I slipped the slim keycard into the door of my room, a smaller satellite just down the hall. The alarm flicked green. It was almost spooky that there wasn't a Watcher waiting at my room. I guess I wasn't quite the priority I'd imagined myself to be. Happy birthday, Harlow. No one noticed you were gone.

I was just wiping the kohl from my eyes when a swift rap at the door jolted me. My thoughts flew directly to Adam. I couldn't think of anyone else who would be knocking on my door in the middle of the night. Still, I hesitated. Adam could be pretty reckless, but he probably wouldn't chance the General's displeasure by lurking outside my room. When a second knock didn't come, I panicked and ran to the door. If he was reaching out to me, the last thing I wanted him to do was leave. With Adam, it could be a limited-time offer. It wasn't like he hadn't just seen me at my worst.

When I flung the door open, I was face-to-face with a cross-armed Watcher dressed like he was running covert ops for the Navy Seals instead of fetching a misbehaving teenager. Faster than I could say *so screwed*, I was standing in front of the General's desk.

He hunched in his beloved high-back chair, under the glow of an antique lamp. He took that chair with him everywhere he traveled; it reeked of the sweet-sour smell of lemon-scented furniture polish. The VisionCrest Patriarch did as he liked. There was a framed picture, on his desk, of him with Eparch Fitz when they were much younger, standing shoulder-to-shoulder in the middle of a busy street in Siem Reap, tuk-tuks darting around them like minnows around a sunfish. Their faces were serious, my father's damaged eye wrapped with a bloody cloth bandage and me swaddled in his arms.

The General's thick fingers drummed at the brass buttons on the chair's armrests, and his lips pressed together like they did when he was trying to solve a particularly complex problem. He didn't even acknowledge my presence. The silent treatment was never a good sign. I expected him to fix me with his deadeye stare—the coldest in his repertoire, the one that meant I was royally flushed. I'd really done it this time. Maybe enough to earn a full-blown quarantine I would never get out from under. Goose bumps rose on my arms. It wasn't just the icebox temperature of this and every room the General stayed in; it was the chill of dread.

Instead, he looked up as if he'd only just registered that I was there. He cracked a weary smile. If he noticed that his daughter looked like something the cat dragged in, it didn't show.

"Harlow."

He sounded surprised. It wouldn't be the first time he'd summoned me only to get absorbed in something else moments later and completely forget about me. His brow wrinkled like dough under a rolling pin.

"Sir?"

He snapped his fingers. "Yes, how could I forget?"

Standing up, he walked around the desk, picking up a small, square package with silver wrapping and an elaborate bow as he came to my side.

"It's your birthday. With all the nonsense earlier, it slipped my mind. I bet you thought I forgot completely, right?" He held the package out to me.

I had officially entered the Twilight Zone. I took the present from him, unable to remember the last time he'd hand-delivered a gift on my birthday.

"Sort of," I whispered feebly. Did he not notice that I was fully dressed, with makeup half-smeared across my face?

I carefully peeled away the wrapping. Inside was a velvet box. I opened it. Nestled on a cushion was a gold band with the crest of the All Seeing Eye stamped into it: my initiate ring. I plucked it from its resting place and turned it over in the light. I hadn't thought that I wanted it, but holding it now it felt like the Rosetta stone, like it would help me to decipher the purpose of my life.

"You're seventeen now. I've arranged everything so you can cross the veil tonight." He beamed. The General didn't beam. "We're going to the Tokyo temple right now."

I stared at him. "I haven't actually been feeling that well. The migraines and all," I hedged. Maybe there was a way to put it off just a little longer. Make sure I really wanted to go through with it.

Disappointment flashed briefly in his eye, then determination. He was not interested in hearing no for an answer.

"I'm sorry if I've been hard on you lately, Harlow. I know it's not easy to be the daughter of the Patriarch. Trust me, taking the Rite will make you forget all that."

I was confused about a lot of things, but one thing was crystal clear: I wanted to be worthy of my father's love. If this was what it took—to take the Rite and wear his love around my finger like an unbreakable promise—I would do it.

He wrapped me in a hug, the first one I could remember in at least a year. Had he hugged me on my last birthday? The familiar cherry smell of tobacco wrapped itself around me. I rested my cheek against the rough material of his suit. If his affection was the reward, I would go along with whatever he wanted.

"I'm honored, sir."

"It's almost the Violet Hour. They're waiting for us—it's time to go."

THE RITE

Fifteen minutes later, we arrived at the VisionCrest temple. The deserted neon glow of pre-dawn Tokyo was the only witness to our convoy of bulletproof sedans slinking through the city streets. We pulled around the back of the temple, where there were two special entrances—one that only the Patriarch could use, and one for the remaining Ministry members and their families. Everyone else had to enter through the grand entrance at the front, which on every VisionCrest temple looked exactly the same: a giant eye that split down the middle and opened to welcome the masses into its mysterious center. As it was nearly the Violet Hour, the temple would be packed with devoted followers assembled for their meditations. Today I would officially become one of them. A slither rolled through my stomach.

"Who will be my second?" I asked as we climbed out of the car. A second was a spiritual mentor, of sorts, from the moment of the Rite forward. I'd always fantasized that mine would be Adam. It was a bond for life, and if there was anyone I wanted to be bonded to, it was Adam Fitz. But he was in his room with Mercy Mayer. Maybe the General had forgotten to tell him and the whole thing would be called off.

Always meticulous in his appearance, the General picked at his sleeve as we walked to the entrances. "One of the British Prelates is passing through town with his son—do you remember Prelate Cantor? He and his son Hayes stayed with us in Twin Falls a few summers ago while the Prelate was taking a survey course."

"A little," I lied.

It was exactly five summers ago. Prelate Cantor was nothing more than a shadowy memory, but I definitely remembered Hayes Cantor. He was my first crush, two years older and impossibly out of reach. Even though he'd barely acknowledged me the entire week he was in my house, I thought about him for years afterward. I couldn't help but feel a little thrill at the possibility of him being my second at the Rite.

"Prelate Cantor's been a little on the fringe lately, and this will be a show of good faith—a strengthening of our alliance, if you will. Having his son second my daughter binds us tighter. Pay attention, Harlow; one day these are the decisions that will belong to you."

My father breezed through his entrance, leaving me standing there dumbstruck. Not at his confirmation that Hayes was my second, but at his allusion to me taking an active role in leading the Fellowship. He'd never done that before. I scrambled through the Ministry entrance, eager to hear more.

My eyes adjusted to the darkness. There was a sliver of

light peeking out from behind a thick velvet curtain that divided the front hall from the inner sanctum where we were. Through the crack, I could see that the hall was full. A thousand heads bowed in prayer.

The Violet Hour was considered sacred, the time when the veil between the Inner Eye and mortal man was the thinnest. With enough meditation, and initiation into the many-leveled mysteries of VisionCrest, True Believers could eventually transcend into the Inner Truth and receive the gift of life everlasting. According to the General, at least. If you asked me, it was thinly veiled all right—a thinly veiled fantasy.

"This way, Harlow," the General instructed.

I tore my eyes away from the worshippers and followed him down a thin, dark hallway. He stopped us in front of a plain wooden door marked with the crest of the Inner Eye and the Roman numeral I. The inner sanctum of every temple had a series of marked doorways. The level you were attempting to attain determined the door you walked through. The first Rite was notoriously simple to pass, but most people never made it beyond that. There was no way of knowing what it would entail. Many gave the Fellowship years of their life and savings for spiritual training to attempt the next mystery, only to fail at whatever awaited behind the door marked II. Sacristans had attained the seventh level, and Prelates the eighth. The Eparch had completed nine, and only the Patriarch had attained all ten. Rumor had it that my father had discovered even higher levels, which so far only he could conquer. Big shocker. I was willing to bet that the General would keep inventing levels until the day he died. It was an insurance policy that kept him and his favorites in power, while everyone else labored for something that remained perpetually out of reach. And here I was, about to willingly participate in the world's biggest lie just to gain my father's approval. The slither rolled through my gut again.

The General passed through the marked door. I pursued him down a frigid hallway lit by the glow of candles mounted along the walls. The air smelled like lavender mixed with sulfur. The murmur of chanting grew louder. I spotted a vent in the ceiling—the voices were coming from the Great Hall, where the VisionCrest faithful were beginning their Violet Hour ablutions.

At the end of the hallway, there was yet another door. The General paused in front of it.

"You will enter alone, signifying the choice you make tonight: to join the Fellowship of your own accord, ready to receive the Inner Truth, or else be severed from it entirely. Do you accept these terms?"

There was no room for hesitation. The mere mention of being severed made my nerves sing with fear. I should have known that was the choice I would face—it must have been how all those lost boys ended up at the Blue House. Nobody really talked about it, or at least not with me. VisionCrest secrets inspired discretion, even from those who didn't believe in them. I wasn't prepared to leave my whole life behind. How could I?

"I accept," I said.

The General's mouth curved up for just a moment. It was the closest thing to outright approval in his repertoire. He pulled a length of fabric out from inside the breast pocket of his jacket and draped it over my head like a veil.

"Proceed," he said.

I placed my hand against the wood and pushed. It was warm to the touch. It swung softly open and I stepped through. The door closed behind me, and the chanting stopped.

The room was a cocoon of dark silence, suffused with a blue light that shone dimly through a series of gauzy panels that hung down from the ceiling. It was a transparent maze. As I passed through the panels, the silky fabric shushed across my shoulders.

Someone whispered behind me. "Closer."

I spun around. No one was there. I thought of Her voice—the terrifying things I had just witnessed inside Mega-Watts—and shivered. I had to make it through this without a meltdown. It might be the most important thing I'd ever done.

Another whisper came, more insistent. "Closer."

It sent me spinning. I searched the darkness, feeling the weight of eyes on me. I was being watched. Up ahead, through the layers, I could see a heavy black curtain. I was pretty sure I knew what it was supposed to be—a kind of dramatic metaphor for the veil between the Inner Eye and the mortal world. The Fellowship wasn't afraid of going heavy on the symbolism.

As I got closer, I could see that there was a small gap between the opaque panels, like the not-quite-drawn curtains of a puppet show. There was a kneeler on the floor in front of it. I stood there examining the curtain, wondering what I was supposed to do next. A hand clamped down on my shoulder. I practically jumped out of my skin. A black-shrouded figure was standing behind me. It pressed me firmly downward, pushing me to kneeling.

"Kneel before the veil and place your right hand inside it, palm up. Behold the first mystery," the figure said. His voice was deeper than when I'd first heard it five years ago, but it had a rasp to it that was impossible to forget. Hayes Cantor was unforgettable on multiple levels. I wished his face wasn't covered—I was curious to know if he lived up to my memories. The deep brown eyes, the lips that quirked up to one side when he smiled…

I had to force myself back to concentration. Of all the times to be thinking about boys, now wasn't one of them.

Gingerly, I placed my hand into the gap in the curtain. Even though it was mostly theatrics, the effect was unsettling, like when they make you touch a bowl of peeled grapes in a haunted house and tell you it's eyeballs. Hayes's hand remained steady on my shoulder. It was oddly reassuring, like he wanted me to know that I wasn't alone. From the other side, a palm lowered down on top of mine.

"This is the way we know one another," Hayes said from over my shoulder. At the same time, the hand within the veil curved my pinky and ring fingers in toward my palm. My thumb, forefinger, and middle finger remained extended, making some kind of sign. Recognition flashed through my brain—I had caught glimpses of Fellowship members making this symbol out of the corner of my eye, but before now I'd never thought anything of it. Then the hand inside the veil straightened my fingers, so that my hand made a flat plane once again.

"Show the sign of the Fellowship," Hayes said.

At first I didn't know what he wanted. Then I curled my pinky and ring fingers in, making the symbol once more behind the veil.

"The first mystery is complete," a voice whispered from the other side. It was impossible to tell if it was male or female. The obscured stranger straightened my fingers again and slipped a band onto my ring finger. I knew it was the one the General had shown me. "Pass through the veil and move to your new life as an initiate of the Fellowship."

The pressure of Hayes's hand on my shoulder disappeared and I stood up. I turned around, but he was already gone, his black robe melting into the shadows. Disappointment stabbed through me, but I followed the instruction and pushed through the curtain.

I was now in an empty room with a single candle burning. The General was standing there, the flicker of the candle below casting a long shadow over his eye-patch. He looked almost ghoulish.

"You've made me proud tonight," he said.

"Thank you for giving me the chance," I said.

"Did you find Hayes a competent second?"

I nodded. "Is he still here? I'd like to thank him."

"No. Seeing your second after a Rite is bad luck."

My heart sank, but being here with my father more than made up for it.

"The Inner Eye has spoken to you tonight, Harlow; may it bring you Inner Peace," the General said.

If the voice that spoke to me was my Inner Eye, then it

wasn't going to give me peace of any kind. And if it wasn't, then my Inner Eye was a lie and so was everyone else's. But the only thing that mattered in that moment was that the General was proud of me.

"Thank you, father," I said.

My voice cracked. I choked back the tears that were pooling in my eyes. For the first time in a long time, I felt loved, like I mattered to him.

"Harlow, are you okay?" he asked.

"There's something I need to tell you," I said. The words tumbled out before I even knew what was happening. "I hear a voice."

The General stiffened. "What did you say?"

"I hear Her speaking to me. Saying terrible things. Showing them to me." The words were like a weight lifting. My father would tell me it was okay—he would help me make it right.

Something sparked in the General's eye. His entire demeanor transformed; it was like watching a grizzly rise up on its hind legs and roar. He grabbed me by the arm, hard.

"What did she show you?" he demanded.

"People dying," I whispered, confused by his reaction.

He backed away, first one step and then another. An all-over body shake transformed him from raging predator to cowering prey.

"How long have you been communicating with her?"

"With who?" I asked.

My father was white as a geisha. He looked legitimately frightened. Reaching his hand back, to find the door I could now see partially obscured in the darkness, he lost his balance and toppled backward onto the floor. I rushed over and reached out to help him, but he crab-walked away from me like I was the Grim Reaper come to claim my next victim.

"Dad?" I heard my voice reaching out from the ghost of my seven-year-old self. It had been years since I'd called the General that.

"You're not my little girl." His words slapped me across the face. My ears rang as if they'd been boxed. "You're an abomination."

A rogue wisp of dark hair broke free from his gel-slicked head and a bead of sweat slid down his forehead. He'd never before looked weak to me, but it was as if the man had been sucked out from inside his suit.

"Watchers! Watchers! Get her out of here!"

Watchers paratroopered in and strong-armed me like they were apprehending a terrorist.

"Sir?" The one in charge helped my father off the floor and awaited instructions.

I held my breath. What would happen next? Would he sever me right here and now?

"Take her back to the hotel," he commanded. "Lock her in her room."

They dragged me out. My heels scraped across the marble floor as I struggled to go to him, to come up with something that would take us back to five minutes before. The General wouldn't look at me. He ran a shaking hand through his thinning hair. He no longer seemed larger-than-life.

The sunrise finished just as we got back to the hotel.

Everything felt upside down. The Watchers pushed me into my room and shut the door behind me. I could hear the squawk of their radios outside, which meant there was no chance of leaving. As if I had anywhere left to go. I crawled into bed, too emotionally and physically exhausted to take off my boots much less try to decode my father's reaction. I looked at the gold ring around my finger, which now felt like a shackle, and floated numbly to sleep.

In my dreams, the voice and I marched side by side. She was next to me, in front of me, above me, inside me. When I turned to identify the footfalls pounding in our wake, I saw an army of eyeless followers: dry sockets unseeing, hollow bodies marching on. They trailed behind us, a battalion of mottled corpses clipping along in perfect time. They spilled out of a forgotten temple clogged with vines, through a million identical doorways, deep into the jungle of my subconscious.

All at once, there was a girl standing right in front of me. She looked exactly like me.

I see you, she whispered over and over.

The more she said it, the closer I drifted toward consciousness. Finally, I realized that I wasn't staring at a girl. I was standing in front of a full-length mirror, whispering *I see you* to my reflection. And my reflection was smiling back.

ALL THE WAY TO CHINA

My tongue tasted like dry lint, and it felt like my teeth were wearing tiny individual fur coats. Anxiety crawled across my skin, then receded by an inch. I turned away from the mirror, rubbing my hand over my eyes. I was only sleepwalking. It was just a bad dream.

My mind turned first to Adam, then to the General. I needed to sort things out with both of them. After the way I'd been ejected from the temple, I was surprised I wasn't already on a one-way express back to Twin Falls. Or worse.

Would the Patriarch sever his own daughter? Ministry children had been made dead in the eyes of the Fellowship before, but I always assumed those rules didn't quite apply to me. But last night, my father was genuinely afraid of me. Like I was a mortal threat. It was almost as if he could see Her inside of me. As if he knew Her somehow.

I popped the top off my new stash of extra-strength Subdueral and crammed a handful in my mouth. Falling apart wasn't going to get me out of this. I reached for the cell on my nightstand to call Dora. The screen was black, battery dead. Freaking perfect.

A sharp rap at the door bolted me upright. I looked around for someplace to hide, the insane thought that I could still find a way out of this mess scrambling my brain.

"Get up, lazy!" Dora yelled. She had the gravely tone of an absolute angel.

I leaped to answer the door.

Dora had chopsticks stuck through the bun in her hair and eyeliner swept dramatically out from the corners of her eyes. Her faded red T-shirt said *China: a really big country with a lot of people.*

She surveyed my disaster of a room.

"Dude, the China express leaves in fifteen minutes and you look like moo goo gai poo. Did you oversleep or what?"

She pushed past me and started to slam things into my suitcase haphazardly. I looked left and right down the hallway, expecting a Watcher to show up any minute.

Nothing.

After Tokyo, the next stop on our tour-de-force was Beijing. China was VisionCrest's closest ally in the East, where with few exceptions the Fellowship was regarded with reverence and respect. Three decades earlier, an anonymous man simply called the Unknown Rebel had stopped the advance of a column of Chinese military tanks following a bloody massacre of government protestors. That event was the tipping point that ultimately led to the downfall of an oppressive dictatorship; China became the most democratic country in the world, and one of the most welcoming to VisionCrest. The fate of an entire country once rested on that silent rebel's delicate shoulders; it was easy to imagine that in some parallel universe, it could have turned out very differently.

In exchange for their support of the Fellowship, China's highest-ranking government officials were ordained as Sacristans and shared in VisionCrest's profits. Many other eastern countries followed suit, but China remained the most powerful of all Ministry satellites. While no country could boast a VisionCrest compound to rival the headquarters in Twin Falls, Beijing came close.

The crumpled itinerary on my nightstand said we were leaving at 11:30 a.m. sharp. Was it remotely possible I wasn't going to be punished?

"Some help here, Messy Marvin?"

"I didn't think I would be coming," I said, dazed. I wasn't sure if it was disbelief or the Subdueral working its black magic.

"What do you mean, you didn't think you were coming?" Dora countered. "We've only been talking about pork buns non-stop for, like, the past week. This is our time, baby! Get moving!" Then she gave me a sharp look that said *I know something's wrong, but you want me to pretend everything's normal, so I'm playing along. For now.*

She was right. This wasn't the time to question my luck. I grabbed a pair of jeans and threw them on, along with a hoodie covered in sewn-on patches of punk bands I loved.

Adam had made it for me back when things were normal. Maybe it would make him remember who I really was.

"I saw the General after we came back last night," I said.

A steely glint of determination flashed in Dora's eyes. It said that I was not going home if she had anything to say about it.

"I don't want to know what happened." She waved her hand in the air. "I just want you to pack up and get your butt down to the lobby. You're not going anywhere but China."

"But—"

She put her hand up to my mouth. "But nothing. I cannot do this trip—this *life*—without you. I refuse. So until you're not, you're here. Now let's go."

There wasn't really any arguing with that. I stuffed the last of my things into an oversized handbag. Dora put my Jackie O glasses on my face.

"There—VisionCrest royalty, ready to rock."

It was impossible to be morose around Dora. I held my breath as we exited the elevator into the lobby, half-expecting Watchers to descend on me as we entered the crowd of Ministry kids. My classmates were buzzing like hornets ready to flee the hive, looking more motley than usual since our VisionCrest uniforms (gray slacks, oxford shirts, ties, and official sweaters for the boys; navy-and-green tartan skirts, oxford shirts, and cardigans for the girls) were optional on travel days. There were Watchers milling around looking bored, but none of them took any more note of my presence than usual.

True to form, Queen Mercy was right at the center of the

action, ordering her consorts around. The way she acted, you would think she was the Patriarch's daughter, not me. She gestured toward the matching set of Louis Vuitton luggage at her side as the scrawny son of a lower-rank Sacristan scrambled to collect it under his arms.

Through the crowd, Adam appeared. His hair was messy and he was wearing an Operation Ivy T-shirt under a fitted gray blazer. My heart clenched. His eyes met mine for a split second. Then he looked away and walked straight to Mercy, leaning over and whispering something in her ear. A smile graced her face that would have made even Mother Theresa weep with jealousy. Then he leaned down and kissed her. He looked up at me, making sure I saw. It was a clear message— *stay away*.

Dora saw it too. "Darling, the world is your oyster. You're going to pry it open and steal its pearl, and no silly boy is going to stop you," she said. It was the Dora version of a pep talk.

I watched Adam and Mercy for a moment longer, unable to tear my eyes away from the train wreck. Mercy tucked her arm inside Adam's and snuggled up against him. He smoothed his hand over the back of her hair. I struggled not to let my knees buckle beneath me.

Dora pulled me along behind her, dragging me toward the waiting buses.

Sayonara, Tokyo. You sucked.

———

The flight to Beijing consisted of me scrunching between Dora and Stubin, the unlikely lovebirds, and trying to disappear. There was no sign of the General's Learjet in the hangar when we boarded our private plane. He must have already headed to China.

Dora insisted on the window so she could keep an eye on the engines "for air safety," and Stubin insisted on the aisle because of his "claustrophobia disorder." No amount of protesting could convince either of them that putting me in a teen-crush sandwich met the standard of cruel and unusual punishment.

I was in no mood to argue, so I succumbed and melted into the thirteen square inches that separated me from a complete mental breakdown. I suspected that Dora was distracting me from what was happening five rows in front of us. Namely, Mercy and Adam sitting with their heads tipped together. As if I wasn't tracking their every move from the corner of my eye.

I considered what it would be like to spill the details of the past day to Dora, in a world where Stubin wasn't butting in every five seconds. Secrets are the ultimate tricksters—they beg not to be kept, promise to behave, but then, let loose upon the world, blaze a trail of mischief and misery. I decided I couldn't do it. The momentary relief of unburdening myself about the Rite would only lead to questions I was too afraid to answer.

On the upside, none of the adults on the plane so much as blinked an eye at me the entire flight. When we disembarked after landing, Brother Howard approached me. He was acting all chummy, the way he always did when he was trying to pump me for information about my father. He was a notorious social climber; if he spent half as much time on our lesson plans as he did on Ministry gossip, I would have my PhD in biochem by now.

"Hi, Harlow. So the Patriarch's attending to some unexpected business, eh?" he said.

"Unexpected business?" My entire body seized up at the mention of the General. I had been waiting for the other shoe-bomb to drop all day.

"I guess that must be why we're changing accommodations at the last minute. It's highly unusual for us to stay in the home of a Sacristan. Don't you agree?" he pressed.

We were supposed to be staying at my father's megamansion in the VisionCrest compound on the outskirts of Beijing. The Patriarch had his own place there, as he did at every compound. Sacristans would never normally be asked to entertain houseguests, especially high-ranking Ministry children from the Twin Falls headquarters. Brother Howard was right—it was strange.

"Uh, yeah. I guess." I played along, eager to get him off my case. It was a common assumption that I knew what the General did and why, but as usual I was as in the dark as everyone else. I had no idea what was going on.

"Excuse me, Brother Howard. I need to talk to Harlow alone for a minute," Dora interrupted, pulling me away by the arm. She looked back at him apologetically and stage whispered, "*Lady business.*"

Brother Howard turned five shades of prune and slunk away.

Where had my father gone? Did his unexpected business have something to do with what happened last night? Why were we staying in the home of a random Ministry official?

A shiver of dread whispered down my spine as we piled into a swarm of industrial-strength, unmarked molester vans. There were more reasons than just my personal ones for being afraid. Many Sacristans were fear-mongers grappling for greater power, and those in China were rumored to be the most corrupt of all. Without the Patriarch and his protections, I wondered if we were safe.

I'd strategically avoided being marooned in the same van as Adam and Mercy, so at least I had that going for me. If I saw another tender moment, I might scratch my own eyeballs out without any help from the crazy voice in my head.

The drive from the airfield to the compound was like traversing a maze. We drove quickly through side streets on the margins of Beijing's urban sprawl, block after block of high-rise apartment buildings that wore pollution like a funeral shroud.

At last, a snaking black driveway leading to the Vision-Crest compound came into view through the front window. The complex was guarded by a massive wrought-iron gate and two surly Watchers with earpieces. We passed through and wound our way up a lush hillside. The occupants of the increasingly massive houses were standing at the ends of their drives, solemnly watching and dropping on bended knee as we passed. It was unsettling.

Near the top of the hill, we reached a sprawling, white marble monstrosity surrounded by a massive wrought-iron fence with giant W's on it. The gates parted and we pulled in. There was only one house bigger than it, perched atop the hill. I figured that was my father's residence, where we ought to be staying.

Dora looked at me and raised her eyebrows. "Is it just me or is this super creepy? I liked the hotel in Japan way better."

All I could do was nod. Attendants ushered us into an entryway that was basically a five-story marble mausoleum. If Chairman Mao, former dictator of China, wasn't so busy being a wax sculpture entombed in Tiananmen Square, he would be chilling somewhere inside the hallowed halls of this house.

"The venerable Sacristan Wang welcomes you to his humble home," an elderly man in a tuxedo announced as we crowded through the doorway.

It was anything but humble. Of course, people who lived in Patriarchs' estates shouldn't throw stones. Sacristan Wang was impeccably dressed, with upturned sausage lips and tight-clipped bangs. I didn't recognize him, but he fit the Ministry part. A gold pin gleamed garishly from his lapel: the All Seeing Eye with a ruby pupil.

Ruby—the gemstone matched the level. Diamond was for Patriarch, emerald for Eparch, sapphire for Prelate, ruby for Sacristan. The All Seeing Eye pins were creepy in general, but the red ones seemed the most forbidding. It was the color of blood. The color of those who've tasted power and are ravenous for more.

The Sacristan's diminutive wife stood behind her husband's equally tiny frame, her eyes like two white marbles with black-pool centers. They were set deep in a catlike countenance that had endured more than one surgical experiment. Her pink Chanel skirt-suit perfectly offset the midnight line of her husband's tailored suit, and she seemed to be looking through our shifty VisionCrest herd rather than at it.

Cowering in their shadow was a slight girl of indiscriminate age. She could just as easily have been eight as twelve. She wore a bell-shaped dress the color of driven snow, which made her look like a tiny letter A, and there was a white satin blindfold across her eyes. Either it was a fashion statement for the blind or her parents were even more twisted than I feared. The General's missing eye had prompted more than one zealot to blind himself in imitation, but surely no one would inflict that upon their child. I immediately thought of my dream from the night before: an army of followers with dry socket eyes.

Brother Howard attempted a bow and said something in muffled Mandarin. He quivered visibly as Sacristan Wang fixed him with a contemptuous stare.

"*Xie xie.*" His wife beckoned to us, her voice as cultured as a petri dish.

"Welcome. This is my wife, Madam Wang, and my daughter, Mei Mei. I am Sacristan Wang, but you may call me Sacristan."

His voice had an air of entitlement that frightened me.

"Enjoy our humble home, but do not wander," his wife admonished. "Behave in a manner befitting of your station."

Roll out the red carpet, why don't you?

Sacristan Wang turned on his heel and clicked out of the room, his wife gliding behind him. Their tiny daughter shuffled in their wake, navigating the room just as easily as if she could see its every detail.

Thus dismissed, Brother Howard split us into two groups, boys and girls. His hands trembled as he motioned us to opposite sides of the staircase. We were politely led in divided lines up the split staircase by house servants.

Dora poked a sharp elbow into my side. "Why do I feel like I'm on a death march?" she snarked.

It might have been funny if I wasn't afraid it might be true. The feeling that I was marching toward something terrible had only grown stronger. I was certain that something wasn't right.

We were parceled out into rooms based on gender and station. The Wangs' home seemed to be bigger than the Imperial Palace. For a Sacristan, he certainly had done well for himself—this type of extravagance was normally reserved for Prelates and above. During the van ride, I'd overheard Brother Howard saying that Sacristan Wang was a virologist and the head of VisionCrest's biolabs, which were located here in China. That would explain the excessive wealth above his station—he was a powerful asset. Ostensibly the labs were doing benevolent things like searching for the cure to cancer, but looking at Sacristan Wang, I suspected there might also be a dark side to that effort.

Not surprisingly, Dora and I were placed with Mercy—it would be unseemly for the daughters of the Patriarch and his two highest-ranking Prelates to stay with lesser mortals. Our room looked like the aftermath of an explosion at the Hostess Sno Ball factory. Madam Wang appeared to have a nauseating affection for the color pink.

"Worst slumber party ever," Mercy complained, heaving her luggage onto one of the frilly twin beds.

Dora looked at me and mimed a gag behind Mercy's back. Mercy spun around with a carefully honed glare. The indignity of bunking with us was scribbled all over her face, and the feeling was mutual.

"We're pretty excited about staying with you too, princess," Dora said.

Mercy rolled her eyes and mumbled under her breath, "Losers."

The stress of the last few days, the thought of Adam kissing her, overcame me. I stepped up close. "Shut up," I said through gritted teeth.

Dora looked at me, shocked but delighted. Mercy froze in the act of unzipping her suitcase. It took every ounce of my self-restraint to not continue further.

Inwardly, I cringed. The last thing I wanted was her reporting back to Adam that I was being mean. It just made me seem jealous. Like I was. Like he obviously wanted me to be, for some reason I couldn't understand.

Dora jabbed her finger in the direction of Mercy. "You know, I don't know what it is, but she's really starting to grow on me."

Mercy twirled around and jumped toward Dora. "Screw you—"

An ominously official knock at the door interrupted what was about to be a full-on girlfight. We all paused, mid-hackle-raise, and stared at each other.

None of us wanted to answer it.

Madam Wang flung open the door, her calculating cat-eyes staring us into submission. Her reflection gleamed from every mirrored surface in the hallway behind her, giving the impression that she was leading an army. She zeroed in on me with laserlike precision.

"Sister Wintergreen. The honor of your company is required in the tea room."

I shook all the way down to my toes. Was this the part where they carted me away and I never came back?

Then, for some unknown reason, Madam Wang turned her stare on Mercy. "Not long for you," she said, her eyes skewering a trembling Mercy.

Then she turned, clicking a retreat across the smooth marble. The three of us stood frozen like wax sculptures of ourselves.

"Crap sandwich," Dora whispered.

I had no choice but to follow Madam Wang. As the daughter of the Patriarch, it was my responsibility to represent the Fellowship. Maybe meeting with Madam Wang would help me find out why we were here, and where my father had gone so suddenly. I took a deep breath and hurried after her retreating footsteps, which were fast fading into the recesses of the labyrinth.

A wind whispered at my back.

Purity.

Oh no. Not now.

CREEPY TEA

Madam Wang dropped a sluggish green ball the size of her fist into a crystal decanter of steaming water. She stubbed out the glowing end of a miniature cigar in a jade ashtray and leveled her feline stare right between my eyes.

I was seated in a lacquered chair directly across from her and her whisper of a daughter, the sharp edge of the chair biting its way into the back of my thighs. A bone china teacup balanced precariously on my knees. Between us, on the table, the mossy bulb dropped like a stone to the bottom of the decanter. It began to writhe as if in pain, spike-tipped green spindles slowly unfurling from its core. Next to it was a tray of blood-red fruits of various shapes and sizes, and a razor-sharp paring knife.

Purity. Promise.

I could swear the hissing voice came from the drowning mass, snaking up from the steam. I'd taken enough Subdueral to sedate an angry rhinoceros, but still Her voice was back and stronger than ever—almost as if Madam Wang herself was amplifying it. The crazy train was officially off the tracks.

Madam Wang's glare did not waver.

I wasn't sure where to look: at my hostess, who appeared to be staring through me; at her daughter, whose head was tilted toward me despite the blindfold across her eyes; or at the creepy talking plant, expanding in the decanter. Pass the crumpets, please.

Vengeance.

I sat up straighter and pinched my teacup tight. The voice was saying things it hadn't before. The squirming mass looked alive, sprouting an appendage from its center that struggled toward the water's surface.

Death.

The stalk exploded into two luminous blossoms—one red and one white—which broke through the liquid's surface. The teacup rattled on my knee.

"It's chrysanthemum." Madam Wang pointed one opalescent nail in my direction. "You have an abundance of yang."

If yang was some kind of mental defect, then yes. I most definitely had too much of it. This was feeling less like tea and more like some multicultural version of *The Stepford Wives.*

A lithe girl in a long red robe tied with an elaborately embroidered swathe of silk padded into the room on velvet slippers. Her silky black hair was coiled on top of her head in two hollow rolls and she was carrying some kind of chime. I slipped a tablet of Subdueral under my tongue. The girl struck the chime with a tiny metal wand, and another identically robed girl appeared to pour the tea.

This new girl picked up the decanter and poured Madam Wang first, then walked around the table to pour me. I lifted my saucer off my lap to make it easier for her.

"Steady her hand," Madam Wang commanded, leaning forward in her chair.

The girl reached out to steady my hand. Squiggly white worms danced their way across my vision as her skin met mine.

An overwhelming urge to cause her suffering reared up inside me. It did not belong to me, it belonged to Her—the voice that owned me from the inside out and was more present in this room than She had ever been before.

Purity. Price. Promise.

My teacup dropped and shattered against the floor. I stood, facing the girl as if to dance. Madam Wang clutched Mei Mei's hand in hers. Mei Mei was shaking like voltage was running through her, and her lips moved as she whispered something over and over.

Was this really happening?

My hands lifted in front of me and clamped around the serving girl's swanlike neck. Boils rose up to meet my touch. My fingers bit into the softness of her flesh, my nails ripping their way across her skin. Tender, blistered flesh ribboned away like tissue paper.

No. Stop, I screamed inside. But my movements were not my own.

The girl twitched and blood spilled across her lips. Dribbled down her chin.

My hand squeezed around her throat, not listening to my desperate command to release. The girl's lips tinted purple.

Kill. Maim. Suffer.

The girl's eyes went wide. I snatched the paring knife off of the fruit plate. It slid across the padded flesh of my thumb with a *shink*. It was perfect.

Purity. Price.

Every inch of my consciousness fought my hand as it moved toward the soft white of her eye. The blade met juicy white flesh, carving into it. The wound gaped. Blood sluiced across her pitch-black iris.

Vengeance mine.

Wedging the blade into the wound, I dug into the spongy tissue like a grapefruit.

Outer blindness, inner sight. Betrayal in the violet light.

The vision raged. I was outside my body and trapped inside it, all at once.

My arm levered down hard, forced by something other than myself, softness giving way to steel. The crystal decanter fell from the girl's hands and exploded in a fantastic array of shards that went skittering across the polished marble, the chrysanthemum blossoms plopping roundly to the floor.

From somewhere beyond the vision, Madam Wang whispered, "Isiris, is it you?"

"It is."

I heard myself say the words, but the voice was not mine. Every molecule within me rebelled.

"No!" I yelled.

Abruptly, everything reversed itself. The decanter reversed

its fall, the girl's eye came back together, the blossoms floated menacingly on the water. All was as it had been moments before. I sat, the empty teacup shaking on my knee. The serving girl poured my tea and shuffled silently out of the room.

It had all been in my head, as usual. But I was certain I'd spoken those words, and although Madam Wang's demeanor remained unchanged, I knew she'd seen what happened when the girl touched my hand. It was almost as if she'd invited the voice into the room. Fear uncoiled like a snake and slithered up my back. Madam Wang was looking at me with half-lidded eyes.

"Who's Isiris?" I croaked.

"I don't understand the question." She sipped her tea matter-of-factly.

"You just said, 'Isiris, is it you?'" I insisted.

"No, I did not. Your tea is getting cold," she replied. "The chrysanthemum will bring your yin in balance."

I sipped the perfumed concoction. We were apparently playing chess and it was my move. If Madam Wang had just spoken to the voice I'd been fighting—and failing—to control, then she was the only person who might be able to help me. Mei Mei sat silently at her mother's side, unmoving.

I was used to playing the part of dutiful daughter, and could fake self-assurance in even the tensest of situations. The General had friends in high places—high, strange places—but there was something ominous afoot here. I could feel it.

"Why are we staying here and not with the Patriarch?" I asked.

"The Ministry has its reasons, I presume." Madam Wang's

lips pinched together like two carefully botoxed slashes of Chinese calligraphy. If I had to guess, I would say they spelled out "creepy."

Her daughter hadn't moved an inch. If I didn't know better, I might think she was a life-size doll. There was something unsettling about not being able to see her eyes.

"When is your birthday, Sister Wintergreen?" Madam Wang asked.

The little girl broke in, her voice tinkling like wind chimes. "On the ninth. It just passed."

"How did you know that?" I asked her.

Madam Wang clamped a hand around her daughter's knee. The girl didn't flinch, but fell silent.

"The ninth day," Madam Wang said. "Like I said, you have too much yang."

"Where is my father?" I countered.

She kept her cat-eyes fixed squarely on me but didn't say anything.

"You want to know why you're here?" she asked.

"Yes," I said.

She ran a finger absently around the rim of her teacup. "It is an honor to have the daughter of the Patriarch in our home. One he would want you to respect, since he himself cannot be here with us."

The subtext was unmistakable. She knew where he was.

"Where is he?" I whispered.

Madam Wang's thin-painted eyebrows rode up a millimeter. "You won't be seeing him for a while. Now let me have your leaves." She thrust her hand across the table.

My stomach dropped.

"Excuse me?"

"Your tea leaves." Mei Mei's voice was like wind whistling through a cave. "She wishes to read them. Summon your spirit."

My spirit? Now we were having a seance? My father would be livid—VisionCrest doctrine expressly forbid the idea of worshipping spiritual beings of any kind. He always said God was inside each of us and there were no such things as spirits; the way he said it always made me think he believed the opposite but desperately wanted not to.

"I don't think the Patriarch would approve of—"

"Give them to me. What the Patriarch would approve of is not my concern, nor is it yours. You have bigger things to worry about." Madam Wang flicked her wrist in impatience.

Now I was sure that something very bad was going on. If there was a spirit to be summoned, it would be the one inhabiting my head. She'd already shown up once at this tea party, and I wasn't eager to have Her back. But maybe this was my way through to Her. To find out what She wanted.

I handed my cup over.

Madam Wang bent over the dregs of my creepy tea, her eyes narrowing.

"Hmm."

I waited for her to elaborate, but for several long minutes she just continued to stare at the cup.

"I see the mirror image of your soul. In it lies your greatest source of power. The voice you hear is your own. She plagues you because she wants you to return." She looked at me expectantly, as if anticipating my reaction to this.

My stomach flipped. "Return where?" I asked.

She snorted. "To the beginning, where bones will turn to blood and ashes."

The words spooked me. Bones, blood, ashes—even if Madam Wang was nothing more than a crazy old zealot, it sounded eerily like a description of my visions.

I stood. "I'd like to go back to my room now."

"There are people you value. It would be unwise to discuss this with them. The girls will show you back."

The fear that rose within me at her threat to Dora and the others was so powerful I thought I might throw up.

Madam Wang stood across from me and tugged on her daughter's hand. Just before they evaporated through the square black doorframe, she turned her cat-eyes back on me one last time.

"Every broken promise exacts a price," she said.

A chill ran down my back. Madam Wang had most certainly heard the voice, and now she'd disappeared, the clicks of her shoes fading into some obscure inner sanctum. I set my saucer down, trembling. Madam Wang also knew where my father was, of that I was certain.

I wanted to get us all the hell out of China, but it wasn't that simple. Even if it was possible for me to leave, I couldn't leave without finding out where the General had gone.

Another servant girl, dressed identically to the first two, materialized and struck the chime. She motioned with her arm for me to follow her out.

"Sister Wintergreen." Mei Mei's voice startled me. She was standing in the doorway. Had she heard me?

"Yes?" I turned back to see her head cocked ever-so-slightly in my direction. Her miniature hand rose to her blindfold and slid it up from her face.

There were empty sockets where her eyes should be. Just like in my dream.

I recoiled.

"May your Inner Eye reveal your Inner Truth."

My stomach churned. The requisite response froze in my throat. I scurried after the servant girl, desperate to see Dora and Adam and even Mercy, to know that they were okay.

The weight of Mei Mei's empty sockets chased me down the hall.

PET SOUNDS

I burst into our room, my body humming with the unpleasant aftershocks of the vision. I'd tried to dial my father's emergency cell on my way there, the number I was forbidden to use except in the most dire of circumstances. The one he promised to always answer no matter what.

It went straight to voicemail.

I had no idea how Madam Wang knew what I experienced, what exactly her cryptic statements were threatening, or whether something had actually happened to my father. I had a terrible feeling about it all, and for the first time, the thought of abduction wormed into my head. It would be nearly impossible to kidnap the Patriarch, but then again, there hadn't been many Watchers around when I visited him the other night in the hotel.

Maybe there'd been some other crisis and my father was pawning us off on the Wangs while he figured out how to handle it. Maybe Madam Wang was just an eccentric in need of a little medication and I'd just had an ill-timed vision. Still, as much as I wanted to rationalize it, it felt like a lot of coincidences.

In the room, Dora was sitting on her bed and Stubin was next to her. Adam and Mercy sat facing them, Mercy's arm draped casually across Adam's knee. Even the sharp tug of jealousy couldn't blunt the ten-ton weight of dread that had settled in my chest. I had to protect them. All of them. And right now that meant acting like everything was normal—there was no way of knowing how serious Madam Wang's threat about not telling them was, and I wasn't going to take any risks.

Stubin was talking animatedly about the Beach Boys again, and as usual only Dora looked interested. The predictability of the scene was comforting.

"I mean, *Pet Sounds* was completely revolutionary. Not only is the layering of vocal harmonies earth-shattering, but the use of classical counterpoint is nothing less than genius."

"Brian Wilson is a god," I interjected.

All four of them turned to look at me.

Stubin nodded so vigorously I thought his head might fly off. "Exactly! That's what I've been telling these guys."

"Where have you been? We've been dying of boredom," Dora said lightly, while the heavy look she gave me asked if I was okay.

I nodded almost imperceptibly. "With Madam Wang."

"Speak for yourself, Dora. *We* haven't been bored." Mercy's hand tightened around Adam's knee.

He looked at me, his leg jiggling nervously. The crease in

his brow showed worry. "You shouldn't have gone by yourself," he said.

This took me by surprise. I'd expected indifference, but instead it was like he knew something wasn't right with the Wangs.

"I'm pretty used to being by myself," I said.

His gaze was unfathomable. He said nothing, his leg bouncing double-time.

Unable to stand the tension, Dora broke in. "Okay, how about you take a quick time-out, right here next to me?" She elbowed Stubin, and they slid over to make room.

I took a deep breath. If it killed me, I had to try to act like everything was relatively normal. Normal for me, at least.

"So what did she want?" Dora asked. "Spill."

"Nothing, really. Madam Weirdo just wanted to welcome me. Over a cup of 'Feed me, Seymour' tea." I shrugged. I could feel Adam's stare but refused to meet it.

"Tea is interesting, but you know what's really interesting? The Beach Boys. Am I right or am I right?" Stubin raised his hand to give Adam a high-five.

Halfheartedly, Adam high-fived him. I sort of loved him for humoring Stubin, even if I officially hated him right now.

Dora raised a brow at me. She knew something was up. I looked down at my shoes. Dora was great at reading my signals—the first moment we were alone she'd be all over me for more info. Adam's eyes tracked every detail of our interaction.

"Well, I'm not sitting here for another hour. I bet Sacristan Wang has some freaky Chinese water torture boards hidden in one of these rooms." Mercy slipped her hand into Adam's. "There's uncharted territory to be discovered."

"No!" I cried out.

A grin of triumph slid across Mercy's face. She thought I was objecting out of jealousy.

"That's a bad idea. I don't think the Wangs want us roaming the halls," Stubin agreed.

Mercy stepped over our legs, Adam reluctantly in tow. "I think we can handle it."

I looked up and met Adam's eyes for a split second. His forehead was pinched. "Are you seriously okay?" he asked.

"I appreciate your sudden concern for my welfare, but I'm fine," I insisted. "Stubin's right, though. It's a bad idea to go wandering around."

Mercy snorted, still assuming I was groveling for attention. If it had to look like I was jealous, then so be it. There were more important things than my pride.

Tugging on Adam's hand, Mercy sighed impatiently. "Come on, baby."

Baby. There it was again.

"Don't go," I said.

Indecision passed over Adam's features. I could see him wavering, seesawing between wanting to make sure I was really okay and wanting to stay angry at me for what happened at MegaWatts. A kernel of hope bloomed inside me.

"I need the distraction," he said, shifting his gaze to the floor.

The bloom wilted. I had to find a way to get back through to him, especially if the situation kept deteriorating.

Adam followed Mercy out the door. I considered jumping up and trying to physically stop them, but I recognized the determined set of Adam's jaw. There was no stopping him when he wanted something. Just ask Mercy.

It only took a second for Dora to snap into mega distraction mode. "So, did the subject of plastic surgery come up? Madam Wang must have had, like, twenty-eight eye lifts." She pulled the skin on her face back with the palms of her hand.

"Is their daughter totally blind? She'd be a great poster child for VisionCrest—I bet she's way in tune with the Inner Eye," Stubin chimed in.

Dora hit him in the arm. I shivered.

"What? She would be," he protested.

"Hey, Stubin? Would you mind giving us a few minutes alone?" Dora asked. "I kind of need Harlow for a minute—you know, girl stuff."

Girl stuff: those magic words sent boys of any age scampering. It was Dora's weapon of choice.

"Yeah, sure, of course, no problem," he stammered, his cheeks reddening. "I'll go burn you a CD of *Pet Sounds*. It'll change your life."

Stubin stumbled to his feet, unable to escape fast enough. He gave Dora an awkward one-armed hug and beelined to the door.

"Later skater," she shouted after him.

Later skater? I mouthed to her questioningly. She shrugged and got a loopy grin on her face. Man, this was dire.

"All right, sister. Park it and give me the 411." Dora patted the spot next to her on the bed.

I sat down and buried my face in my hands, then ran them back through my hair.

"Is this charades?" Dora asked. "Wait, don't tell me—exasperation station?"

"The Wangs' daughter isn't just blind. She doesn't have any eyes at all. Just empty sockets," I whispered.

"Shut the front door."

"No kidding. If I tell you more, you can't repeat any of it. To anyone. Swearsies."

"Swearsies," she said.

"I think Madam Wang might be a little mental. She told me I had too much yang and then tried to read my tea leaves." I wanted to tell her more, but didn't want to put her in danger.

"Like, Psychic Sue style?" she asked.

"Yeah, exactly."

Dora chewed on the inside of her cheek. Then she said, "You're not telling me everything."

My best friend knew me too well. I didn't want to lie to her.

"No, I'm not. And I can't. All I can say is, I'm pretty sure she was threatening me."

"Why would she do that?"

"I don't know yet. But I think it has something to do with my father."

"It *is* weird that he left us. Wasn't the whole point for us to be his adorable entourage? Show the entire world that everything is perfectly normal in VisionCrest land?"

I nodded.

Once again, I considered telling Dora everything. The

Rite. The voice. The visions. The uncontrollable way I fantasized about digging the sight and the soul out of innocent people, no matter how hard I fought not to. All of it.

Dora gathered me into a hug. The secret stayed locked in its cage and the moment passed.

"It's the Violet Hour somewhere in the world," she said. "Do you want to meditate together? It might make you feel better."

The difference in our beliefs had never come between us, and the fact that it hadn't spoke volumes. We respected each other and loved each other, no matter what. I thought about her offer, and was surprised to find that it sounded kind of soothing.

"I would love that, actually," I said.

We got down on our knees and steepled our hands over the beds.

"It's just not right, D. Us being here, the General leaving, Madam Wang—the whole thing," I whispered.

"You know what I think? That woman is one microdermabrasion short of a lobotomy, true, but you're overtired and stressing yourself *way* too hard lately. You feel me?" Dora put her head up and looked me hard in the eye. "Everything is fine. Swizzle Stick. Say it with me."

"Everything is fine."

"And?"

"Swizzle Stick."

Dora began the humming incantations of the Violet Hour meditation. I wanted to find solace, but I couldn't quiet my mind. Everything wasn't Swizzle Stick, and there was a sneaking feeling twisting its way through my guts that we were about to find out just how not Swizzle Stick it really was.

I gasped awake in the middle of the night, an iron fist of panic gripping my heart. The bedroom had an eerie glow. It was silent except for the soft moaning sounds Mercy made in her sleep, as if her conscience awoke in the night to cry for release.

A shuffle sounded outside our door. Every muscle in my body froze in place, as if that might protect me from whatever dark shadow was blocking the light of the door crack.

A palm beat against the door—*swap, swap*. Someone was out there. And it was as if they knew I was awake; the soft beat was barely audible. I wanted to fake sleep and pretend this wasn't happening.

Swap. Swap.

Dora's leg thrashed in her bed and her glasses shmooshed up against the pillow. She was always forgetting to take them off before going to sleep. Other than that, nobody stirred.

What was the worst it could be? Madam Wang offering me more tea? Adam coming to apologize for dropping Mercy off at our room past midnight, her hair messed up and cheeks glowing?

Swap. Swap.

Whoever it was, they weren't going away. I climbed out of bed and padded softly to the door. *Swap.*

The thump vibrated through the wood. It hadn't come

from the height where my hand was, I realized. It was much lower. Why would someone bang against the bottom of the—

Mei Mei. It had to be the Wangs' ghost of a daughter.

I turned the doorknob and heard the soft scrape of feet moving back. There was Mei Mei, looking up at me. Her eye sockets were uncovered and her black hair was a reverse halo over her head. Slipping into the hallway, I let the door click closed behind me.

Mei Mei held her hands out in front of her, silently, like she was reaching for me. There was something unnatural about her movements. Her mouth ticked nervously to the side. The salty scent of childish exertion mixed with the pungent odor of fear.

She began to mumble something, but I couldn't make out what it was. It sounded like her mouth was full of marbles. I crouched down, coming face-to-face with this little girl who seemed more like a caged and beaten animal than a human being.

"Mei Mei, what is it?" I asked softly.

She raised her finger, thin as a matchstick, and pressed it to the center of my forehead. I flinched, my forehead burning under her touch.

"Help," she said. The word sounded foreign in her mouth, as if she couldn't quite form the shape of it.

She was sleepwalking, as if in a trance.

Her finger stayed pressed against my forehead. I was afraid to even breathe, lest I send her scattering to the wind. Whatever she had come to tell me, it was important.

"Help who?" I asked.

She shook her head. I gently grabbed her hand and moved it away from my forehead, clasping it in my own in what I hoped was a gesture of comfort. "Mei Mei. Help what?" I whispered.

Her voice hitched. "Everyone will die."

It took a monumental effort for her to form these words, as if she were fighting every syllable. Her face went completely still. The two black craters where her eyes should be drilled into me. "She is coming. Bringing death. You see it. The virus."

A chill deeper than an empty well radiated through me. Mei Mei knew what I had seen. The visions. The boils, the vomiting of blood, the flesh falling from bone. Was it possible everything I'd seen was some grim portent of an impending future?

Mei Mei again struggled to form words, wrestling them out. It seemed she was trying to break out of the trance. What had the Wangs done to her?

"You hear her. Isiris wants you to return. You must fight or all will perish."

Isiris ... the unseen presence Madam Wang had addressed. My heart was a kickdrum in my chest. "Who is Isiris?" I whispered.

"You are not safe. None of us are."

I reached out to touch her shoulder. "Mei Mei. I'll help you. But you have to tell me who Isiris is."

She darted out from under my touch faster than a minnow, slipping into the pitch-dark hall. I tried to stop her, but she was vapor through my fingers. A far-off echo stirred in another part of the fathomless house. I leaped to my feet, sweating with panic and fear. I slipped back into the bedroom, frightened of what might happen next in the Wang Tea Shop of Terror. My pulse raced.

She is coming. Bringing death.

I leaned back against the door and exhaled, willing my body to slow down. Death. Just like the voice in my visions had promised.

You see it. The virus.

Madam Wang and Mei Mei knew about my visions. They were more than just freakozoidal followers of the Inner Eye. Sacristan Wang was a virologist, with the access and ability to create a bioweapon, but he wasn't the voice in my head. Madam Wang was threatening, but she wasn't the voice either. Was Isiris the key? Everything was getting worse.

A terrible momentum was gathering.

I snuck quietly back into the bedroom. My eyes roamed over the sleeping girls. Dora was still as a statue in her bed, completely undisturbed. But when I looked at Mercy, I could see her blue eyes shining, taking me in, evaluating. Making sure I saw her, but making no move to learn what was the matter. Just watching. Like a sentinel. Or a spy. The memory of her sneaking in just hours ago washed over me. All that time, she'd been somewhere in this house with Adam doing who knows what.

I felt ill. I went into the bathroom, flipping on the light and shutting the door behind me. Dark rings around my eyes reflected my own exhaustion back at me in the mirror over the sink.

You must fight or all will perish.

I turned the faucet on and splashed water over my face. When I stood up, my reflection was already there, as if I had never bent down. While I stood there, frozen, it turned and walked out of the open door of the bathroom, reflected behind me. I spun around, frightened. The door was closed. When I looked back at the mirror, it was just me, the closed bathroom door beyond me.

I hurried out of the bathroom and over to my bed, climbing under the covers in a panic. Mercy's eyes tracked me all the way. She was probably gleeful, plotting the ways she could break the news of yet another weird incident involving Harlow the Freak to Adam. Little did she know how right she was.

My hand reached for the Subdueral I'd slipped under my pillow when we first settled in the room, but I grasped at nothing. I patted around for a second. It was gone. I had a feeling the Wangs were behind it—not even Mercy was mean enough for that move.

Dora coughed. I knew that cough. It was an *I'm awake and I know you are too* Dora special. I turned my head and opened my eyes. I couldn't see hers through the reflection off her glasses, but I knew they were wide open. She slid her hand out from under her comforter and reached it out to mine. I took it, more grateful for the comfort than she could ever know.

I wasn't able to sleep—the crushing weight of impending doom would not fade to black. Holding Dora's hand made the uncertainty bearable until the tentative light of morning peeked through the window shades. Whatever the next day would bring, I knew with dread certainty it would be something awful.

GREAT WALL

Brother Howard burst in, sending all three of us flying from our beds. His hand was shielding his eyes so he wouldn't see anything illegal.

"Get up, girls! Today is a big day! It's not every day you get to see the Great Wall of Chi-i-i-ina!" He sang the word "China" like he was Julie Andrews on a mountaintop.

"It's not day. Not even close," Dora grumbled from her bed.

Brother Howard was undeterred. "Lots of people never even get the chance to see the wall. It's something you'll remember for the rest of your lives," he said reverently. "Not only that, but I have a very exciting project for you today. Something that will help awaken your inner eyes!"

Mercy and Dora groaned. Even the believers thought that VisionCrest should give it a break atop the Great Wall of China. I was too preoccupied with worrying about what the hidden motive behind this outing might be—a decoy, perhaps, broadcasting to the world that everything was business as usual with VisionCrest? The Wangs were calling the shots here, that much was for sure.

Mercy threw back her covers and rose like the Phoenix from her bed. It never ceased to amaze me how she could emerge fully formed and polished like some kind of beautiful robot.

I looked over at Dora, who had the impression of her glasses branded into her cheek and looked like she was housing a family of sparrows in her hair. She did a little *whoop-de-do* twirl with her finger.

"Go Team Inner Eye," she deadpanned.

The desperate urge to tell her about Mei Mei rose in my throat. I swallowed it down. Telling her any more risked endangering her further. I'd already put her at risk by telling her a tiny bit of what had happened with Madam Wackadoo.

"Be downstairs in forty minutes, girls. Forty, and not a second more."

Brother Howard tried to sound authoritative, but Mercy flicked him away with her hand as if she were swatting a gnat.

"It would be a lot easier to get ready without you here," she said.

Brother Howard turned puce and ducked his head. He scrambled out of the room like a whipped dog.

Sixty minutes later, the entire entourage of Ministry offspring was standing in the entryway of Casa de Wang. Brother Howard gave us a look but thought better of chastising us. The daughters of the Ministry elite could take a few extra minutes if they liked.

I combed through the bleary-eyed crowd of students, still evenly divided by boys and girls, for Adam. Stubin was standing across the room doing his usual limber-up leg-shaking maneuvers. His sweater today was Colonel Mustard yellow with a custom-embroidered VisionCrest logo. Stubin seemed to have a monopoly on uniform flair—while everyone else was rocking the boring rotation of predictable grays, greens, and blues, Stubin was always out there. I was also ninety percent sure he was rocking guyliner. Somewhere between Tokyo and Beijing, I'd grown kind of fond of him.

Stubin shifted an inch to the right and there was Adam, burning me with the intensity of his stare. His sleeves were rolled up and his tie a little askew under his navy sweater—recklessly beautiful, as always. I thought of Mercy sneaking in last night and looked away. It was time to forget him, or at least pretend to until I actually could.

"All right, everyone!" Brother Howard's over-enthusiastic bellow got the group's attention. "Today is going to be a wonderful day full of history and mystery as you work in pairs to discover one of the wonders of the world."

I knew what "work in pairs" meant—the Patriarch's daughter was always put with the next-highest-ranking offspring. My stomach clenched.

"Sister Wintergreen with Brother Fitz." Howard started yelling out names, organizing us for whatever harebrained project he'd cooked up.

I tried to remain stoic, as if being paired with Adam didn't send my heart into panicked palpitations. I could feel the sizzle of Mercy's laser beams on my back. At least he would be forced to finally talk to me.

One by one, disgruntled pairs were formed; it was like they'd designed it as a social experiment to see how quickly we would kill and eat each other at a national monument. Sacristan and Madam Wang were nowhere to be seen, nor was there any sign of Mei Mei. I wished we were sticking around so I could try to track her down for some daylight interrogation.

Brother Howard was calling off the last few names. A nervous cloud settled over me.

"So, are you going to call a truce or hang him by his ankles and hope a terracotta warrior reanimates and comes to finish him off?" Dora asked, reading the worry on my face.

"I don't know. What's your plan for keeping that Mercy-clone's manicured claws out of your Mansfield?" I jutted my chin toward Stubin, who was paired with a girl who was desperately trying to cop Mercy's style.

Dora cracked a sardonic smile. "No plan—look at him, he's miserable already."

"Totally Swizzle Stick, right?"

Dora put her arm around my shoulder, clearly pleased at my use of her trademarked term.

"You with Adam, me with Mercy. I'd say this is the second coming of the Anti-Swizzle. But we can pretend."

Brother Howard raised his VisionCrest flag and speared it into the air. Someone needed to burn that friggin' thing.

"Everyone grab a handout and head to the vans with your partner. Your project begins now and will take you on an adventure through history—and through your own inner eyes!"

My inner eyes were already rolling, but there was no evading the inevitable.

"Tear him up, Tiger," Dora said.

I took a deep breath and walked out to a van, not bothering to check if Adam was coming. He could follow me for once. I thought of my missing bottle of Subdueral. It practically guaranteed the voice and the visions were coming along for the ride, but the medicine hadn't been doing much to help lately anyway. I would just have to take my chances.

———————

Adam remained mute for the entire ride to Simatai, one of the oldest and steepest sections of the Great Wall, seventy-five miles outside of Beijing. We were squeezed into a van with nine Sacristan kids I didn't know very well, and four members of the Watch who worked for Sacristan Wang. The Ministry kids had been divided into three groups that were traveling to different sections of the wall, all with an unusually high number of Watchers. I guessed that whoever orchestrated this trip wanted to ensure maximum media exposure but wasn't taking any chances on an abduction. Mercy and Dora were sent to the section at Mutianyu, which left Adam and me on our own. My palms were sweating.

The handout Brother Howard gave us had a bunch of

"thought prompts," which was VisionCrest speak for questions that are supposed to help you learn something valuable about your Inner Self but really just read like lame high school essay questions: *This section of the Great Wall was begun in AD 550 under Emperor Wenxuan, who declared Buddhism to be the one true religion of his realm. Discuss why VisionCrest Fellowship is the one true religion of the realm in modern day.* Whatever.

Since I wasn't in a giant hurry to complete Brother Howard's bullshit assignment, Adam's silence was fine by me. There were a million things I wanted to say to him and exactly zero ways I could imagine saying them, and I needed to collect my thoughts. Through hooded lashes, Adam watched the landscape slide by as we began the twisting, turning ascent into the mountainous Chinese countryside.

When we arrived at the Great Wall two hours later, I still had no idea how I was going to begin the conversation. Adam slid the van door open and jumped out. I got out and stood next to him, both of us looking up at the massive mountain with the Great Wall snaking across its top. The other kids ambled ahead, eager to get in line for the gondola that ferried people up the mountainside. There were tourists everywhere, and several vans full of Watchers had arrived as reinforcements, dotting the crowd and unsuccessfully trying to blend in.

My eyes traced the snaking line of the rickety lift that ascended the face of the ridge. It was the only way to reach the wall itself, which looked like a series of tiny upended puzzle pieces from way down here.

"This is all so surreal, isn't it?" Adam asked.

As majestic as it was, I knew he wasn't just talking about the Great Wall. Being in the eye of the VisionCrest storm was like living inside a Dalí painting. After all my angst about how to start a conversation with him, he'd been the first to begin.

"And getting weirder all the time," I said.

"Sorry for being a jerk. Leaving you at the club like that was a dick move. I was scared." He still wasn't looking at me.

"Yeah. Me too."

His jaw clenched. "I'm not sure I'm ready to talk about it yet."

"I'm not sure I can wait for you to be ready."

That got his attention. He looked at me. There was something new in his face—respect, maybe.

"We better get going, then," he said.

We walked on in silence toward the base of the mountain. The multicolored gondolas were strung precariously from a cable, like a child's candy necklace. The cable snaked its way vertically up the mountain, and a vast chasm cut through the earth far below. I could imagine that if a gondola were to fall, it might keep on falling, straight to the center of the earth. The others in our group were way ahead of us now, climbing into the open-air cars. My knees quivered and my stomach did a queasy flop. Heights scared the hell out of me.

When we reached the front of the line, the attendant opened our door as the car rushed past. Adam jumped in and then held his hand out to me. I held my breath and jumped. The little half-door swung close and I glued myself to the hard plastic seat, facing Adam.

"You're as white as that sheet of paper you're clutching," he said with a smirk.

I barely registered that I was still holding the homework assignment in my hands. Bouncing by a thread over a bottomless abyss, I felt like that sheet of paper was holding me and not the other way around.

Adam put his hand on my knee, grounding me. "Breathe. Just focus on me."

I zeroed in on him, staring into his eyes like my life depended on it and not letting the tilting horizon in my peripheral vision filter in. The blue of his iris was slashed through with silver behind his dark lashes. Slowly, my hands and feet reattached to my body and the four-by-four world inside our little teacup slid into focus.

Now that I was back, the feel of his hand on my knee drew my attention. I could see the spot where his tattoos began their winding path, right at the wrist. I gently turned his forearm over to get a closer look. He didn't flinch.

There were two strings of numbers, stacked one on top of the other. The first line read 135738.6022, and the second 104213.2076. They were different from the other tattoos— solid black font, no florid colors or grandiose ornamentation.

"What do they mean?" I asked, sliding my thumb over his skin.

He pulled his hand lightly out of my grip. A fleeting look darkened his face. "Uh-uh. You first. What happened in the club?"

My heart tilted, and it wasn't because of the gondola.

I was standing on the edge of a cliff, and at that moment I knew I was going to jump.

"If I'm going to tell you things, they have to stay between us. I need to be sure I can trust you," I said.

He looked out over the horizon. I traced the line of his jaw as he clenched and unclenched it.

"You don't trust me?" His eyes returned to me, disarming.

I wanted to say that I did, but the truth was, I didn't know him anymore.

"I want to. I used to," I said. "Why won't you tell me about your tattoos?"

"Is this about Mercy?" he asked.

"This isn't about her. It's about us. How you've been, since you came back. How you've been to *me*."

"What do you want me to say, Harlow?" There was a wild look in his eyes.

"I just want you to tell me the truth. Why are you treating me like a stranger?"

"Do you want me to tell you about being blindfolded? About being beaten? About how I heard my mother crying in the cell next to me and couldn't do anything to help her? If I'm different, maybe it has nothing to do with you. Have you considered that?"

The words lacerated me. He'd clearly singled me out for punishment, but it had nothing to do with me at all? I shouldn't have given up so easily. I felt relieved and angry and ashamed all at the same time.

"I'm sorry. You're my best friend. I wanted to be there for you. I didn't think you wanted me to."

He ran his hand through his hair. There was a flush on his cheeks. I wanted to kiss him so badly.

"I didn't," he said.

My throat constricted.

"You want Mercy?" I managed.

"Does it matter?"

I bit back the tears. He wasn't denying it.

As crushing as this conversation was, what I needed was an ally, not a boyfriend. Adam had seen what I'd seen in the Tokyo club and things were getting worse. If there was something going on with the Wangs and my father, then I needed to make sure someone else was on guard for it.

"Everything I tell you has to stay between us. I mean it—it could be dangerous if it doesn't," I said.

"I haven't told a soul about the club. Now tell me what happened in there."

Secret.

I swallowed past the fear in my chest. Past the voice rising up inside me.

Secret. Price.

"I'm not sure, exactly—"

"Dammit, Harlow. Tell me the truth!" Adam smacked his hand so hard against the side of the car that it sent us bouncing on the cable, which was now beginning the near-vertical ascent up to Simatai.

DeathSecretDeathSecretKillSecretDeath.

My arms gripped the sides of the car and I squeezed my eyes shut, shoving down the voice that was razoring through my brain.

"I have visions!" I blurted out.

"Visions," Adam repeated.

I opened my eyes. He was studying me like he wasn't sure what to make of me anymore.

I nodded, talking fast before I could change my mind. "You know how I have those little episodes? Migraines? Pass-out scenes? Well, that's not really what they are. They're visions of horrible things. They've gotten way worse since we arrived in Asia. Like the signal's been amplified or something."

"So you … what? You can put what you see into other people's minds? Is that what you did to me?"

"No! I can't control them. And I would never do that to you. I don't know how that happened. I don't know why."

My fingers curled around the sides of the cable car, gripping for dear life as the truth spilled out. Divulging this secret was one of my life's greatest fears, one I'd worked hard to suppress. I'd barely had a chance to tell my father before he flipped out. Yet somehow, telling Adam wasn't as terrible as I'd imagined it would be. In fact, as awful as it was, it was sort of liberating to finally talk to someone who could understand what I was experiencing.

"People were dying," he said.

"Yes."

"Not just dying. Vomiting blood. Skin melting from their bones."

I could only nod.

"Is there more?"

Secret.

It was on the tip of my tongue. The voice wanted me to leave it there.

Well, the voice could go screw herself.

"There's this voice that whispers to me. She whispers things, mostly really ominous but cryptic things. I think She's the one who causes the visions."

I expected Adam to lean away, to look away, to do almost anything but what he did. He crossed the space between us and sat down next to me, taking me in his arms.

He smelled like dryer sheets, just like the smell that filtered into my subconscious when he carried me in his arms from Yoyogi Park.

It felt so good to set the truth free, however crazy it was, to someone who would listen. The tears flowed out of me, inevitable as the tide.

"I know. I heard her too," he said into my hair. "That voice made me think I was going crazy."

Price.

"Me too. Believe me, for the longest time I thought I was insane. But now I think it might mean something—I have the awful feeling that something bad is going to actually happen."

"Do you recognize it? The voice?" he asked.

"No. Why, do you?" I perked up.

His eyes shifted away from mine. "It sounded like you," he said.

We were in the final moments of our ascent now, but I'd forgotten all about us being suspended over oblivion. I felt like I'd already fallen.

"It wasn't me," I said.

The sudden thought that he might tell Mercy overwhelmed me with dread. She would crucify me. Rat me out to the Ministry and have me severed before I could even make it down off this mountain. Adam had admitted he wanted her. Kind of. For all I knew, he was spying for her right now.

"If you tell Mercy, I'll have you castrated."

"You'll—" He started to sputter a protest, but then burst into uncontrollable laughter.

I realized how ridiculous that threat sounded. Even though it felt like I should do anything—*anything*—but laugh, I couldn't help myself.

"Too much?" I asked when I could finally breathe again.

"You've always been too much," he said. "In a good way."

Our laughter died down, like both of us were realizing how different things were between us than they used to be. The cable car bounced up and down, struggling its way up the steepest part of the vertical rise.

Adam looked at me. I could almost see the gears of his mind clicking and whirring.

"What?" I asked.

"Whatever happens now, we're in this together. You're not alone."

His words knocked the air from my lungs. The gondola slowed as we glided into the turnabout. An attendant swung open our car door.

"Good. Because I still have more to tell you," I said.

"Awesome, can't wait. Come on, let's go." He grabbed my hand and pulled me onto the platform after him.

FAIRY TOWER

The view that was waiting for me when I stumbled out of the cable car swallowed me whole. My eyes blinked against the light, which was intensified by the smudgy layer of gray-white clouds that crowned the mountaintop. One look at the expanse of jade-colored foliage cascading below me sent the world spinning topsy-turvy. I dropped to my knees and put my hands on the stone floor of the Great Wall. The ground felt like it was rolling beneath me.

I'd always thought the wall was a walkway with high walls on each side, like an open-air tunnel. Instead, I found myself standing on the back of a stone serpent that snaked on as far as the eye could see. The edges of the wall rose only inches on each side of me—beyond which the wall dropped into a precipitous decline as steep as the south face of Mt. Everest. Instead of being comfortably ensconced like a rat in a maze, one false move would send me plunging over the side to my death. I'd rather be a rat.

The shouts and laughter of tourists mingled as if through some long tunnel and the landscape waved before my eyes like a watercolor. A new wave of terror rode through me: I didn't want anyone to see me—or worse, photograph me—like this. It was important for the Patriarch's daughter to project an air of strength, especially since the kidnappings had put Vision-Crest in a precarious situation. A situation that seemed more uncertain all the time.

The polished toe of an expensive wing-tip boot came into view beneath my nose. I couldn't look up—physically couldn't—but I knew it was Adam's. He always gave the VisionCrest uniform a sophisticated indie edge, right down to the footwear.

"Give me your hand," he said gently. I could see his long fingers dangling in the upper periphery of my vision.

"I can't—" I could barely eke out the strangled words. This was bad.

"Yes, you can." His fingers closed carefully around my arm, supporting me. "One foot at a time. Just look at me."

I put one foot underneath me and let my eyes slide up to his shin. I fixated on his pant leg like it was the only thing standing between me and certain destruction.

He pulled me to my feet and I leaned into him, my face buried against his chest. The wind whistled softly past us, making me queasy all over again.

"Did anyone see me?"

He leaned his cheek against mine for an instant and

whispered in my ear, "Nobody but me. It's okay, Harlow. We're only human."

Something about the feel of him so solid against me, the way his words were calming yet not denying me my fear, something so uniquely *Adam*, made me feel like everything was okay. Like being perched precariously atop a dangerously high mountaintop, seconds away from toppling to my death, wasn't such a big thing after all. Not if I wasn't alone.

"You should look around—take it in. You never know when you'll see something like this again."

I looked up into Adam's face. He was holding me tightly against him, one hand on the small of my back. The wind was whipping against us. He squinted into it, looking out over the horizon.

Following his gaze, I looked out on the scene with new eyes. The gray-brown stone serpent snaked across the crest of the ridge. Puffs of cottony trees clung to its edges, then rapidly dropped away on each side of the mountain. Hazy patches of fog hung lazily under the thin sky—spotty wisps that had drifted below their natural elevation. In the far-off distance, the wall's turrets were still visible, popping up at intervals along what seemed from here to be a never-ending stretch of stone.

The little dots of the Sacristan kids in their sweaters and tartan crept along the back of the beast, interspersed with Watchers. How they'd managed to get so far away in so little time astounded me. I didn't think my feet would move forward more than an inch at a time.

"You okay?" Adam asked.

I drew away from him, rooting myself in place on my legs and willing my body not to rebel. It worked. I was shaky but I was still on my feet, and the world around me was coming into sharper focus. I looked over my shoulder and saw a Watcher hovering at a discreet distance, just out of earshot.

"Will you tell me what your tattoo means now—the numbers on your wrist?" I asked.

Adam hesitated for a moment, then answered. "I put it there. After I came back. My dad whispered those numbers to me before the kidnappers let me go. The last time I saw him."

"Oh, Adam. I'm so sorry," I said. Although I was dying to ask if his father had told him what they meant, I waited for Adam to volunteer the information. He didn't.

"Did he tell you anything else?" I prodded.

Adam hesitated. "A few things. But he was in pretty bad shape." His voice cracked a little. He wasn't ready to tell me the whole story yet.

I looked at the numbers again. "If the Eparch told them to you, they mean something," I assured him.

Adam nodded, then sighed. "Come on," he said. "Let's go that way." He pointed behind us, in the opposite direction from where the Sacristan kids had gone. Turning, I saw that the wall became a steep incline.

I pulled the crumpled "thought prompts" out of my bag. "But this says we're supposed to find the twelfth watchtower, which is over there." I pointed toward our group.

Adam grabbed the paper and wadded it into a ball, then threw it over the side of the wall. "Screw the homework."

Why hadn't I thought of that first?

"You're right—screw it," I said.

Adam slipped his arm around my waist and pulled me close to him. A wave of warmth rolled through me. "I've got you," he said. "Just follow my lead."

We walked slowly and deliberately, traversing the vertical climb to what was apparently the highest physical location on the planet. The Watcher who'd been trailing us stayed at the bottom of the incline, probably working up the courage to follow. I tried to concentrate on my shoes against the stones, zoom lens only. Still, even with the distraction of looming death, it was impossible to ignore the solid feel of Adam's arm pressed against my hip.

The last hundred feet of the climb was brutal. Crumbly stones gave way beneath us as we ascended, sending miniature avalanches of ancient stone cascading over the sides of the wall. Every pebble that dropped over the edge robbed me of a little piece of my sanity, and I couldn't afford to waste the precious little I had left. Even so, Adam somehow managed to take us the rest of the way without me freezing in panic. Having him next to me made all the difference.

Finally, we reached the tower. Above the cloudbank, nobody was visible. It was like we were alone at the top of the world.

I wrinkled my nose. Inside the four walls of the tower the air smelled like thousand-year-old boiled cabbage sprinkled in dust. It was a simple four-by-four room, but it was still so much bigger than anything I'd ever experienced before. There was one window, a keyhole framing the lush green expanse beyond the walls. I loved it. It felt like our own hidden shelter from the world: an ivory tower from which I never wanted to climb down.

"What is this place?"

"It's Fairy Tower, the most famous part of Simatai. And you just climbed up the second most famous—and death-defying—part. The Heavenly Ladder."

"What? I tell you I'm terrified, so you take me to the scariest place possible?"

"And you made it just fine. Nothing to be afraid of. You had it in you all along." He reached out and grabbed my hand, pulling me to him. "You just needed someone to show you."

Adam's voice was low and raw with something electric. Out of nowhere, we were drawn together like a moth to a five-thousand-megawatt bug zapper. I put my arms around his neck and he bent down to meet me with a hungry kiss. Grabbing my hips, he lifted me onto the ledge of the window. His palms slid along my bare thighs, fingertips slipping beneath the hem of my skirt and sending shivers over my body. He leaned into me, and our mouths pressed together so hard that his teeth cut into my lip. Months of fear, desperation, anger, and loneliness wound together in this one moment.

Mercy's face popped into my head. I pulled away.

"Wait. Stop. We can't do this."

Adam ran his lips lightly along my jaw, then groaned. "Why not?"

"Mercy. There's something going on between you two, right?"

Adam's eyes searched mine. "I don't want to hurt you."

"Just don't lie to me."

"She's my friend. We're helping each other out," he said.

"Your friend?"

He grimaced, the dimple in his cheek flashing. Here came the knife. "Harlow…"

"Are you hooking up with her?"

He scrutinized my face. "Can we talk about something else, please?"

"I guess I'm just wondering what happened. Before you went away, things were so different between us."

"Before I went away, a lot of things were different," he said, his voice raw. Clearly it was a painful topic.

"I don't want to be anyone's consolation prize, Adam. Can we just start back as friends and go from there?"

He sighed and backed away, leaning against the wall across the room from me. He rubbed his hand over his face and his shoulders slumped. "You're right. I'm sorry, I just miss you so much sometimes, I can barely take it."

"Yeah. I know the feeling," I said.

We were silent for a few minutes.

"How did you know this was here?" I asked, trying to get us back to semi-normal.

He shrugged, shoving his hands in his pockets. "Internet."

"It's really cool."

He looked down at his feet. "You said there was more you needed to tell me."

"I'm worried about my father. He's supposed to be with us, but I haven't seen him since Tokyo."

"Before we went to the club?" he asked. "Dora said he stopped by your room."

"After, actually. I thought I was going to be busted for going out, but instead he took me to the temple. We had a fight."

Adam's eyebrows raised. "You got initiated?"

I nodded. "The first Rite."

He looked conflicted. "I always thought I'd be there—I wanted to be your second."

I didn't say anything at first, just looked into his eyes. The moment hung between us.

"I was hoping it would be you, too," I finally whispered.

I decided not to mention that it was Hayes Cantor. By the way Adam was pursing and unpursing his lips, I could tell he wanted to ask, but he didn't.

"So, did the fight happen after you got initiated?"

"Yeah. At first we were having this, like, father-daughter moment. Talking in a way we haven't in a long time. Then I made the mistake of telling him about the voice," I said.

This revelation had a bigger impact than I thought it would. Adam straightened up and took his hands out of his pockets. "What did he say?"

"He freaked out and had the Watch lock me in my room. I was sure he would send me home, but then we all came to China and the General was nowhere to be found."

Adam crossed the room toward me, only this time he looked alarmed, not amorous. "What did he say to you? Exactly?" He put his hand on my shoulder and gripped it tightly.

"Let go. That hurts," I said, wriggling away and scooting off the window ledge.

I walked to the door, my back to Adam but careful not to get close to the descent. He walked up behind me. So close yet so far; the warmth of his body was heartbreaking.

"Harlow, you have to tell me what he said," he repeated, his voice low.

"He wanted to know how long I'd been communicating with Her," I said. "At the time, I thought it was just an odd choice of words. Now, after yesterday with Madam Wang, I'm not so sure."

"What really happened with Madam Wang?"

"She said I wouldn't be seeing my father for a while."

Adam put his hands on my shoulders and gently turned me around. "And?"

"And then she read my tea leaves. She knew about the voice—said it wants me to 'return' somewhere. I have no idea where."

"Crap," he said, dropping his hands.

"Adam." I looked up at him. "What happened to you when you were kidnapped?"

His face stayed stone-still but his shoulders flinched a little. "I don't want to talk about it."

"Can't you see that this is all somehow tied together? If

we don't trust each other, something bad is going to happen. I know it."

He just looked at me. Stone-faced. Silent.

"You do trust me, don't you? You believe I'm not behind whatever's happening?" I asked.

His silence was the only answer I needed. It was like being kicked in the stomach.

"Fine. If that's what you think, then we're done," I said.

I turned to face the doorway again. The stone path fell vertically away from the tower, like an ancient slide of doom.

"Harlow, don't go," he said.

A part of me wanted to just fall into his arms. But that was the old part. The new part of me was just pissed that after everything we'd been through, after baring every part of my soul to him, he still couldn't do the same.

"For your information, Sacristan Wang is a virologist," I snapped. "Head of the VisionCrest biolabs. Given the kind of visions I've been having, that seems like a pretty convenient coincidence. Thought that tidbit might be of interest to you."

I took a deep breath and put one tentative Mary Jane down sideways onto the so-called Heavenly Ladder, trying to approach it like a ski slope and sidestep my way down. I willed my eyes to focus only on crisscrossing my feet, one over the other, down the slope. I'd made it six steps when I noticed my shadow stretching out below me. Although I remained standing, my silhouette crouched down, then slowly rose to standing again.

Startled, I felt my downslope foot begin to slide. It rolled smoothly over a miniscule handful of pebbles that I knew were going to be my undoing. I tried to turn my body and fall to the ground, wishing I hadn't been above the indignity of crawling on all fours to begin with. But it was too late.

The momentum of those few stones was enough to send me sliding, faster and faster, down the wall. My fingers grasped at the smooth-worn crevasses, trying to find something to hold on to. I screamed out and looked up at the doorway, where Adam was watching. The panic on his face was a mirror of my own.

Then my knee hit a protruding stone and the shift in balance upended me, sending me rolling toward the side of the wall even as I picked up speed. I caught a flash of the expanse of nothingness stretched out before me just before I barreled sideways over the edge.

This wasn't happening. My hands grasped, hoping for a last-minute miracle. I managed to catch the rim of the wall.

I was dangling like a wind chime off one of the wonders of the world.

Loose pebbles hit me in the face as Adam's shoes slid into focus. A split second later he was on his stomach and reaching his hand out to me.

"Take it!" he yelled.

I wasn't really in a position to wait for an engraved invitation, so I let go of the wall and grasped his forearm. I was eye-to-eye with the swirl of his tattoos, the things that branded his body as property—that marked it as still belonging to whoever had kidnapped him. In my desperate state, I suddenly saw images of blood and terror buried in the jungle of colors and symbols.

Something clicked in my brain. I gasped, forgetting for a moment that I was dangling in mortal peril. His kidnapping was related to my visions. "They let you go for a reason!"

It was more an accusation than a declaration. But before Adam could say anything, I heard voices of Chinese tourists chattering and yelling near us. People had noticed that something was going on and were closing in to get a look, even as a white-hot tunnel of pain was shrinking them to tiny dots of nothingness.

Death.

Adam jerked like he'd touched a downed power line. But unlike last time, at least, this time he didn't let me go.

Obliterate.

The world went white and we were swallowed by the vision.

Decimate.

It was like I'd fallen through the looking glass, and the only thing anchoring me to reality was Adam.

Exsanguinate.

I was still dangling over the precipice, and Adam was still holding on to my arm, but at the same time I was watching the whole scene unfold before us as if I were floating outside of my body. It was impossible to tell from Adam's face what was happening to him, whether he too had disconnected from reality, but I just hoped he held on tight.

The smell of burning tires and something meaty filled

the air. Behind Adam, flesh dripped from the bones of the unlucky onlookers. Clothes hung tattered from their birdcage torsos, and their stripped-bare femurs clattered like marionettes. This was just like the last vision Adam and I had shared—gruesome and unreal. I could feel his fear coursing through me, feel our connection even as I felt completely disconnected from my own body.

This was going to happen—these deaths would become real. The voice was going to make sure of that. Something terrible was coming, and Adam knew more than he was letting on. The whispering of the voice rushed through my ears, at first far away and then pounding over me like an air-raid siren, the words blending together: *PurityDeathObliterateDecimateExsanguinatePurityDeathObliterateDecimateExsanguinate.*

Adam yanked me hard, and I was simultaneously pulled back into my body and up over the edge of the wall. Then Adam ripped his arm from mine, shoving me away. The voice was abruptly silenced.

We lay on the ground, side-by-side, breathing hard and shallow. Two Watchers pushed past the people around us, yelling.

Adam looked at me and whispered, "Harlow, I've done something horrible. I need to tell you—"

The Watchers pulled me away from him, the flashbulbs of the tourist cameras documenting everything for the next day's news.

I had no clue what Adam had done, or if we'd get another chance to be alone so he could tell me. But somewhere in my heart I knew that it was the reason he could barely look me in the eyes.

After revealing my innermost secret, I felt like I was more completely on my own than ever before.

MERCY

I halfway expected to be greeted by the Watch and carted to a padded cell when we arrived back at the Wangs', but instead was escorted to my room without a word. Adam was taken to some other part of the building by a burly Watcher who looked like he might have him for a snack. If we were going to ever get a chance to talk, it would have to be later.

Dora returned to the room hours after I did, during one of the knockout slumbers that frequently followed my most intense visions. She shook me awake.

"Hey, cheekie monkey ... are you okay? I heard you took a swan dive off the Great Wall. Ten points for style."

It took me a minute to clear the sludge from my brain. The whole scene unfolded in my memory. I forced myself to sitting, my head pounding.

"I slipped."

"I sense there's more to that story, morning glory."

I rubbed my temples. "How much time do you have?"

"Why don't you just hit me with the highlights?" Dora smiled her most reassuring smile.

"Here we go: Adam and I had a heart-to-heart. Then he flipped out. Then I flipped out. I fell over the side of the Great Wall. He saved me. The end."

"Oh, is that all? Gosh, girl. Normally we'd just call that Wednesday."

"I have to find him," I said.

Dora looked down. I could see the avoidance all over her face.

"What is it?" I asked.

"Mercy took off a few minutes ago to find him. Did you get the scoop on what's up with them?"

I groaned, falling back onto my pillow and putting my arms over my head. "He wouldn't give me a straight answer, so it's safe to conclude they're hooking up."

"So you're involved in a real-life love triangle, eh? It's so *telenovela* of you. I'm *muy* impressed." Dora poked at my arm, trying to make light of it.

"Honestly, that's the least of my worries right now," I said.

"Spill it, sister. Guts on the table."

It was time to let her in. I didn't even know where to begin. How do you tell your best friend you're hearing voices that want you to kill people?

"D, this is going to sound a little strange. Actually, it's going to sound a lot strange."

A knock at the door interrupted us.

"Dinner, misses," a soft voice called. A demure girl poked

her head in. It was the maid whose eye I'd dreamed of cutting out during tea.

"What is it?" Dora's brows knit together in concern.

"It can wait until after dinner," I said, giving Dora a meaningful look and tilting my head toward the maid, who I was unable to look at directly.

Dora nodded and held out her hand, hefting me out of bed.

"Okay, but we're having salacious confessions for dessert," she said. Then, unexpectedly, she leaned in, pretending to kiss me on the cheek, and whispered in my ear. "They took our cell phones away from us when we came back. And they rifled through our luggage while we were gone."

My eyes went wide. I looked around our room, panicked. She was right—things weren't exactly as we'd left them. They had clearly been gone through.

A Watcher pushed the door wide. "Your presence is requested downstairs, Miss Wintergreen." He looked at Dora dismissively. "You too."

Panic uncoiled in my belly. Dora beamed her sunniest fake smile at him. "Ready or not, here we come."

They had taken away our means of communicating with the outside world. We were now prisoners. Not that anyone could defend us from the Ministry itself—no government, no politician, no one would dare.

When we got downstairs, all thirty-odd Ministry kids were already there, looking stunned and frightened. Everyone could feel that something had shifted. It was silent

137

as a cemetery. Stubin found us like a heat-seeking missile and for once kept his mouth shut. Watchers flanked two massive doors. My eyes combed the crowd for Adam, but I didn't see him. He was probably off with Mercy somewhere, doing who knew what; the thought made me want to tear my hair out by the fistful.

The doors opened before us. The Watchers herded us into two regimented lines—shooing me to the front of one and Stubin to the front of the other—and into the cavernous dining hall.

The world's longest table was laid out for dinner. Sacristan Wang stood rigid, like a five-foot-tall military general, at the other end of the room, in front of an elaborately carved chair that could only be described as a throne.

"You know what they say—big chair, huge ass," Dora whispered. But I wasn't in the mood for joking.

"Welcome back from the beyond." Wang's voice boomed across the great hall. "If Sister Wintergreen and Brother Fitz would please sit at the head of the table."

My ears perked at the sound of Adam's name, and I swiveled. Like magic, there he was next to me, a burly Watcher shoving him in front of Stubin.

Adam looked at me, his gaze heavy. A million unspoken words passed between us. There was no sign of the good Madam or their pallid paper cutout of a daughter. It seemed weird that they weren't here. Speaking of no sign, Mercy wasn't around either. Knowing her, she would saunter in halfway through dinner demanding a gluten-free option. Still, given the most recent developments, I was genuinely worried.

Adam and I led the two solemn lines down opposite sides of the table, like death row inmates marching toward the electric chair. The usual tittering and jostling was replaced with gravity. Everyone sensed the zero-tolerance vibes practically oozing from Sacristan Wang's pores. The atrocious bowl cut he was rocking made him look like an overgrown child. It gave the smug look of satisfaction on his face an ominous edge. He had the look of someone who would stop at nothing to elbow his way to the top of the VisionCrest ladder. Or the look of someone who already had; there was still no word from the General.

The table was impeccably set—china plates featuring fire-breathing dragons, silver platters piled high with succulent goodies, goblets filled with murky-looking liquid—the works. It was like a dinner party at Count Dracula's castle.

"Think that's water in his glass or does he prefer to drink baby tears?" Dora whispered.

Wang's sausage lips turned down at the corners; no detail escaped his notice. A pang of fear ran through me.

"Shhh," I hissed. I didn't want Dora singling herself out.

Wang picked a pewter bell up off the table and rang it like a petulant child. Servants skittered from all directions to pull out my chair, and Adam's on the other side of the table. Everyone else could apparently suck it. I knew weird, and this was over the line even for me.

"Daughter of the Patriarch and Son of the Eparch." Wang

raised a golden goblet. There was a wet, burbling gargle in his pronunciation. "It feels good to have you at my side."

He said it like we were his subjects. A knot of foreboding lodged behind my sternum. The Sacristan nodded to me and then to Adam. His Jimmy Dean lips stretched into a bowed smile.

"Everyone! Take your seats!" he yelled, so loudly that spit flew out of his mouth and plopped into his soup bowl. Everyone flinched, then dutifully pulled out their chairs and sat down.

"*Bon appétit,*" he said, garnishing it with a gap-toothed sneer.

I'd thought that even sitting next to Creepy Creeperton wouldn't make me less hungry, but then the servants pulled the silver covers off the dinner platters. Chicken feet.

Dora's face went white as she looked at the pale steamy pile of knuckles and claws in front of her.

"In China, chicken feet are a delicacy," Stubin whispered, loud enough for people in Taiwan to hear.

The whole table was waiting to see what I was going to do, except for Wang, who was feasting with voracity. I needed to project composure, so I picked up my chopsticks. The rest of the table took my cue and reluctantly followed suit.

It dawned on me just how much everyone was looking to me for leadership. I was all they had. There was no choice but to step up, which right now meant playing along until I could figure a way out of whatever this was.

I had just wrangled the first slippery toes into my mouth

when there was a commotion near the doorway. Servants scattered as they were pushed aside by the frantic windmilling of Mercy's arms as she barreled into the dining room.

Halfway between the door and the table, she collided with a wheeled serving cart and sent china platters and silver toppers clattering to the floor like shrapnel from a roadside bomb. Her hands were grabbing her throat and she was running around in crazed circles.

Everyone's chopsticks froze midair. Adam jumped out of his seat, his chair tipping over and crashing to the floor behind him. He ran toward Mercy. Amidst her choking and gurgling, she spotted him. Her eyes cleared as she recognized help. Stumbling toward him, she pitched headlong into the dining table. Everyone jumped back from their seats in unison, as if she were a felled electrical wire. Everyone except for Adam, who grabbed her arm and put a hand on her back as she leaned over the table, face-first over a steaming pot of soup, convulsing.

"Are you choking?" he asked her, panicked.

She jerked frantically, clutching at her neck. Her eyes jumped like a frightened rabbit's. I ran around the table to help them.

"What do we do?" I asked.

"Hold her up," Adam commanded, his voice shaking. Mercy's joints were like Jell-O. I draped her arm over my shoulder and did my best to shoulder her weight. Adam moved behind her and wrapped his arms around her, about to administer the Heimlich.

Sacristan Wang watched from the far end of the table, his sausage mouth methodically crunching on chicken feet as if this was a spectacle for his amusement.

Adam clenched his hands into a fist at Mercy's diaphragm, then jerked them back hard. What happened next was horrifying. Even though I'd seen it coming, in real life it was ten times worse than in my visions.

Mercy spewed a fountain of blood from her mouth; it splattered into the soup pot. Black boils erupted on her face. A sick popping sound rose from her. She was infected with the virus from my visions. Only this was absolutely real.

The room exploded in chaos. Kids ran and servants crashed into one another. Only Sacristan Wang stayed still, a spooky grin fixed to his lifeless face.

I couldn't support Mercy's weight anymore; I draped her body over the table. Adam moved to grab her as she crumpled to the floor.

"Don't touch her! Back away! It's contagious, Adam! Get away!"

He heard me yelling and looked up, confused and horrified, his arms wrapping around Mercy's waist. I clamped a hand over my mouth, equally horrified by my own words. I fell to my knees beside her, drawing my arm around her quivering shoulders. Trying to give her some comfort, someone to be with. If this was the end, she wouldn't have to face it alone.

Mercy looked up at me like a drowning puppy and fixed me with a look that seared itself into my memory. I could see the blood vessels bloom in the whites of her eyes just as the light left them. Exactly like the Harajuku girl's had.

It felt as if my heart had ceased to beat. Adam stumbled back, then ran from the room. My brain could only think of one thing to do. I gathered Mercy in my arms and cried.

DEARLY DEPARTED

It took me an hour of searching the grounds before I finally found Adam.

"Hold up!" I yelled. He froze, his back to me, the gravel of the Wangs' manicured drive crunching under our feet.

Four black-clad Watchers snapped to attention, gripping their semi-automatics tighter like they might knock a round into the chamber and fire a warning spray into the sky. You'd think the Wangs were preparing for a militant apocalypse instead of holding teenagers hostage. For the first time, I felt truly afraid.

Adam turned to me, his face a tempest of ragged emotion, and the reality of what had happened slammed into me. Mercy was dead. The Watchers had taken her, limp, from my arms. Maybe I could have stopped it if I'd told someone about my visions sooner.

Then Adam bent double, the way I'd seen him do the time he got sucker-punched by some gutter punks outside the Blue House who were harassing a townie girl on her way home from school.

"Tell me it was a vision," he said to the ground. His voice cracked, and it looked like he wasn't far behind.

My fingers and toes felt numb. This watered-down reality belonged in a REM cycle, not my life. I wanted to lie to him. But what would be the point?

"It wasn't a vision. I wish it was," I said.

"This is my fault." The words wrenched themselves from his body.

I put my hand on his back. His body was wracked with silent sobs as he tried to swallow his sorrow. Tears traced rivers down my cheeks. Mercy shouldn't have died.

"No. It's not," I said. "If it's anyone's fault, it's mine."

He stood up, his head in hands, and let out a primal scream of anger and frustration. Then he looked at his hands like they belonged to someone else. They were covered in Mercy's blood.

"Here." I took my cardigan off and handed it to him, "Wipe it off."

I watched him smear the VisionCrest logo red. It somehow seemed fitting. His eyes were red-rimmed.

"I can't believe this is happening," he said.

Taking a step closer to him, I placed my hand against his chest.

"You couldn't have stopped it," I said.

A storm cloud descended over his features; the tortured look of defiance and solitude he'd been carrying for the past few months returned. I could see him physically shutting me out, and it made my heart constrict.

"Why didn't you tell me sooner about Sacristan Wang being a virologist?" he hissed.

"You didn't give me a chance! And *why* won't you tell me what happened to you when you were kidnapped? What's the terrible thing you did?" I countered. His hypocrisy was infuriating.

"I'm not playing this game with you right now, Harlow. Mercy's dead. Talking isn't going to bring her back."

"Adam, it's important. I need to know what you know."

He shook his head, "I'm going to see if I can help. Someone who cares about her should be taking care of things."

He might as well have slapped me across the face. As he turned from me, I reached out and grabbed his arm, feeling the muscle tense against my touch.

"Don't go. We might not have a lot of time."

"Harlow! Harlow!" Dora's breathless cries reached across the lawn, closing in.

Adam's brow furrowed and he looked over my shoulder toward Dora. "All I care about right now is Mercy," he said.

Before I could object, he stalked off across the grounds, shoving his hands into his pockets, his back rigid. I was left standing there alone, drowning in dread, confusion, and hopelessness. Dora came panting up behind me. As I turned, she crushed me into a mama-bear hug. She was crying.

"I wish I could take back every time I said Mercy Mayer should die in a fire. I was only joking," she said. Stubin stood next to her and put a comforting hand on her shoulder.

I could tell by the desperate wrinkles around Dora's eyes that she was taking this really hard. "It's not your fault," I mumbled, watching Adam's silhouette fade into shadowed edges of the woods beyond the house. Several Watchers followed him closely. As if there was any way to escape this place.

"What's going on?" Stubin asked. "This is getting scary."

It was a question with no answer. All three of us looked down at our feet.

"Do you think the Wangs have something to do with it?" Dora asked, hiccuping. It seemed like it was a thousand years ago that I'd talked to her about my spooky tête-à-tête with the Queen of Creepy.

"Not something," I answered. "Everything."

"That's a serious accusation, Harlow." Stubin was completely in denial. "Dora told me you think the Wangs are up to something bad, but an esteemed member of the Ministry like Sacristan Wang would never hurt any of us. Mercy must have eaten something rotten."

"Oh really, Stubin? I didn't realize you were such an expert on Sacristan Wang's character. And last time I checked, rancid fish won't make you puke up your intestines," I snapped.

Dora stepped in front of me, wiping tears off her cheeks. "Hey! Put the crab claws away. This isn't Stubin's fault."

"Well, Stubin Mansfield doesn't need to know every detail I share with you in confidence."

Turning on my heel, I strode back toward the house. Instantly, I felt awful for venting at Dora and Stubin; they had no idea about all the other stuff going on. The voice, the visions, the nighttime encounter with Mei Mei. I wanted to tell her now, but I couldn't do it with Stubin there. I was terrified he would dismiss me and she would take his side. I couldn't bear the thought of it.

It seemed I'd officially alienated my only three allies, all in the space of a few hours and right when I needed them most. I kicked at the gravel, watching the white rocks scurry over their neat borders and into the lawn. Take that, landscaping.

The grounds were starting to look a little like *The Walking Dead*, kids ambling around like zombies. I guessed the adults must be dealing with the forensic situation inside, but things were rapidly devolving. As I neared the front of the house, more confused students wove their way uncertainly out the front door and congregated in cowed little groups on the lawn. Everyone was retelling the story of what they'd seen, as if there was some fresh angle or insight that was going to make it all make sense.

"She was clutching her chest when she ran in, like she was having an asthma attack."

"I heard if you get bitten by a flea here, you'll for sure get a hantavirus. I bet that's what it was."

"She's probably in the iris of the Inner Eye right now. My father said you circle it for a while, and only when you unlock the last secret do you proceed into the pupil."

"Did you see the way Adam ran to help her? There's something so romantic about it, like Marc Antony and Cleopatra."

Only children of the Fellowship could mind-warp barfing

up your entrails into dying a poetic death, sealed with a righteous kiss. Their commentary was a revolting reminder of how twisted the world inside the Fellowship bubble really was.

A hush came over the group as Brother Howard emerged from inside, looking haggard. He clapped his hands once really loud and everyone fell silent. For a second, there was only the sound of crickets in the fading twilight.

"Everyone." He gulped at the air like a fish, trying not to cry. Brother Howard was not the right man for this job.

A tear rolled down his cheek. He cleared his throat and his voice cracked. His body trembled, and he looked over his shoulder. Watchers stood behind him; one of them nodded. I realized that he wasn't just shaken up. He was scared.

"Mercy Mayer was a precious snowflake, beautiful and special, too soon to melt from this world. She has now transcended the Eye and resides within the infinite truth."

He was reciting the words as if reading from a script. My throat constricted. I wanted to find Adam and force him to talk to me; I wanted to make up with Dora; I wanted to know what the hell was going on here. Instead, I was struck just as useless as everyone around me.

Brother Howard held both of his hands up over our heads like he was healing the lame, then intoned the Vision-Crest mantra, his voice shaking. "From your Inner Eye—"

"Attain your Inner Truth," the crowd responded, me included. After seventeen years of conditioning, it was like tapping my knee with a plastic mallet.

"For now, return to your rooms and remain there to await

instructions. Use this time to reflect on your Inner Truth. It's what Mercy would have wanted."

Yes, I'm sure that would've been a top priority for her.

A Watcher behind Brother Howard cleared his throat. Brother Howard fumbled to find words. It seemed like he had been coached on what to say, and, from the looks of it, threatened to the point of terror to deliver it right.

"There's no cause for worry. Mercy was a very sick girl, with a rare blood disorder. She didn't want her peers to know because she didn't want to be treated differently. It's not contagious. You have no reason to be concerned."

Translation: *commence panic now*. I'd never seen Mercy so much as sneeze. She would have done almost anything to maintain her spot at the top of the social food chain, but I didn't think chronic illness was within her power to disguise.

"Now return to your rooms. Send positive energy for a speedy passage into the infinite truth for our dear departed Mercy."

Like lost sheep, everyone started to trickle back inside.

"From now on, I'm calling this place the Tainted Wang," Dora said morosely, walking up behind me. The joke was her olive branch, her way of calling a truce. We had never been able to stay mad at each other. Our longest fight was two hours.

I was so relieved, tears came to my eyes. Stubin walked up on the other side of me and put a reassuring hand on my arm.

"That sounds like a bed and breakfast for pedophiles," I said.

"This is so screwed," Dora said.

"Completely," I agreed.

We stood at the foot of the staircase. I turned behind me to look across the lawn for any sign of Adam. Nothing. Boys funneled left, girls funneled right. I had no choice but to fall in line. This time it was definitely like a funeral march. Dora pecked Stubin on the lips and hooked her arm into mine. He turned the color of a beet.

"See you later, alligator," she said, then tugged me behind her up the staircase.

"I need to tell you something, D," I said as we entered our room, closing the door behind us. Mercy's clothes hanging in the closet were unbearably depressing.

"No apologies," Dora said. "Our friendship defies convention. We're the best thing we've got going, sugarpie." She tapped the tip of my nose with her finger.

"There's something else."

"So let it out, sister. I know you've been holding out on me—tell me everything. Spill it."

I told her everything. For our entire friendship, I'd never trusted her enough to tell her what was happening to me. I'd never trusted anyone enough. I always expected them to judge me the way I judged myself. To blame me, call me crazy, and reject me.

Instead, Dora put her hand over mine.

"I'm so sorry this is happening to you. We'll figure it out. It's not your fault," she said.

The wall I'd built around my heart crumbled. I hadn't given my best friend enough credit. I hadn't given Adam enough credit. They were compassionate and kind. And they loved me. I let the tears go, and Dora let me rest my head against her shoulder.

Of all the moments of our friendship, this was the sweetest of all.

There was a stiff rap at the door. We both looked up as a Watcher let himself in.

"Sister Wintergreen, I need you to come with me. The situation is urgent," he said.

Thanks for the newsflash, CNN.

Irritated at being treated like an idiot, I didn't even look at him. "Yeah, I know. We were kind of eyewitnesses, so thanks for the update, but it's a little late."

The Watcher didn't budge. "I'm afraid I have to insist."

I followed him to the hall, irritated. "What's this about?" I asked. "I really need to be with Sister Elber right now."

"It concerns your father."

My blood turned to ice. The other shoe had dropped.

"My father? What about him?"

Oh, please no.

"Come with me."

TREACHERY

Snick-snick-snick-snick-snick.

The seconds ticked by on the grandfather clock in the Wangs' library. My thighs were cling-wrapped to the calfskin chair facing Sacristan Wang's massive desk. The shadows of unread books towered over me on all sides. I'd been sitting here for over an hour, just waiting.

Finally, the door clicked open and the two Wangs entered. Sacristan Wang was dressed like some kind of ship's captain, an elaborate paisley ascot tied around his neck and gold tassels perching at the shoulders of his navy, brass-buttoned blazer. A white captain's hat, with gold-leaf detail and an embroidered homage to the Inner Eye in its center, completed the outfit. Madam Wang looked even more bizarre, if that was possible. She was dressed in full bedroom regalia: ivory silk nightie tied with a cape, powder-puff kitten heels, mint-green face mask, thick red lipstick, zebra-print headscarf, and a miniature cigar.

The Sacristan took his seat at the desk and Madam

Wang stood behind him. She puffed on her slim torpedo, emitting a noxious cloud worthy of government regulation.

I coughed, choking a little on the fumes of her traveling smokestack. The Sacristan's fingers drummed against the top of his desk as his eyes stayed fixed on me.

"Sacristan Wang," I tried to sound confident. "I want to know where—"

"Silence!" he yelled, slamming his hand down hard on the desk. Madam Wang puffed away behind him. "I will ask the questions and you, Sister Wintergreen, will answer them."

He steepled his fingers and reclined in the leather wingback. "First of all, Brother Howard has been sent away. You and the other Ministry children are in my care now."

I thought of poor Brother Howard—the jackrabbit panic in his eyes after Mercy's death. "Lucky us," I said.

"Are you aware that your father is an apostate of the true faith?" Wang asked.

"What does that even mean?" I said, clenching my hands in my lap to keep from leaping across the table at him.

Fzzzzzzzzzzzztt. The dull buzz of the voice started in. Turning my concentration inward, I forced it down. Madam Wang snorted, like she knew what I was doing and how futile the effort was.

"Apostasy is the act of renouncing the faith," he told me with a condescending smile.

"Nobody is more devout than my father. It would be ridiculous for him to renounce a religion he made up himself," I said.

From outer blindness, inner sight.

"Like father like daughter, I see. The Patriarch began his abnegation of the true faith of the Inner Eye from the moment he formed VisionCrest. The organization is built on a foundation of lies, and there are those of us within the Ministry who have long worked to subvert his attempt to pervert it."

Betrayal in the violet light.

"Did you kidnap my father?" I asked, clenching my teeth.

"The sect of the True Believers answers only to the Inner Eye herself," he said.

"Herself?"

"Don't play dumb, girl. You know exactly who I mean. My wife tells me you are well acquainted with Isiris," Wang said.

That name again. It resonated with some deep part of me; a memory that taunted, just out of reach. I wanted to ask who she was, but that would mean admitting they were right.

"Hers is the voice you hear. The eyes with which you see, and which see you." Madam Wang answered my unasked question, smoke curling from her nostrils.

"Why on earth would the Inner Eye be speaking to me?" I asked.

A promise and a sacrifice. Purity exacts a price.

The voice was coming through clearer every minute that passed. My stomach writhed like a snake charmer's basket.

Sacristan Wang tilted his head back, looking up at Madam Wang puffing away. "Was I unclear about who was asking the questions?"

A gray cloud billowed around Madam Wang's silk turban.

"You were not," she answered, even though the question was clearly rhetorical.

He tapped his cocktail weenie fingers together at his chin. The ruby in his VisionCrest pin glinted, as if winking at me.

"Very well. Here is what is going to happen next, Sister Wintergreen. Tomorrow morning, the Patriarch is scheduled to give a press conference at the Forbidden City in Beijing. Many members of the Ministry will be in attendance, and you will speak in your father's place. You are going to indicate that your father has decided to take a short leave from his duties, and that in his place he has named me as his successor."

It was impossible not to notice the surprised arch of Madam Wang's overplucked eyebrows. It seemed that this was news even to her. The buzzing in my brain became a keening wail, microphone feedback and a crossword jumble of words stampeding over each other.

I stood up out of my chair, holding my hands to my head. "Where is my father? I'm not doing anything until I speak to him," I managed to say.

A Watcher strode over and pressed my shoulder, forcing me back into my chair. The keening stopped.

There was no way I was going to let Sacristan Wang have VisionCrest.

"You are not in a position to negotiate," Wang said. "And he is not in a position to entertain guests."

He smiled. A chill whispered up the back of my neck.

"The Prelates would never allow it, not to mention the rest of the Sacristans," I said.

"We'll take care of that part, not to worry. You just do your part," he said.

"And if I say no?"

Both the Sacristan and Madam Wang chuckled. "We have your father," Wang said. "We have your friends. We have the virus that we tested so successfully on Prelate Mayer's precious daughter. I think you will say yes."

A cold sweat broke out on my forehead. I thought of Dora and Adam, Stubin and the others. I couldn't let what happened to Mercy happen to them, too.

"I'll only do it if you let the others go—send them away or I say nothing," I said, trying my best to sound confident.

Wang's eyebrows raised a millimeter. "Never accept the opening offer, eh?"

I tilted my chin up.

"I'll send the others back to Twin Falls in the morning," he said. "I have no use for them. They are like so much vermin crawling through the halls of my home."

I exhaled. It seemed too good to be true that my request was granted so easily.

Wang lifted a finger. "Except . . . there are two or three that I have grown fond of. I couldn't possibly part with them."

His words landed like a punch to my stomach. I may have saved my classmates, but my friends weren't going anywhere.

"And what happens after this press conference?" I asked.

"Isiris chose us. We honored her with the blinding of Mei Mei, and she ordained us as her emissaries."

"How do you know what she wants?"

"Madam Wang, as you already know, is gifted in the sight," the Sacristan said. "Isiris communicates her wishes through my wife. What happens next, Sister Wintergreen, is that we embody Isiris's will."

"As it should be," added Madam Wang.

My heartbeat whooshed in my ears. Isiris was the voice in my head, and now the Wangs said she was the Inner Eye. I'd never believed there was such a thing; I always assumed the General had just made it all up. Now I wasn't so sure, but the only person who could clear it up for me was either in the Wangs' possession or—well, I couldn't think about the other alternatives.

"You're both traitors to VisionCrest. You're a disgrace to the Ministry," I said.

"The Patriarch is the traitor! He corrupts the purity of the Inner Eye with every breath he takes. But not for long." Wang stood up, the military creases in his white polyester pants straightening. He walked around the desk and stood right in front of me. He was so small that he was precisely at eye level. "You underestimate me, Sister. It would be wise to be fearful." His breath was sour.

"Oh, I know exactly what you're worth. And believe me, I'm not afraid of you," I said. It was a total lie, but the only power I had left here was the illusion of it.

"You should be afraid. Not of me, but of Isiris," he intoned.

"Screw Isiris," I spat back.

"It seems you would benefit from some time to reflect. Think of your friends, sleeping just over your head"—he motioned up to the ceiling—"unaware that their fate is in your hands. I hope tonight their dreams are sweet."

He did a sharp about-face and marched from the room. Madam Wang eyed me lazily and walked around the desk. She blew a smoke ring in the air, then leaned down, her face so close to mine I could smell the minty-clay smell of her face mask.

"I told you not to tell your friends anything—now you have endangered them even more. Let us hope for all our sakes that they are keeping their mouths shut," she hissed.

I had no idea how she knew I'd spoken to Adam and Dora about what happened at our tea, or why on earth she was suddenly speaking as if her lot was cast with us. All I could do was stare in stunned silence.

"Listen for Mei Mei. She will take you to see your father," Madam Wang whispered, the thick sweetness of cigar smoke on her breath. Before I could react, she swept from the room in a dervish of silk.

I had no idea what to make of it, but she clearly hadn't wanted the Sacristan to hear her. Maybe there was more to Madam Wang than met the eye.

The click of the lock felt like the lid of a coffin closing over me.

Five hours later, I was still listening to the *snick-snick-snick* of the clock ticking off the seconds, each one bringing me closer to the press conference. Five hours of isolation, worry, and torment. Five hours of not knowing what the hell I was supposed to do next.

I considered looking for a way out of the library. Maybe if I could find the others and warn them, we could escape from the Wang mansion and go for help. But I knew that was a pipe dream; there was absolutely no way any of us would get past the Watch unnoticed. And Madam Wang had said Mei Mei was going to take me to see my father. I desperately needed to see him; if he was okay, then there was still hope. And he was the one person who could confirm or deny Sacristan Wang's assertions about the Inner Eye. He might be able to help me fix this mess.

I realized that Sacristan Wang had implied that he was not alone, that there were more traitors inside the Ministry. They were almost certainly behind the kidnappings— but was there really some larger force guiding their actions?

Pieces of my last exchange with Madam Wang kept coming back to me. I tried to decide if her words were a threat or a warning. I couldn't tell if she was an enemy or some kind of twisted ally.

The voice you hear is your own. She plagues you because she wants you to return.

She'd been talking, at our tea, about the leader of the so-called True Believers. Was it possible that whoever this leader was, she was speaking to me? Invading my mind? It sounded crazy, but crazy was the new normal.

I see the mirror image of your soul.

The words suddenly clicked into place. All the times I'd thought I was hallucinating, seeing things in my reflection— it was Her, Isiris, becoming stronger. Breaking through to me. Seeing the world through my eyes. The mirror image of my soul.

Snick-snick-snick. The room swam around me as the realization hit: there was some sort of truth buried in VisionCrest. It felt like the circumstances for this insight ought to be more dramatic, but it was in the quiet of an empty library, alone with my thoughts, that it happened.

The moment when I first believed.

It was both unremarkable and profound. I was the daughter of the Patriarch, and daughters didn't have any power. And yet the General was a normal person—unremarkable—before he found me. I was the axis around which his life had changed. Around which the world changed.

Shrrrrk.

A scraping sound grated from the blockade of books on the wall next to me. One section of them began to move. I hopped out of my chair and cowered behind the side of the Sacristan's behemoth desk. Was it Isiris? By accepting the truth of her existence, had I somehow conjured her? Or maybe I had officially lost my mind. Perhaps this entire day had been a figment of my corrupt imagination.

Shrrrrk.

My spine stiffened. I peeked over the edge of the desk, which reeked of lemon-scented furniture polish and made me homesick for my father.

The bookcase was cracked open; where a solid wall had been before, there was now the sliver of a darkened doorway to something beyond. I stood up slowly, an inch at a time.

Breath rushed from my lungs. Standing there, tiny and ethereal as ever in her white satin blindfold and crepe dress, was Mei Mei. Even though she couldn't possibly see me, she beckoned me forward as if she could.

Just like Madam Wang had promised, Mei Mei was taking me to see the General.

THE HISTORY OF HARLOW

Mei Mei held her tiny hand out to me. My palm slid against hers, and she guided me through the break in the bookcase. She paused as we crossed the threshold. I knew she was waiting for me to close the bookcase behind us. I didn't want to— we would be entombed in blackness. But I did it anyway.

It shut with a *skreeek* that echoed down the blank expanse stretching in front of us. These must be servant passageways, but judging from the dank smell of them, they didn't get much use. Mei Mei ushered us forward and I shuffled behind her. The tunnel got narrower and narrower, and my shoulders began to bump against the sides.

"Are you taking me to see my father?" I asked in hushed tones.

Mei Mei didn't respond. I wondered if she only spoke when sleepwalking.

We continued on for what seemed like an eternity, Mei Mei making confident turns at every twist and juncture.

There was no way I would find my way back from this trip into the dark unknown.

Finally Mei Mei stopped short. She placed my hand on something cool and round. A doorknob. All was silent. I turned the knob and entered a smooth white world suffused with blue light. It reminded me of the inner sanctum of the Tokyo temple where I'd taken the Rite.

I looked behind me in time to see Mei Mei pulling the door softly shut, her satin blindfold shining in the darkness and then disappearing. I was alone.

I was in what looked like some kind of wacked-out mental institution. The hallway curved around in a semi-circle, a series of identical white doors with small observation windows dotting its length. Muffled beeps and the rhythmic sound of air compressions floated from somewhere beyond the doors. This must be Sacristan Wang's personal lab. I stood perfectly still, pricking my ears for any sound of footfalls. Nothing.

I approached the door in front of me, going up on my tiptoes to peek through the narrow window. Inside, a man was curled up on a cot under a thin blanket, wearing a pale blue hospital gown. There was a clear plastic barrier partitioning him from the rest of the room, which held odd equipment and a sink lined with suspicious instruments. There was nothing behind the barrier other than the man, the blanket, and the cot, all under the ever-present glow of soft blue light.

The man writhed and gave a feeble cough, and I got a look at the crown of his head. The once-thick hair was now thinning, as was the blocklike bone structure I'd once assumed was indestructible.

It was the General. I barely recognized him lying there, stripped and isolated. He'd lost considerable weight in only a few days. There was a thin thread of blood crusted between one nostril and the frayed skin at the edge of his lips. His signature eye-patch was gone; the angry, puckered skin over his missing eye looked as if it were burning.

Without hesitation or thought to what infection might lie beyond, I pushed my way into the room. The General flinched, curling into the blanket tighter and rasping something that sounded like a protest. There was some kind of speaker system that piped the sounds from behind his plastic partition into the rest of the room.

The metal door slammed behind me and we both jumped. The General's good eye opened and fixed on me. The black of his pupil consumed nearly his entire eye.

"Isiris?" His voice was scratchy.

My stomach turned. "It's me, dad. It's Harlow."

He blinked once in confusion, then seemed to startle back to himself. He used what appeared to be the last of his energy to push up to sitting. He looked like an orphaned child—bare feet, bewildered gaze. It felt as if a weight were literally crushing my heart. I put my hand up to the partition; as far as I could tell, there was no way through it.

"Harlow?" he asked, his voice catching. "Is it really you?"

"Yes. The Wangs' daughter brought me here," I said.

"The Wangs?" he asked, clearly disoriented.

I wanted to sob and wail, seeing my larger-than-life father broken like this. But I didn't have that luxury. I had no idea if the General would be able to tell me anything of use, but I had to try. Information was the only weapon I had, and my only hope for ultimately getting my father and the rest of us out of here.

"Sacristan Wang. We're in his house. He's behind the abductions," I said.

This seemed to register with the General, to bring him a shade closer to his normal self. "I have to stop him," he said.

"That's why I'm here. I need you to tell me some things. It's very important, Dad."

He nodded, but I wasn't confident he understood. Still, there was very little time and no option but to try.

"Who is Isiris?" I asked.

He physically recoiled at the name, but also became more lucid. He put his hand over his eyes for a moment, as if what he was about to say was too painful to bear.

"I had a family before you, Harlow. A wife and a baby daughter," he said.

This revelation hit me like a grenade. I'd had no idea that the General had another family before me.

"What happened to them?" I asked.

"A van hit their car head-on. I was supposed to be with them, and I wasn't, and they died. Eparch Fitz was a passenger in the van that hit them—he was the sole survivor, and racked with guilt because of it. Survivor's guilt, they call it. It sounds strange, but we became friends. Brothers in arms, of a sort. Initially, we set out to destroy ourselves; we took crazy risks, inviting death to come and take us."

Even though it was totally twisted, I resented my father's real family. I was just a replacement, and a dubious one. The loss he'd suffered made him human—destructible—and it was their fault.

"I'm sorry," was all I could manage to say.

He nodded. "Eparch Fitz and I traveled the world for nearly a year, doing things I don't even want to speak of. Then, deep in the Cambodian jungle, we happened upon the crumbling ruin of a temple. It was buried in strangler figs and looked old—it didn't quite look Khmer, but at the time I didn't think much of it. I left Eparch Fitz, wandered around the temple a bit. I felt drawn to it somehow. Out of nowhere, a doorway appeared."

I knew what would be coming next. The part where all the puzzle pieces fell together. The General's eyes glazed over and he looked off into the corner.

"What happened then?" I prompted him. It seemed to snap him back, at least part of him.

"There was a girl there. Standing in the doorway, holding an infant. She invited me in." His eye zeroed in on me. His voice hitched and a wrinkle appeared on his brow. "She looked exactly like you."

"Isiris," I whispered. I thought of the girl in the mirror.

He nodded. "Walking into the temple was like stepping through to another plane of existence. It was round, endless, levels going up as far up as the eye could see, corridors and doorways everywhere I looked."

If I wasn't someone who heard voices in her head, I'd have assumed the General had lost it, right there in the Cambodian jungle.

"What did she want from you?" I asked.

"She said she'd been waiting for me—that all the tragedy in my life had not been without purpose, and it had all been leading up to this."

"Like she knew you were coming," I said. A little part of me wondered whether, if she knew so much, maybe she had somehow orchestrated it all.

"She handed me you. Said I should raise you as my own."

There was more dangling at the end of that sentence. "In exchange for what?" I asked.

"For greatness beyond my imagination," he said. "Power, wealth, money, respect … and love."

I felt as though a stone had lodged itself in my throat. I was just a bargain he'd made for something better.

The General caught the look on my face and shook his head. "Harlow, it was the last one that sealed it for me. Love. All I saw was your beautiful, perfect face. I didn't care about the rest of it. All I saw was you."

I swallowed the stone. This was the closest my father had ever come to saying he loved me. He seemed like a dying man giving his last will and testament.

"But there was a catch, wasn't there?" I asked.

"She said I need only sacrifice one of my eyes as a sign of my faith. Then I would return to the world and listen for her voice in my head. Do as she asked, obeying every word with purity of heart."

The memory of Isiris's voice rang in my mind. *Sacrifice. Purity.* That was her, all right.

"Did she tell you what was supposed to happen then?" I asked.

"I would establish her kingdom in the physical world, and then she would join us and give all her believers immortal life," he said. "At the time, I didn't really buy it. Despite what I was seeing right in front of me, I was completely transfixed by you. I would have done anything to have you in my arms."

I looked at my father now, at his missing eye.

"That was how you lost your eye? In exchange for me?" I whispered.

He nodded. "It was worth it."

"Did you hear her voice like she said you would?" I asked, my throat going dry.

The General rubbed his eyes. I didn't know what was wrong with him, but he was fading.

"I did. She told me what to do—how to make Vision-Crest. She dictated the scripture of the Inner Eye, which I hid from all but the innermost circle of the Ministry because it was so outlandish. She fed me the mysteries and Rites. Her voice was strong when you were close to me, and unreachable when you were far." He ducked his head as if ashamed. "I got scared, convinced myself the whole thing was a dream. I kept you away from me, and over time her voice faded. I did what I wanted with VisionCrest. Created a mythology that was more believable. And for a while, it worked. Everything was great—"

"Until I started having visions," I said.

His shoulders slumped. "I didn't mean for any of this to happen."

"What am I?" I asked.

He looked up at me, his eye meeting mine. He tilted his chin up. "You're my daughter."

"Yes, I am. But that's not what I mean."

"I don't know, Harlow. But you look exactly like her."

"Is that why you've been so distant?" I asked. "Because I look like her?"

"Harlow, you don't just look like her. You *are* her. Exactly."

My stomach plummeted to my feet. He was wrong. I wasn't her, not even remotely.

"Do you believe Isiris is everything you've preached? Is Isiris the Inner Eye?" I needed to know more, before it was too late.

"I don't know what she is, Harlow. She has immense power and is without mercy. I didn't want to bring that to the world. She lives in a temple with a thousand doors, but she doesn't seem to have a way out. So I chose to make VisionCrest something else, something better. And in doing that, I may have condemned us all. I'm so sorry."

A thread of blood issued from his nose. His body began to shake.

"Harlow. They've done something to me. I don't feel like myself anymore," he said, seeming to slip back into his bewildered state.

I pressed my hands up against the glass, looking for a way to push through.

"Dad," I croaked, helpless.

He lay back down on the cot, his eye going blank into the far distance, his breathing shallow. I didn't know if it was the same affliction that had taken Mercy down, but I could tell he wasn't going to last much longer.

"I'll get you out of here," I promised.

I knew it wasn't true—he was near the end. Still, he deserved to have the comfort of hope. He closed his eye. The urge to break the glass so I could lay my head on his shoulder and never leave was overwhelming. But I had to keep going.

Reluctantly, I turned away.

"Harlow?" His voice was barely audible.

I tipped my forehead against the cold metal of the door to the room, unable to turn back and look at him. "Yes?"

"I love you," he said.

"I love you too, Dad." I barely managed the words.

My heart felt like it was being turned inside out. My father had finally revealed the truth about who I was, and simultaneously confirmed my deepest-held fears. My brain still wanted to deny it, but I knew in my heart it was true. On top of everything else, he'd told me he loved me for the first and last time. My heart felt like it was being mixed an industrial-strength blender.

I pushed through the door, knowing I would never see him again. It clicked shut behind me. My feet felt like they were poured in concrete. I doubled over, sobbing. My pain echoed down the hallway in both directions. I had finally made a real connection with my father, and I was still completely alone. I had no idea what to do next. But I had to do something.

I wiped the tears from my face and forced myself upright. Unsure of what else to do, I decided to look in the other nearby windows. Maybe I would learn something useful. I approached the first one, feeling as if my guts had been torn to ribbons.

I looked in, my eyes bleary. There was a very young boy I didn't recognize, playing with a small red ball behind a partition identical to the General's. I moved on to the next room: a young girl, lying on a bed with a canopy of plastic draped over it, a veil of wires emanating from her bald head. I looked into the next one, expecting yet another stranger. Instead, I saw something that made me straighten up and snap out of my wallow.

Mercy.

Holy crap—she wasn't dead. I stepped inside. The room was hung in plastic—walls, floors, ceiling. There was no partition. It was just a white-marble cube that had served who-knows-what purpose prior to becoming Sacristan Wang's playground of pain. Mercy was enshrined at the center, encased in a transparent plastic bullet, tubes running in and out of her. She was alive, but by the looks of it just barely. Foreboding skittered up my arms.

Last time I saw her, Mercy was flailing like a guppy on the floor beneath my feet. Even if I had no great love for the girl, she didn't deserve to end like this.

I approached her bed slowly, the soft whirring of the machines disguising the click of my shoes on the marble floor. Even from afar, I could see that this was not the Mercy I knew. It was her sunken shell—skin draped across bone. I stopped at the foot of the capsule and steadied my hand against it. I couldn't bring myself to look at her face.

The blankets were tucked so tightly around her legs that

if she were awake, she'd be immobile. I moved along the length of the container, my nemesis's withered body laid out before me. The awkward bend in her arms, the clockwork rise of her machine-operated lungs, the lily-white neck that had exchanged its pearls for plastic tubing.

I closed my eyes and took a breath, gathering the strength to look at Mercy's face. To really see what had been done to her, possibly by the evil thing that lurked inside my head. The thing that looked just like me. Who haunted my reflection. Isiris.

Purity.

The word whispered underneath the door.

My eyes flew open. Mercy was staring up at me, terror tightening her blue-tinged lips. My reflection echoed back at me, hovering over the incubator. A slow, wicked smile turned up the corners of my mouth. But it wasn't me who was smiling. It was my reflection in the plastic case that surrounded Mercy. It was Isiris. And she was taking over my body.

Obliterate.

My hand moved to the latch that held the capsule closed. I was trapped, motionless, inside my body. I wasn't going to let her take control of me. I couldn't.

Exsanguinate.

As my hand lifted the plastic cover, the needles and tubes pulled, tearing through the tissue-thinness of Mercy's neck. Her skin broke with satisfying pops. Blood flowed, soaking her corn-silk hair and pooling like a crown behind her. Tears slipped in streams from the watery corners of her eyes. She shuddered inside her blanket restraint.

From outer blindness, inner sight.

I leaned over her.

The reflection's head cocked to the side, mirrored back at me in the irises of Mercy's wild eyes. Isiris's pursed lips taunted me. Hands that were not mine ran along Mercy's shoulders, tangling themselves in the mess of hair and gore. They moved over Mercy's cheekbones, thumbs following the skull-hollow contour of her eye sockets. Slippery with blood, my thumbs met with the fleshy perfection of Mercy's sky-blue eyes. They pressed, hard.

Revulsion swept through me. I strained against the invasion, every muscle in my body tensing for a fight. I hovered over Mercy, lips nearly touching lips. I concentrated every ounce of my being on shoving Isiris out, pushing her back for good.

The pressure from my fingers eased, and I thought I had won. Beaten Isiris at her own game. Then my thumbs pressed down doubly hard, and a puff of breath pushed from Mercy as her optic nerves broke loose. Her head thrashed back and forth, spattering blood across the walls.

My fingers tugged her eyeballs free; two perfect orbs glistened in the palms of my hand. I screamed inside my brain, horror overtaking me. This was not me. I did not want this. The reflection smiled sweetly, gleaming up at me from the lifeless sheen of Mercy's extracted gaze.

You cannot stop me. You are part of me.

Isiris raised her prizes to my mouth, shoved them between my protesting lips. She bit down.

The click of the door sounded behind me. I spun around. Mei Mei was standing there.

I looked down at my hands. They were empty. The latch on Mercy's capsule was still secure, tubes running in and out of her body as before. Her eyelids were closed, lashes fluttering lightly against her sallow cheeks. No blood. No empty sockets. No smooth, round firmness against my tongue. Not a trace of what Isiris had done. Or what I thought she had done.

Mei Mei tilted her pale face up to mine. "Isiris was here."

A chill ran over my skin. It was a harbinger. Isiris's hold on me was getting stronger— she was inhabiting me from the inside out. My time was running out.

FORBIDDEN CITY

Mei Mei deposited me back in the library, returning to the tunnel without a word. The room was silent except for the *snick snick* of the clock, which told me it was past three a.m. I paced the room, unable to get the images of my father and Mercy out of my head. Finally, sometime after four a.m., I collapsed onto the couch and fell into a fitful sleep.

I dreamt I was wandering through a temple with a thousand doors. Every time I opened one, I stepped into yet another endless hallway. No matter how fast I ran, I never found what I was looking for. No matter which way I went, I could never escape. A voice followed me down each passage: *Harlow… Harlow…*

"Harlow." The word sounded from some far-off place. My brain felt like it was stuffed with cotton.

"Harlow," Adam's voice whispered in my ear. His touch ran down the length of my arm.

Reality slammed into focus. I bolted upright. Adam was sitting on the couch next to me.

"Am I dreaming?" I asked.

His eyes traced the lines of my body. It was like he was seeing me for the first time since those distant days in the carriage house.

"No."

As I tried to get oriented, the memory of what I'd seen in the lab came drifting back. Adam slid his arm behind me and drew me close. I leaned my head against his chest, tears dampening my cheeks.

I was overwhelmed by the irrational desire to return to Twin Falls and pretend that none of this had ever happened. I'd always hoped that one day the noose of the Fellowship would slip off my neck and I could just be normal; but right now, I would give anything to be back at the VisionCrest compound, sitting in the carriage house listening to punk rock records with Adam.

"How did you find me?" I asked.

He ran his hand over my hair. "Mei Mei," he said.

"Sacristan Wang is behind the abductions."

Adam leaned away from me. His face became pale. "How do you know that?" he asked.

"He told me."

Adam released me and leaned forward, elbows on knees and head in hands. "Harlow—that thing I needed to tell you," he started. His voice was tortured.

I held my breath. This was going to be bad.

"Remember when I told you yesterday that I'd heard the voice?"

I recalled his words in the gondola: *I heard her, too. That voice made me think I was going crazy.*

"Yeah," I said.

He looked up at me. "That night at the club wasn't the first time I heard it. I recognized it because it isn't just in your mind. It's real. And it belongs to someone I know."

My scalp tingled. "Who?" I asked, even though I already knew the answer.

"Her name is Isiris. I think she's your twin."

I couldn't breathe. Adam thought she was my twin, but she wasn't. I didn't know *what* she was to me, but after what the General had described, I knew she was something infinitely more terrifying than a long-lost sibling.

Adam seemed to think I was confused. "My family was abducted out of our home, by strangers, in the middle of the night. At least I thought it was by strangers." His voice was urgent, heart-wrenching. "When I came to, I was blindfolded. I screamed and screamed until I had no voice left. After days of isolation, the first thing I heard was *your* voice. Giving the orders to cut out my father's eyes."

He paused, getting choked up. I felt sick.

"And you already know what she did to me after that," he said.

He pulled his shirt up over his head and turned his body to the side. The blaze of reds, greens, and blues twisted up his arms and over his chest. My eyes followed the lines of ink down the ridges of his rib cage, across his stomach. I'd seen the tattoos before, of course, but I'd never been able to really study them. There were signs and symbols embedded in them. Hidden things. Secrets. They reminded me of the renderings of the Inner Eye that filled the sacred texts my father once claimed were dictated to him by our version of God. In the tattoos, repeated over and over, was a rougher version of the slick VisionCrest logo that hung watchful on walls across the world.

"I was strapped to a table. It took days to finish the tattoos. Isiris was there the entire time, hovering over me, rambling about VisionCrest destroying the purity of the Inner Eye. It was horrible, but nothing compared to what came next," he said.

The way Adam looked at me was like a silent apology. Like he needed to make a confession that might break things between us in a way that couldn't be repaired.

"You can tell me," I whispered.

"They removed my blindfold, and she was there. Isiris. She looks exactly like you, but there's this vacancy behind her eyes. Like she has no soul."

"Where were you?" I asked, shifting the topic. I wasn't ready to tell him what my father had revealed to me about Isiris giving me to him. I couldn't bear the thought that it might make Adam feel differently about me.

"Inside a temple. Isiris's temple. I don't know where it is, and I didn't see much of it, but it was old. VisionCrest inscriptions all over it, just like my tattoos. Doors everywhere," he said. His words validated what my father had told me only hours earlier. "She was surrounded by these... things. Some of them were like zombies—they'd been blinded, but moved around like they could see. The way Mei Mei does, except not human. Some of them were more like wraiths."

"Ghosts?" I asked, incredulous.

"I guess, kind of," he said. "I don't know—I was really disoriented. Maybe I imagined it."

"So if you weren't kidnapped by strangers, then who took you there?" I asked. "Was it the Wangs?"

He shook his head and his shoulders slumped a little. "It was my father. When he whispered the numbers that are on my wrist, he told me what he'd done. Apologized to me. But it was already too late."

"Why would your father kidnap you?" I asked, incredulous.

"To cover up his defection, and to make sure we couldn't be used as leverage against him. Sacristan Wang recruited my father—said that he and Madam Wang were uncovering the most sacred secrets of VisionCrest. Things only the Patriarch knew, the source of his power. Wang said that with that knowledge, he and my father could gain control of the Fellowship. All he wanted in exchange was for my dad to tell him where the temple was." Adam paused bitterly. "Maybe my father should've wondered why Isiris didn't just tell Wang directly, if she was so ready to give up her secrets."

"So your father and the Wangs were working together."

"Not exactly. My father was greedy—he was the only person besides the Patriarch who knew how to find the temple. He wrongly assumed that all he needed to do was show up and Isiris would bestow some great power upon him. So he figured, why not bypass Wang and have it all for himself? Cut out the middleman. He staged my family's disappearance—took us with him in case the Patriarch found him out, or the Wangs tried to get revenge. He actually thought that my mother and I would thank him, once we had the world at our fingertips."

My father's best friend had betrayed him. I was torn between feeling furious at the Eparch's selfishness and hurt for Adam. His father's actions had torn his family to shreds and endangered us all.

"Why didn't your father just kidnap me? I'm sure that's what Wang had planned," I said.

"Wang didn't tell him that Isiris wanted you. My dad only found that out once we got there. I hate to say it, but if he'd known, he probably *would* have taken you." Adam hung his head.

I let that sink in. If the Eparch and Wang hadn't been so busy double-crossing each another, I might already be in Isiris's clutches.

"I don't understand why the one secret Wang couldn't figure out was where the temple was," I finally said.

"Who knows? Maybe his connection to Isiris wasn't as strong as he made it out to be. Or maybe something else was standing in his way."

"What happened when your father showed up instead of Wang, and without me?" I asked.

Adam swallowed hard. "She decided to use me as her weapon."

My stomach did a flip-flop. My throat went dry. "What do you mean?"

"Isiris said she needed you to be whole. To remake the

world—purify it. Some of her followers brought my mother into the room. She was frail—couldn't even stand up on her own. Isiris put the tip of the blade right up to her eye. My mother was crying, telling me it was okay, that I shouldn't give Isiris what she wanted. Isiris said that every promise exacts a price."

Tears stung my eyes. "Adam, I'm so sorry. I would give anything to take this hurt away."

He shook his head sharply, his voice thick with emotion. "Don't. Don't apologize. I'm the one who should apologize."

"Why?" I asked. "You don't have anything to be sorry for. None of this was your fault."

"Harlow, I didn't have another choice," he said.

There was something in his eyes. Something terrible. My heart started to race. "What do you mean? Adam, *what did you do?*"

I didn't want to hear it, but I had to. Even if it was something that would change things between us, irreparably and forever.

"Isiris said that if I convinced the Patriarch to bring you to Asia, she would let my mother keep her eyes," he whispered. "She might let my father live." His cheeks tinged red.

"She sent you back to get me," I said.

He hung his head. "Yes."

My limbs began to shake as the realization of what he'd done set in. Just like my father, I'd been betrayed.

"How did you convince my father to bring us here?" I asked, my voice dead calm. I needed to hear it all.

"Mercy did it. I convinced her to talk to her mother—

persuade her that the Patriarch was overdue for a diplomatic trip to Asia, and that he should bring the Ministry children along to keep us safely in the public eye. It didn't take long for Prelate Mayer to sell the idea to your father. What Mercy wants, Mercy gets."

An anger like none I'd ever felt before bubbled up to the surface. "There's clearly more to your relationship with Mercy than convincing her mother to recommend a PR trip to Asia," I spat. "You kept hanging out with her long after that was done."

Adam's jaw clenched. "It was the best way to keep you away from me. I couldn't look you in the eye, knowing what I had to do."

The lid blew off my fury and I jumped to my feet. "What you *had* to do? No, Adam. What you *chose* to do."

"What else *could* I do?" he asked.

"Anything! I loved you!"

"I loved you too. I love you now," he pleaded.

"Screw you. You don't get to say that to me. Not ever."

Adam looked up at me, the corners of his eyes tight with pain. I was so angry with him I could barely see straight, but there were things much bigger than me in motion, and lives were in danger.

"Mercy isn't dead," I said.

"What?" he asked, his voice hoarse.

"Sacristan Wang is keeping her alive. My father, too. He's using them for some kind of experiment. I saw both of them. If they die, it's your..."

I wanted to say it would be his fault, but I couldn't bring myself to do it.

Disbelief mingled with relief in his voice. "She's alive?"

"Yes, no thanks to you."

His voice cracked. "Harlow, I'm so sorry. Isiris was going to murder my parents. What was I supposed to do?"

He was right, in a way. But it didn't matter. He'd hand-delivered me to someone who wanted to hurt me. He'd created the situation that now left my father dying in an underground lab. There was no getting around that.

"I don't know, Adam. Maybe trust me? The girl you supposedly love? We could have figured it out together."

"I'm so sorry," he said.

"It's not enough."

He stood up. "What do you want me to do, Harlow? I'll do anything to make this right."

For the first time in my life, I looked at him and felt nothing. No, that wasn't exactly true. I felt disgusted and betrayed.

"Nothing will ever make this right. There's no coming back from what you've done, Adam."

The latch on the library door rattled and Madam Wang slipped in, a cloud of sickly sweet smoke preceding her. She'd discarded her sleepwear for an elaborate silk cheongsam dress that made her look like a 1920s film star. Her hair was twisted into a pretzel bun and her lips were painted red. She glanced back and forth between us.

"It is time for you to leave Sister Wintergreen and her preponderance of yang, Brother Fitz," she said. Taking a long drag of her miniature cigar, she ground the butt into an ash-tray on the Sacristan's desk.

"I haven't told her everything yet," Adam said. They shared a conspiratorial glance.

"I will see to it. Go with Mei Mei. It's nearly time," Madam Wang commanded. Her chimeric daughter appeared behind her.

Adam hesitated, looking at me. I couldn't look him in the eye.

"Harlow, I'm not your enemy," he said. Then he followed Mei Mei out of the room.

I sat back down on the couch. Madam Wang seated herself behind the Sacristan's desk and pulled out another cigar. She didn't smoke it, just twirled it between her fingers. I'd once seen a feral cat catch a mouse and slowly kill it between its paws—letting it escape just often enough that the light of survival stayed in its little eyes until just before it was dead. That was exactly the way I felt right now.

"The stars are aligned against you, girl," she said. "Your father died an hour ago."

Like a dagger, the words slipped between my ribs and pierced my heart, cold and inevitable. If I hadn't seen the empty look in my father's eye myself, I would have wondered if she was lying. But I knew she wasn't. He was gone.

"But not all the stars," she added.

I could only blink at her, an icy sadness laboring in my veins.

"There is power that lives in you. I've seen it. And a willing army that waits to stand behind it."

"If you're talking about Isiris, I know all about her. You can spare yourself the cryptic declarations," I said, the words bitter in my mouth.

Madam Wang stood up, rounding the desk and bending down on one knee in front of me. The move was so unexpected that I startled back.

"I'm not talking about Isiris. I'm talking about the Resistance," she said.

"Resistance?"

"A network of the non-corrupt. In this moment, you are our leader. The Matriarch. What you do with it will define everything that comes after. Choose wisely today. We need you to be strong," she said. Then she bowed her head.

It struck me, in that moment, what she was saying. Madam Wang was secretly working against her husband, subverting his efforts while pretending to be his loyal aid. She was likely the reason Wang didn't know how to find Isiris's temple. And now she was telling me what I had to do. I was the leader of VisionCrest now that my father was dead.

"This underground is ready to stand behind you as you claim VisionCrest for your own," she said, her voice barely a whisper. "Myself among them. But we have done all that we can do. The rest is up to you."

I was going to have to defy Sacristan Wang and take on Isiris. Stop her, somehow. There was no other option.

"I won't have enough support," I said weakly. "I'm not— I've only had the first Rite. If I try to claim VisionCrest, there's no telling how the Ministry will react. They might try to imprison me—or worse."

"You cannot imprison something you do not have," she said.

"So, at this press conference, I'm supposed to claim leadership of VisionCrest instead of giving it to Sacristan Wang? And then disappear out from under everyone's noses?" I asked, incredulous. It sounded absolutely ridiculous. Ridiculous and impossible.

Madam Wang didn't seem to think so. She looked gravely up at me and nodded. "Mei Mei will be your guide."

———

When dawn broke an hour later, an army of servant girls flooded the room to help get me ready for the press conference. Madam Wang had abandoned me after our conversation, and the moment she departed, my anxiety doubled. There was no static in my head, no sign of Isiris's voice. All was uncharacteristically silent, and that was even more unsettling.

When we were ready to leave, I was ushered to a town car waiting in the drive. I expected to be greeted by the Sacristan's sneer, but instead came face-to-face with Dora and Stubin's nervous grins. Adam sat across from them, stone-faced.

Part of me was relieved and the other part horrified. Whatever was going to happen at the press conference, there was a good chance it was going to be bad. I reluctantly took the empty seat beside Adam.

"Isn't this exciting? A private tour of *Zijin Cheng*—the Forbidden City!" Stubin said.

"After what happened to Mercy last night, I wouldn't exactly call it exciting," Dora replied. Stubin's smile sagged.

"Where's everyone else?" I asked.

"They left in vans this morning," Adam said, his voice monotone.

I hoped that Sacristan Wang had been true to his bargain and sent them home; right now I desperately needed to believe that he had.

"I was so worried about you, but then they told me the good news about your father finally arriving. It's awesome, but I didn't think you would be gone all freakin' night," Dora said.

"Yeah," I said, not sure what to say.

Dora looked at me funny. As usual, she knew something was off.

"Did you know the Ministry modeled the VisionCrest compound off the Imperial Palace design—a walled city with North, South, East, and West gates?" Stubin asked.

"Four gates and a wall. What a novel concept." Dora's eyes were steady on me, gauging my reaction. "We got a message from my father. According to Madam Wang, 'the illustrious Prelate Elber is holding down the Ministry fort in Twin Falls, but he says the General's press conference is going to be a veritable who's who of the VisionCrest elite.'"

I thanked the universe for small favors—Dora's father would be absent, which meant one less loved one to stress over.

"Most of the other Ministry officials will be there because of what happened to Mercy. Out of respect for her family . . ." Stubin said, trailing off at the end of the sentence as he looked at the hard lines of Adam's face.

Dora gave Stubin a conciliatory kiss on the cheek. "Or maybe just to see your adorable face," she said.

I gave them the most enthusiastic smile I could muster, determined not to set off Dora's friend-dar any further. Adam sat stiffly next to me, but as far as Dora knew, he was still grieving Mercy's death and on the outs with me.

Everyone I cared about—who was still alive, that is—was in this car. Today would be a success if they all got out of China by the end of it, no matter what else happened. I needed to stay focused on that. I had no idea how Mei Mei was going to get us past the Watch, or what I planned to do if we managed to miracle up some kind of escape.

When we arrived outside the red-walled fortress of the Forbidden City, I expected to be swarmed by the usual menagerie of VisionCrest devotees. The General's press conferences were a big deal, tirelessly promoted by the VisonCrest marketing machine and attracting thousands of people. Instead of being mobbed, however, we pulled up next to a vacant sidewalk. A massive structure towered overhead, its blood-red base topped with a crimson colonnade and two-tiered sloping roof that looked like a multicolored marzipan. Hidden at ground level were several sets of immense, weather-worn red wooden doors, twenty feet high and adorned with gold rivets. The doors on the left creaked open, revealing a phalanx of Watchers on the other side.

As the doors shut behind us, I realized that our arrival was truly unnoticed. Not even the inevitable pocket of haranguers who followed the Ministry around, accusing them of being false prophets, was present. It was eerie.

According to Sacristan Wang, most if not all of the Ministry would be in attendance today to witness his coronation. For all their sophistication, the Ministry was so self-involved that they apparently hadn't noticed the corruption within their ranks. Just like they'd missed the fact that the Patriarch had disappeared and their children had been taken hostage. I wondered if any of them were part of the army Madam Wang had alluded to, or how many of them knew of the plot and had sided with Sacristan Wang. Either way, they considered themselves invincible.

They could think again.

The Watchers escorted us across the grounds. We wound our way along a tree-lined path, the heels of the Watchers' boots clicking against the concrete like an ominous metronome. We came to a ramp that led to a second gate, several stories tall and even brighter red than the first we'd passed through. Another massive set of riveted double doors stood open, and waiting on the other side of them was Sacristan Wang, Madam Wang impassive at his side. When we reached them, Sacristan Wang greeted us with an expansive sweep of his arm.

"Welcome to the Forbidden City. You have just entered through the East Glorious Gate. Over there is the Meridian Gate, which marks the official entrance to the former city of the Emperors." He nodded his head in the direction of a structure that towered to our left—if the first gate was a marzipan confection, the Meridian Gate was a many-tiered wedding cake, its sloping roofs a horizontal stairway to heaven. "The press conference will take place beyond the Meridian Gate, on the balcony of the Gate of Heavenly Peace overlooking Tiananmen Square. Some people call the Gate of Heavenly Peace the entrance to the Forbidden City, but some people are wrong. The Meridian is the true entrance."

"Thanks for the history lesson," I said, smiling like I absolutely did not mean it. Wang's eyebrows fell together in an irritated V.

"The preparations will take a bit more time," Madam Wang said. "We invite you to take a look around. Take in the culture." She raised an eyebrow at me as Wang hitched his cuff and glanced at his watch. "We must go. The Watch will be radioed to retrieve you when everything is ready for your announcement."

The Wangs retreated, heading through the Meridian Gate. A pack of Watchers escorted them, and a few stayed behind to watch over us.

I surveyed the abandoned grounds—they must have closed it to tourists. I knew exactly why the Sacristan was keeping us isolated; he didn't want me near any Ministry members until the very last moment, just in case I might betray his true intentions

"What does he mean, your announcement?" Dora looked hard at me, her suspicions suddenly raised.

No words came. I didn't want to lie to her.

"Harlow's introducing the Patriarch," Adam answered, rescuing me. If I didn't hate his guts, I might have been grateful.

"I realize I'm risking my teen-angst image by saying this, but this is actually sort of badass. Harlow's finally getting credit for her awesomeness, against a backdrop of Forbidden City Meets Nuclear Winter," Dora said, appraising the scene.

She was right. Slate-gray clouds tumbled over buildings so grandiose they looked fake—like cardboard cutouts of ancient Imperial palaces. There wasn't a soul in sight. It was a little Armageddony.

The Sacristan's black-clad minions hovered near us, our inevitable shadows. It occurred to me that these might be my final moments with my friends—the last semi-normal thing to ever happen to us; or the last thing to ever happen to us, period.

"Would you guys mind if I whisked my concubine off on a private tour?" Stubin asked.

"Oh, um. Sure. Of course not," I lied.

Dora looked at me warily. "You seem like something's up," she said. "Is everything okay?"

"Harlow and I got in a little argument. We could use the time alone to talk," Adam said.

I shot him a scathing glance. But I wanted Dora to have this time with Stubin; she might need something good to hold on to later.

"Nothing's up. But listen," I said, lowering my voice to a whisper. "If I don't get a chance to talk to you guys before the press conference, I just want to say how much you mean to me."

"Okay," Dora said hesitantly, narrowing her eyes. "Is there any particular reason you feel compelled to share that right now?"

I looked at the ground, and then back up to her. "No. Just—you know—after what happened to Mercy, I'm feeling a little shaken up. I just want you to know how much I love you."

She grabbed me and hugged me so hard I couldn't breathe.

"Okay, okay. We'll see you in bit. Have *fun*," I insisted.

"Twist my arm." Dora broke into a smile. "We'll see you in two shakes."

She tugged at Stubin's sleeve and they started over a limestone bridge that led up to the squat, slope-roofed buildings of the Forbidden City's inner courtyards. They created a perfect silhouette against the sky, Dora tilting her head toward Stubin's shoulder. Adam and I stood there in silence watching them skip off, their clasped hands swinging between them.

For the first time in my life, I did not want to be alone with Adam. I set out across the plaza—with Adam, and then the Watchers, trailing at a distance.

MIRROR, MIRROR

Two enormous jade lion statues flanked the building in front of me. The tiered, red-tiled roof made it look like a giant Asian gingerbread house with a huge, square cutout in the middle.

"It's the Gate of Supreme Harmony," Adam said from behind me.

I ignored him and kept walking. He could take his Supreme Harmony and shove it.

I approached the building and trudged up the steps. A pang of heartache stung me as I heard Adam's footsteps following. Cresting the staircase, I froze. The arch I was passing through was a gateway, and stretching out before me was an immense plaza, open to the sky. The stone that once covered it was now just a worn patchwork of gray poking its way out of a mossy green sea.

On the far side of the plaza, there was another building, similar to the gateway I'd just passed through, only much more massive. It looked like a buxom Chinese mistress squatting on a stool. Her sloped, tiled red roof was ninety percent of the building, with just a bare suggestion of arching entryways peeking out from beneath her skirts.

"It's beautiful," I said. It just slipped out.

"Yes, it is," Adam agreed.

"I was talking to myself, not you." I scanned the width of the plaza and took in the dozens of smaller pavilions that matched the mother ship. It would take a month to see all there was to see.

"You hate me, Harlow. I get it. Believe me, I hate myself." Adam tilted his head down toward me and I permitted myself a glance back up at him.

"I don't hate you," I said. "You're just not the person I thought you were."

"We're standing in the Gate of Supreme Harmony," he said, choosing to ignore the venom in my words. "And that . . . " He pointed. I hated the way my traitorous eyes still tracked the sinewy curve of his arm. "That's the Hall of Supreme Harmony. The central axis of the Forbidden City, where the Emperors were enthroned and married."

His stare was the same deep blue sea of mystery it always was, which contained no answers. There was no possibility of understanding what he had done, but maybe I had it in me to forgive him. Then again, maybe not.

I started out of the pavilion, crossing the plaza toward the Hall without a word. I heard Adam's steps behind me again, and farther behind, those of the Watchers. I wished Adam would just go away, and at the same time I needed to not be alone.

I walked inside the Hall. A bronze cylinder with markings on it in a language I didn't recognize towered before me. It looked like a giant spool on a sewing machine, except it had the aura of something mystical. Without ever having seen this before, I knew it was holy. A thick scent of burning cedar filled the room.

"This is a Tibetan prayer wheel. You put your hand on it and walk around it in a circle. And then you send your prayers up to Heaven," Adam said.

"When did you become the expert on Chinese history?" I asked.

"I've been reading a lot the last few months. Anything to keep my mind off what I've done."

"How's that been working for you?" I asked.

"Not very well," he said.

I put my hand on the wheel and walked in a circle. Adam did the same, on the opposite side. I glanced over my shoulder—the Watchers were at the bottom of the stairs, within sight but out of earshot.

"Those Watchers are on our side," Adam said.

I looked at him. In the half-light of the pavilion, his features seemed sharper. "Our side?"

"Didn't Madam Wang tell you about the Resistance?" he asked.

"Does Madam Wang ever speak in anything but riddles?"

He chuckled, even though there was nothing joking about my tone. "No, I guess not," he said.

"You obviously want to tell me something, so just tell me already," I said.

He sighed. "I don't know that much. I was contacted by a lower-level Sacristan in Twin Falls several months ago on behalf of Madam Wang. She'd turned on Isiris once she realized it wasn't the Inner Eye speaking through her, but something malevolent. It was too late to stop what had been set in motion. Isiris was communicating through her, and she couldn't control it. Plotting with Sacristan Wang and a network of conspirators—people at the highest levels of the Ministry. But whenever Isiris was absent, Madam Wang worked with a shadow network, a group of believers who'd rallied to stop it. They're underground, but according to Madam Wang, they have means. They call themselves the Resistance."

"So you want me to believe that you're a member of some sort of benevolent shadow organization called the Resistance, instead of a traitor?" I asked.

"No," Adam said. "I refused to hear her emissary out. I only started to listen after what happened to Mercy."

"Are you in love with Mercy?" I asked.

"You should know by now."

He couldn't have caught my heart in my throat more effectively if he'd had it on the end of a spear.

"The only girl I've ever loved is you," he said.

"You have a funny definition of love." I fixated on the letters of the prayer wheel. Somehow, slowly turning circles around this wheel with Adam was suffusing me with a gradual peace.

"I wonder what the inscription means," I added.

"It's Sanskrit. *Om mani padme hum*. If you recite it, you approach enlightenment."

"*Om mani padme hum*," I said, pressing my hand against the prayer wheel. *Om mani padme hum*. I was definitely feeling a resonant vibration, but it wasn't enlightenment. The buzz was back—Isiris was near.

My breath caught in my throat. The prayer wheel shushed to a stop.

"Let me help you, Harlow."

The weight of Adam's words pressed down on me. I couldn't accept his help; there was no way to trust him. The darkness of the pavilion stood between us like a ghost. Still, I could see the blue of Adam's eyes looking into mine.

"Did Isiris say what she intends to do with me?" I asked.

Adam looked wounded. "Just that you belonged inside the temple."

The thought of being trapped somewhere with the person who had tormented me my entire life was unbearable.

"If it saved the people that I loved, I'd have to give it some serious thought," I said.

"I wouldn't let you do that," he said.

"It's not a matter of *letting* me anything, Adam," I countered. A question sparked in my mind. "Do you think the reason she tattooed you is so you'll always remember you belong to her?"

"I don't belong to her," he said, quiet but angry.

I only raised my eyebrows in response.

"I think she did it to protect me," he said.

"Protect you from what?"

"She didn't say, but I've thought about it a lot. At first, I thought Isiris meant the tattoos as a talisman. But then I thought about all her talk of purifying the world. About your bloody visions, and what happened to Mercy. I've been putting it all together ... and I wonder if, maybe, the tattoos actually make me an inoculated carrier of whatever thing she plans to unleash ... "

"What's an inoculated carrier?" I asked.

"Someone who's been injected with an attenuated version of the virus, a version that's been mutated to make it non-lethal. Basically that's what a vaccine is. Maybe that's what I am—a carrier."

My knees went weak at the thought. But that couldn't be it.

"Wang's a virologist," I said. "If anyone's making a virus, it's him. He has a lab in the basement of his house. It's massive—he's definitely not working alone. Whatever they're making down there is what infected Mercy. I'm sure of it."

"Maybe it's only a matter of time. Or maybe it needs some kind of catalyst to set it off," Adam said.

I thought of Mercy's meltdown, perfectly choreographed to coincide with the Wangs' takeover.

"A lot of stuff is your fault, but not that," I said. Still, I wondered if there was something to what he was saying, and the tattoos served some sort of purpose.

Harlow, Isiris's voice whispered, as if carried on the wind through the hall.

My heart sped up to a hummingbird's beat.

Over here.

"Did you hear that?" I asked, looking around.

"What? Are the Watchers coming?" Adam craned to see down into the plaza.

The room swam out of focus.

In the mirror.

"Harlow?" Adam's voice was a million miles away.

Isiris's fingers wrapped around my mind, blotting out everything real.

I want to show you something.

My head jerked toward her voice. My voice. On the far side of the hall, there was a wall made of mirrors. Even at a distance, I could see the image of myself standing there. The reflection beckoned me with her hand.

Some distant part of me felt Adam's fingers grip my arm. I shook him off.

My reflection crooked her finger.

Closer.

I stepped forward. The reflection stayed still.

Come to me.

As I reached her, she raised her arms, hands reaching through the glass. She clasped my wrists.

The force of her grip stirred a hurricane inside of me. The center of my chest was like a magnet, pulling me into the reflection. I fought against it, refusing to succumb to the tornado vortex of my mirror image.

You cannot fight me. I am stronger. I am your creator.

"Harlow!" Adam's voice was panicked.

In the mirror, I saw him grab my uplifted arms. The tattoo on his wrist—the one he'd added to remember the numbers his father whispered to him—was reflected back at me. I saw Isiris's eyes dart up to them.

Return to me.

I knew, then, what the numbers meant. As surely as if Isiris had whispered in my ear, I knew. They were latitude and longitude coordinates. Adam's father had given him the location of the temple.

+13° 57' 38.6022"

+104° 21' 3.2076"

She was telling me where to find her.

Isiris closed her eyes, and when she opened them they were just empty black sockets. She was surrounded by hundreds of lifeless bodies, their eyes also removed.

I found my voice where none had been before and let loose a bellowing scream that tore the vision apart at the seams.

Snap. Silence.

I was standing there. Right where I had been at the beginning: Adam's arms wrapped around me, staring at my reflection in the mirror. Only Isiris was gone. It was just me reflected back.

I collapsed into his arms.

"What was that?" Adam asked.

"I know where to find her. I know where we have to go to get your parents back," I said.

"Harlow, we can't. It's too dangerous, I won't let you—"

I stood up and pushed him away. "It's not up to you."

The clomp of boots silenced us as a cluster of Watchers crowned the staircase.

"The press conference is starting. We need you to come with us," one of them said.

"Just a second," Adam said. His hand at the small of my back was my only anchor to sanity. "What are you planning to do?" he whispered to me, frantic.

It was time to take control of this situation. If Isiris wanted a showdown, that was what I would give her. This was my moment to make things right.

"Whatever it takes," I said.

STANDING ALONE

The dull roar of the crowd and the popping of the paparazzi's flashbulbs overwhelmed me. So this was where the crowd was. I stepped onto the upper pavilion of the Gate of Heavenly Peace. The massive balcony stretched the full length of the imposing structure, looming out over Tiananmen Square. It was once used by ancient Chinese emperors to survey their troops, assembled below. Today there was an assemblage of reporters. Separated from the rest of the crowd by barricades, they circled like hungry hyenas, howling for scraps of flesh. The rest of the square was filled with wall-to-wall believers. VisionCrest followers must have traveled from all over China to get a glimpse of the Patriarch, and, more importantly, the freedom of belief he represented.

Dora, Stubin, and Adam stood awkwardly behind me, flanked by Watchers. They looked as shell-shocked as I felt, any traces of enthusiasm wiped away. Directly to my left, Sacristan Wang stood with Madam Wang and Mei Mei—

it was the privilege of the hosting Sacristan to announce the Patriarch. Beyond him stretched a line of Prelates and Sacristans from all over the world, Mercy's father among them. Many of them met my eye and nodded respectfully; some of them looked at me quizzically, no doubt wondering why my father had not appeared with me; a few of them acted as if I weren't there at all. I knew those were the traitors, too ashamed to look me in the eye. To our right was a vast assembly of Chinese dignitaries; being allied with VisionCrest was a major deposit in the bank of political capital. Interspersed throughout were Watchers, every one of them with an assault rifle cradled in his arms.

"Harlow, where's the General?" Dora whispered, her voice shaking.

We had been friends too long for her not to see the worry in my eyes or the determined set of my jaw. I reached my hand out behind me and she slipped her palm into mine. I squeezed it as reassuringly as I could.

"Everything's Swizzle Stick. Just stick close to me and I'll explain later," I answered.

I watched the teeming crowd below, wondering how Mei Mei was ever going to get us out of here. Even if we made it past the Watchers, and that was a stretch, there was no way we would make it through a hundred thousand people unobstructed.

Sacristan Wang stepped up to the microphone in front of him. He shot me a glare of calculated confidence.

"Attention! Attention! It is my duty and privilege to welcome you, True Believers of the VisionCrest Fellowship, worshipers of the Inner Eye, to this most historic of events. As your Sacristan and humble servant, I invite you to receive the tidings of the day with an open heart."

The words boomed out over the crowd. Little beads of sweat were forming at the Sacristan's hairline as he worked himself into a melodramatic frenzy. I noticed that the Ministry delegates who were not part of Wang's traitorous circle were eyeing each other nervously, vaguely aware of a loose cannon in their midst and no doubt wondering how he dared get things underway before the Patriarch arrived.

"Look upon the revelations with the infinite wisdom of the Inner Eye, which resides within each of you until the day She comes to walk among us and give us the infinite grace of everlasting life."

There was a collective gasp from the crowd below at Wang's use of the female pronoun. Wang got visibly flustered at this, but stumbled through to the end of his ridiculous speech. The Ministry members on the balcony began to murmur to one another, or else began to sweat as well. It occurred to me that Wang's alliance wasn't as solid as he supposed; the shadiest among the Ministry looked ready to deny the whole thing at the first sign of trouble.

"And so, with that, I introduce to you the daughter of the Patriarch, Sister Harlow Wintergreen, who will make a monumental announcement of vital importance to the Fellowship." Wang's stumpy arm swept out to the side.

The crowd broke into reluctant applause, clearly confused as to why the first daughter of the Fellowship would speak in her father's place. For all the hundreds of press conferences I'd attended as a showpiece, never once had I spoken in public. I looked out over the endless sea of bodies below, their upturned faces looking to me for guidance. It struck me hard, in that moment—these people were counting on me. This wasn't about me, or Adam, or Dora, or even my father. This was about them; if I failed, they would lose every bit as much as I would. What I was about to do was contrary to the foundational tenets of VisionCrest.

"Hello," I said. My words echoed across the square as I spoke into the microphone in front of me. "It's so humbling to see all of you here. Thank you for coming to support the Patriarch and the Fellowship. You are our family."

The silence was deafening. I swallowed hard and continued on.

"We are embarking on dark days. Days that will test our faith, days that will call upon each of us to sacrifice. I stand before you bearing a message from the Patriarch."

A restless wave rolled through the crowd. I glanced sideways at Sacristan Wang, who was already tugging the hem of his jacket straight and puffing himself up like a peacock, ready to take the reigns of the organization. I glanced briefly over the heads of the Ministry to see a phalanx of Watchers trying to push their way onto the balcony. Madam Wang caught my eye. She tilted her head ever so slightly, telling me to look to my right. I noticed Mei Mei had slipped away from her parents and was now standing next to a small cluster of Watchers among the political dignitaries. It suddenly hit me that the Watchers on the balcony with us were part of the Resistance—loyal to Madam Wang. The Watchers trying to push their way in no doubt were not. I took a deep breath. There was no turning back now.

"The Patriarch has passed into the endless peace of the Inner Eye and named me as his successor," I declared. "You should know that there are traitors here today—Sacristan Wang chief among them. He is my father's murderer and is plotting to take the Fellowship for his own. The proof of this lies in the basement of his own home, where he is housing a laboratory. VisionCrest abductees—"

The entire square, which had seemed to collapse under the news of the Patriarch's death, erupted in complete chaos one beat later at the contradiction of it all. I was just barely an initiate to the first mystery, so I couldn't technically be named as my father's successor. And yet the Patriarch was infallible, so if he had named me, there must be a way to make it legitimate. The masses churned in grief and confusion, stumbling over each other at a loss for what to do. I could see that I wasn't going to get a chance to provide the damning litany of Wang's transgressions. The situation was devolving.

Sensing an opportunity to prevent me from saying anything more, Wang flew at me, his sausage lip curled into a furious sneer. Adam pulled me back and Wang just missed me, his hands instead closing around Stubin. He spun Stubin around and clutched him to his chest, as though he planned to use him as a human shield. The sun caught the edge of something shiny in Wang's hand and my stomach dropped out from beneath me. He was holding a knife. Stubin looked back at us, wild-eyed.

"Help me," he said feebly, putting his hands up to Wang's arm, which held him in a chokehold.

Dora screamed, trying to launch herself at Wang. Adam stopped her. The Watchers who were struggling to fight their way onto the mezzanine broke through the crowd and began threading their way toward us. Ministry members either ran for the door or stood frozen in stunned disbelief. Someone tugged at my hand, and I looked down to see Mei Mei. She motioned hurriedly for me to follow her, then jutted her chin toward the advancing Watchers. Several of them had zeroed in on me—they would be here within moments, and they did not look friendly. I looked up at Adam.

"Get Dora out of here. Follow Mei Mei," I told him.

"I'm not leaving you here," he said.

"We're not leaving Stubin," Dora said to me, her words panicked.

"Sister Wintergreen, this blood is on your hands. I offer this boy as a sacrifice to Isiris. There will be a million more like him, as payment for your betrayal," Sacristan Wang said.

Dora let loose a scream so primal it didn't sound human. Without even thinking, I ran at Wang, closing my hand over the knife in his hand and feeling the sharp sting of it as it sliced against my palm. Dora flew in and bit down on his arm as hard as she could. Wang let out a squeal of pain, releasing

Stubin but pivoting to turn the weapon on me. He came directly at me, and I was sure it was the end. All I could see was the flash of sunlight on metal.

Then Adam barreled into Wang's side, out of nowhere. He hit him so hard that he picked him up off his feet and sent him tumbling over the edge of the balcony. Wang caught the rail and held on with one hand, dangling precariously stories above the crowd.

Adam and I looked at each other, paralyzed for a moment. Then I noticed Wang's Watchers seizing the remaining Ministry members and Madam Wang. They were only steps away from us. Madam Wang looked at me as the brute who had her by the arm homed in on an even better target. Me.

She mouthed one word: *Run.*

———

We ran—with Mei Mei and four Watchers who were loyal to Madam Wang and the Resistance—down a back staircase, while another contingent of Watchers stayed on the mezzanine to fight off Wang's dogs. Our side was outnumbered by Wang's, ten to one; our head start was going to be a small one. One of our Watchers was carrying tiny Mei Mei in his arms as we made it to the ground floor and hustled back into the Forbidden City. There was no way we would be able to escape through the crowd outside the Gate of Heavenly Peace—even though it would provide great cover, people would recognize me immediately and we would be mobbed by grieving Fellowship members wishing to kiss the hand of VisionCrest's new leader. One of the Watchers held his hand up to his ear-piece.

"This way, Sister Wintergreen! There's a car waiting at the side gate, the one past the Gate of Prosperous Harmony," he yelled, breaking right.

My hand was sluicing a blood-offering onto the stones of the Forbidden City.

"You're going the wrong way! The Gate of Prosperous Harmony is over there!" Adam screamed, pointing to a squat red gateway on our left that had a gold-tile roof with tiny ceramic animals lining its center.

"I'm in charge here. We go right," the Watcher said, ignoring him.

"Stop!" I yelled. Everyone froze.

"Adam, are you sure?" I asked. I hated having to rely on him, but he clearly knew a lot about this place.

"Sister Wintergreen, with all due—" the Watcher started.

I looked at him, hard. "Actually, I'm the one who's in charge here. Adam?"

"I swear on my life that's it on the left," he said.

"Are you sure you wouldn't rather swear on mine?" I asked. He winced.

I looked at the group, everyone panting and waiting for me to make a call.

"We go left. Come on," I said, and started running toward the gate. I refused to look behind me but I could hear the rhythmic thud of boots on stone across the plaza. The head start was over; our pursuers were closing in.

The path to the Gate of Prosperous Harmony sloped upward, forming a kind of waterless bridge. We were at a full-out sprint, Adam leading the way as we passed through the gateway and down the other side, descending into a lush green garden with winding walks. All but one of the Watchers, the man carrying Mei Mei, fell back to hold off the coming attack.

Stubin was breathing in horrible wheezing puffs, his pace slowing. I could see the wall of the Forbidden City ahead of us, less than a hundred yards. When I looked over my shoulder, a battalion of Watchers crested the rise of the Gate of Prosperous Harmony. Stubin came to a halt, doubling over and going into an all-out asthma attack. Dora stood with her hand on his back, panic written on her face.

"He can't breathe," Dora yelled. "He forgot his inhaler—he told me in the car this morning."

Without hesitating, Adam shot back to Stubin and threw him over his shoulder, beginning to run toward the outer gate but lumbering under Stubin's weight.

"Take Dora and go ahead! Don't wait for us!" Adam yelled.

Dora shook her head no, but the sight of enemy Watchers running toward us made me grab her hand and force her to run. "Adam's got him. We have to get out of here or we'll all end up like Mercy," I told her. Incredibly, she began to run again.

When we reached the outer gate, our Watcher was holding open a small door, Mei Mei still perched in his arms. We ran out and down the pathway, over the medieval moat that surrounded the red walls of the Forbidden City. There were beat-up cars, scooters, and rickshaws zooming by on the busy thoroughfare. Regular life was carrying on as if nothing unusual were happening. Parked on the sidewalk was a run-down coupe with its battered doors flung open—our escape vehicle. It looked like the million other cars that were whizzing by: ancient and nondescript.

As I reached the car I looked back, just in time to see Adam stumble through the gate. The Watcher whispered something in Mei Mei's ear and then set her on the ground, facing her in the direction of the car. Alongside Adam, she ran in a straight line toward us.

The Watcher, whose name I didn't even know, met my eyes. He tilted his head and briefly genuflected, one knee brushing the ground. Then he pulled out a pistol from the holster at his hip, turned, and shut himself inside the Forbidden City. He was sacrificing his life to save ours.

It felt like the axis of the earth moved underneath me. People were going to die for me.

Dora and I squeezed into the front seat together next to the driver, a thin, middle-aged Chinese man who simply nodded at me sedately. The minute it took for Adam, Stubin, and Mei Mei to reach us felt like an eternity. Sweat rolled down Adam's face as he finally put a hyperventilating Stubin down and helped him into the car.

"Hurry!" I said, knowing that any minute the door to the Forbidden City would open. The Watchers would certainly open fire, at the very least to shoot out the tires so we couldn't get away. If this fell through, there was no chance we'd all be able to escape on foot. I couldn't bear the thought of anyone being left behind.

Dora turned around and started talking Stubin down from the ledge, putting her hand on his knee and soothing him with whispered words. Mei Mei and then Adam squeezed in and shut the doors, just as the door to the Forbidden City swung open and Watchers streamed out, stepping over the limp body of the Watcher who'd brought us to freedom. Several of them already had their guns drawn, taking aim. I thought our driver was just going to remain parked there— that we had made some horrible miscalculation—but then he nodded, fired up the engine, and swerved the car recklessly off the sidewalk, into the chaotic stream of traffic.

A single bullet glanced off the side of the car as we turned a sharp corner. The Forbidden City receded into the distance. I closed my eyes and breathed in, for what felt like the first time since I'd spoken those first words to the crowd. It was crazy—I'd staked my claim as leader of VisionCrest, yet I could never go back. Sacristan Wang and his coconspirators would undoubtedly capture me and invalidate my right to the Fellowship on the grounds that I was not yet an advanced initiate. None of us would ever see the light of day again, on the off chance we were allowed to live at all. At the same time, I was the leader of the most powerful religion the world had ever seen.

Stubin's labored breathing grew marginally calmer in the backseat, and our driver grunted as he stepped on the accelerator. I heard the rip of fabric, and then Adam quietly reached around from the backseat and wrapped my hand in the tattered remnants of his shirt's hem.

The sting of the knife wound was nothing compared to the sting of what I had just done. I had no idea where we were going, but there was definitely no going back.

THE RESISTANCE

The dull roar of the engines couldn't drown out the static buzz of Isiris's presence growing nearer. Our mystery chauffeur had driven us to a small corporate airfield; there was a Gulfstream jet waiting on the runway, already humming and ready to go. It had a giant eye in an upside-down triangle emblazoned on its side—it was the General's personal plane, The Flying Eye. I had no idea how they'd done it, but the Resistance clearly had connections. The driver pulled right up to the stairway, grunted, and pointed.

I was the last one to board. The captain of the plane went down to one knee, then rose back up with his eyes cast down in deference.

"I'll be taking you to the Resistance, Sister Wintergreen. They'll take care of everything," he said.

"Actually, I want you to take us to Rota—it's an island in the Pacific Ocean, south of Japan," I said. "The Fellowship has a small compound there, and it's a U.S. Commonwealth, so we'll get a little more protection." I glanced over my shoulder. It would only be a matter of minutes before our enemies tracked us here, if they weren't already en route.

The captain met my eye with an apologetic grimace. "I'm sorry, Sister. But I'm under strict orders to bring you to the Resistance."

"They can just come meet us at Rota—I'd be happy to meet with them and figure out how we can work together."

The set of his jaw got firmer. It dawned on me that I wasn't calling the shots here, either; I had just traded one prison for another.

"I see. Then will you at least tell me where we're going?" I asked.

He shook his head.

"Fine. Let's just get in the freaking air before we all get killed." I stormed away. It took every ounce of strength I had to bite back the tears of frustration, but all that mattered in that moment was getting in the air. Figuring out how to escape yet another group of nefarious strangers would have to wait.

Once we were above the clouds, I turned to look at my battle-weary group, assembled on the leather couches that flanked both sides of the plane. Every surface gleamed with cherrywood paneling. There was a wet bar in the corner. Stubin was stretched out on a couch, his head resting in Dora's lap. His asthma attack was under control for now, but I worried about what lay ahead. I doubted he could withstand another episode. One lens of Dora's glasses was smashed from her tussle with the Watchers, and she was absently stroking Stubin's hair, shell-shocked. Mei Mei sat sideways, mute and mysterious as ever, seeming to look out the window even though blindfolded. Adam was hunched over, his head in his hands.

Only one of them deserved to face what came next, at my side. I knew what I had to do.

I cleared my throat. "Adam, we need to talk. In private."

He looked up slowly, his blue eyes burning into mine, and a thousand thoughts were laid bare. Shared grief for the loss of our fathers. Fear for the terror that surely awaited us. A mutual inability to forgive him for what he'd done.

Dora stirred back to awareness long enough to give me a blank look.

I attempted a smile, but my parchment-paper lips wouldn't cooperate. My bones felt like I'd slept a hundred years and needed a hundred more before they would hold me up again. She drifted away, looking back into the distance.

Adam stood, and I walked to the back of the plane, conscious of his presence behind me. I slipped into the stateroom—my father's former bedroom—and heard Adam click the door shut behind him. I turned to face him.

Standing in front of him like this, I realized how tall and solid he was. Part of me wanted him to fold me into his arms and tell me it was all just a bad dream.

The corners of his mouth turned down. "I'm sorry," he said, reaching out for me.

I stepped away.

"Please," he said, his voice hoarse. I relented, just for a moment, letting him pull me close.

I could hear his heartbeat through the thin cotton of his T-shirt, rough against my cheek. He was warm, just like on those summer days behind the carriage house. It was a reminder of everything he'd ruined, and I couldn't keep the tears from spilling over.

"We need to make an escape plan," I said.

"What do you mean? I thought the pilot was taking us to the Resistance."

I pushed him away. "Exactly! We have no idea who the hell these people are, but I guarantee you they're not looking to throw me a parade. Madam Wang is charming and all, but I seriously doubt that she or her cronies have my best interests, or the Fellowship's, at heart. Don't forget—they're traitors, too."

"They're the only protection we've got. The entire Ministry was just ripped apart at the seams," he said.

"For all we know, they're just as bad as Wang. People do all kinds of twisted things for power. To them I'm just a pawn, but there's a much larger game than control of the Fellowship in play."

"You're not a pawn," Adam said.

"No, I'm not. Isiris is planning a genocide, and I'm the only one who can stop her. That means I'm now the Queen."

"You were always the Queen," he said.

I didn't have anything to say in response.

"We're never going to find her," Adam finally said. "Our fathers were the only ones who knew how to find her, and they're both … gone."

The words hung heavy in the air between us.

"Your father didn't let that happen," I told him. "The

words he whispered to you—that tattoo on your wrist—it's the latitude and longitude of Isiris's temple."

Adam instinctively grabbed for the ink on his skin, as if covering it from view could erase its existence. "Who told you that?" he asked, his eyes narrowing.

"Isiris did," I said. "We're going to find her and stop her."

"Stubin needs a hospital. Mei Mei's just a little girl. You can't ask them to do that." His eyes were wild.

"I don't plan to. They're not coming with us."

Understanding dawned on his face.

"Us," he repeated. His searching eyes rested only on mine.

"Yep. You and me," I said.

I walked over to the headboard of my father's bed. Inlaid in gold filigree was the VisionCrest logo. Only my father and I knew that it was also a safe—the General was fond of stashing valuables in hidden places, just in case. I always thought he was just being paranoid, but apparently he was onto something. I twisted the iris of the eye counterclockwise, and a springloaded lock snapped open.

"When we get wherever we're going, you're going to do two things: figure out where exactly those coordinates point to, and sell these to fund our getaway. I don't know how—you're just going to have to improvise. When the time comes, we'll make a run for it together." I reached into the eye and pulled out a wad of cash and loose gems.

"There's no way that's going to work. Dora will never let you go without her," he said.

He was right about Dora—she wouldn't step back willingly. A plan to leave her behind was already forming in my mind, but I couldn't bring myself to say it; it was too awful to verbalize.

"Let me worry about that part. You worry about keeping this safe until you can hock it," I said, dumping the goods into his hands. "And just for the record, I still don't trust you. You're just the best of my bad options."

"Thanks for the reminder," he said.

I felt a little hypocritical. Dora was in the next room and I was planning to betray her, just like Adam had betrayed me. Well, maybe not *just* like, but what I was planning would hurt her. Under normal circumstances, I'd never be able to pull the wool over Dora's eyes. But right now she was in tatters. Not knowing I was eventually going to give her the slip was for her own good. At least that's what I told myself.

"Where do you think they're taking us?" Adam asked.

I shook my head, hopelessness writhing in the pit of my stomach. "I have no idea. It could be anywhere."

"Let's just hope we get lucky. You're not exactly inconspicuous. Even if we manage to get away from the Resistance, pretty much everyone in the world is going to be looking for you."

Six hours later, the plane bumped to a landing on an abandoned airstrip, in the midst of a tropical jungle. Vegetation was swallowing the asphalt by inches, and the carcasses of corrugated metal hangars littered the surroundings like cockroach shells. Hazy mountains loomed in the near distance. The whole place had the bombed-out resonance of a forgotten war.

Dora looked at me, her eyes accusatory. "Where are we? Stubin needs a hospital."

Stubin winced, his ears getting red. "I'm fine now. We should just worry about getting everyone to a safe place."

Dora set her shoulders back and looked out the window, putting an invisible wall between herself and me. Adam was squinting at a tattered flag hanging limp in the torpid air. He looked at me with grim determination.

"Danang," he said. "Vietnam."

It felt like my skin was too tight across my forehead. Vietnam was just about the worst place we could be, other than back in Beijing. It was the only country from which the Fellowship had ever been expelled. Its extreme danger for Vision-Crest devotees was probably what made it a great place for the Resistance to hide out in. Here we were, landing the Flying Eye on an unused runway—we might as well announce our presence with a fireworks display.

As the plane taxied to a halt, I waited for alarms to sound or troops to flood out of hiding. But the engines powered down and the tarmac remained still. The cockpit door opened and the captain emerged, taking his hat off and mopping his sweaty brow with his forearm.

"We made it," he said, leaning against the doorway and sighing.

"Isn't this, like, the least safe place we could be?" I asked.

"Other than with you, you mean," Dora said. There was a very un-Dora bite of bitterness in her voice.

The captain tipped his head toward the window. "I'll let them explain all that."

A gray van with tinted windows was idling outside. It had practically materialized out of nowhere. The captain hoisted himself upright and set about opening the door. Adam and I exchanged a heavy look. There was no telling how things would go from here—if we'd be separated or even remotely capable of escaping.

Mei Mei stood up and walked over to me, taking my hand as if she knew what to do. I stood up, knowing exactly why she'd done it and appreciating the show of solidarity from the only person who held any political sway with the people waiting on the tarmac.

Right before we descended the stairs, I turned and met the stares of Dora, Stubin, and Adam. They'd risen, unsure whether to follow.

"I'll do whatever it takes to make sure you're all safe. That much I promise," I said.

Then we walked out together—me and my tiny emissary—to the Resistance, ready to face our new frenemies together.

———————

We drove for twenty minutes along a two-lane highway, sandwiched, on bench seats in the back of the van, between four paramilitary-looking dudes in gray camo. Nobody said a word to us the entire ride, opting to grunt their instructions instead. The driver and the person in the passenger seat were wearing hoodies and sunglasses, so I couldn't get a good look at them other than to determine that the driver was a woman. I tried to ask where we were going, but they maintained a monastic silence. Mei Mei squeezed my hand.

"Not exactly my idea of a welcome wagon," Dora said. Her eyes darted to mine before looking away. If things went my way, she would remain spitting mad at me. It was for the best.

The highway gave way to city roads as we entered a ramshackle district of slope-roofed houses that looked like they'd been built hundreds of years before. They were illuminated by the light of colored silk lanterns, which were strung from every cornice and balcony. The further we pushed into the heart of the city, the more brightly lit the buildings became. The entire town was one giant flaming torch.

Finally, we turned down a narrow alley and the van slowed to a crawl. We took a sudden, sharp turn and pulled up onto the sidewalk.

"Everybody out," the driver instructed.

The gray-suit dudes hustled us onto the darkened street. On a balcony above us, the glowing red tip of a cigarette made the rhythmic journey to and from an old man's mouth, lighting his face up like a ghoul in ten-second intervals.

The driver walked around the front of the van and whipped off her hood. Her face was illuminated by the thin light coming from inside the dilapidated apartments above us. She was blond, shorter than I'd realized, and older. The person in the passenger seat climbed out too, and a vague bell of recognition sounded in my brain. The last time I'd seen him, he was wearing a shroud and helping initiate me into the first mystery.

All the feelings from that night came rushing back, mixed with the confused feelings of my twelve-year-old crush, as Hayes pulled off his hood and slid his sunglasses up on his head. His sandy hair was disheveled, and his brown eyes were flecked with gold. I couldn't help but notice how tall and athletic he was now—something I couldn't appreciate in the darkness of the Tokyo temple.

"Hayes Cantor," he said, his lips quirking into that half smile as he extended his hand to me. "We've met before." He arched one dark brow, and a meaningful look passed between us. Adam's posture stiffened as he sensed a rival.

"I remember," I said.

"I'm Adam, and this is Stubin, Dora, and Mei Mei," Adam broke in, his voice tight.

"Oh, we know Mei Mei," the blond lady said, putting her arm around Mei Mei's shoulders. "I'm Sister Cantor, Hayes's mother. Welcome to Hoi An." The clipped edges of her British accent somehow made me feel more secure than I really was.

"Sister Cantor! You're the architect who designed the All Knowing, at the compound," Stubin said.

She ducked her head, clearly uncomfortable. "Please, call me Emily. And I was once, yes. Now I have a far greater purpose." Her eyes moved to Hayes, who stood up a little straighter.

"Right. Well, the channel is this way," Hayes said. "We'll boat the rest of the way. Almost there." He motioned ahead of us down the dark alleyway and began to walk.

The gray-suits nudged us from behind.

"Dude, call off the dogs," Adam said.

"They're for protection," Hayes replied, not bothering to turn around. "The Southern Vietnamese army grants us asylum, but you can't be too careful."

"We're not your prisoners," Adam said through gritted teeth.

I was painfully aware of Adam's hand inside his pocket, palming the gems that would secure our escape. I wished he would just shut up.

We picked our way down the walkway to the water's edge, where a thin, flat boat wavered on the glassy surface. The boat's front and back edges curved upward, but its middle rose only inches above the water. To me it looked more like a floating platform; one that was potentially not seaworthy. I could hear string music threading through the air from an open-air restaurant on the opposite bank.

Hayes helped Dora, then Stubin, climb into the boat. Emily lifted the diminutive Mei Mei and carried her on. Two of the four henchmen climbed aboard. Adam placed a protective hand on the small of my back, sheltering me from the rest of the muscle hovering behind us. His eyes were locked on Hayes, who stepped out of the boat and held his hand out to me as if Adam weren't even there.

"After you," Hayes said.

Adam's fingers curled around my waist. "I've got her."

I shot Adam a dirty look and ignored Hayes's hand as I stepped into the boat.

"I've got myself," I said.

It was impossible not to feel a flutter in my stomach at Hayes's appreciative smile.

"My kind of girl," he said.

Adam snorted in disgust and climbed in after me, his shoulder bumping Hayes as he passed. He sat down next to me, protectively close. Hayes's smile didn't falter as he pushed us away from the bank and hopped in. The other two men stayed on land, watching us float away.

Hayes stood at the back of the boat, manning the oars that were lashed to posts on each side. He was graceful and strong. The flutter came again. As if he could feel me watching him, he met my stare and gave me the half smile again. The fluttering intensified.

The boat glided along at a steady speed, passing makeshift docks and dark buildings that extended on stilts out into the water. Hayes expertly navigated around the myriad boats moored along the banks. The channel finally gave way to open ocean as we left Hoi An behind. I dropped my hand over the side of the boat and let it skim over the dark water, just inches below us.

We rowed for a while, out into the darkness.

"Almost there," Emily said in a low voice. "The island's just ahead."

A few minutes later, a stretch of glowing beachfront came into view, partially obscured by jungle foliage. As we got closer I could see there was a pathway, lit by votives inside red paper bags, snaking into the dense vegetation. Hayes let out a three-toned whistle that reverberated through the night. Through the trees, set back in the distance, the tiled roof of a vast cluster of buildings peeked through. Hayes repeated the whistle pattern. People emerged from the border of the jungle, lining the beach like silent sentinels.

Hayes rowed us toward the shore and several onlookers

rushed to help pull us in. Once we were safely wedged on the sand, I stood up on unsteady feet.

The people standing on the beach all dropped to one knee, bowing their heads.

"Welcome to Bên Trong Mắt," Hayes said. "We're honored to have you."

LAST FIRST KISS

A soft knock roused me out of my sleep.

"Harlow? Are you awake?" It was Hayes. His adorable accent was unmistakable.

I sat up abruptly, looking around in alarm, as the details of my surroundings came into focus. I was by myself on a low-slung bed in an elegant room. Everything in this place was made of gleaming teak: floors, walls, ceiling. A teak fan spun determinedly overhead as daylight filtered through the windows. The silk pajamas I'd been given by Emily slid against my skin and the mattress was incredibly soft. Part of me wanted to slip under the covers and never emerge again. There was too much to face.

"I'm not dressed," I said, climbing out of bed. I looked down at my hand, freshly bandaged by Emily the night before. She said there would be a scar, but at least I wouldn't have to worry about infection.

Hayes cleared his throat. "I'll just wait out here, then, yeah?"

Apparently he wasn't leaving. The floor was cool against the soles of my feet as I spotted a red silk robe laid carefully across the Papasan loveseat across the room. There was a full-length mirror against the wall—I averted my eyes as I picked the robe up, afraid of what I might see.

I cracked the door just a millimeter. Hayes had his back turned, pacing in the light-filled hallway.

"Yes?" I asked.

He spun around, his hand automatically rising to rake through his hair, which was perfectly beach-tossed. The daylight was even kinder to his features than the night had been—sharp jaw, brownish-gold eyes, a cute little mole beneath his lower lip. He raised his eyebrows, like I'd caught him by surprise and he was momentarily unsure what to say.

"I was wondering if you'd like to come down to the beach with me," he said. He was wearing a tank top and board shorts.

"Where are my friends?" I asked.

"We brought a doctor for Stubin, and Dora's with him in the infirmary. He's going to be fine, but they're doing a nebulizer treatment right now. The doc says he's lucky to have made it, and he's going to need to take it easy for a while."

"What about Adam?" I asked.

Hayes scratched the back of his neck, the gesture making him weirdly hotter.

"He took a surf board out earlier with one of the local

guys who helps out around here. I'm sure he'll be back when the swell dies down."

My heart instantly began to race. Adam was resourceful, so I shouldn't be surprised that he was already well on his way to arranging our escape; there was absolutely no doubt in my mind that that was what he was up to. He had a way of manipulating people into getting what he wanted, which was a skill both Mercy and I had paid the price for.

The thought of Mercy helped me refocus on my bigger purpose—getting out of here and finding Isiris.

"Since I know you're about to ask, Mei Mei is playing cards with my mother on the lanai," Hayes continued. "And to answer the other question you're thinking, yes, you slept incredibly late and everyone else has gone about their day." He cracked his classic half smile, half smirk. I could tell he was working overtime to put me at ease.

"Very funny," I said. "Okay, give me a minute to pull myself together. But after the beach I want to see Dora."

"No problem. She's staying down the hall, right there," he said, pointing. "You can see her anytime you like."

I closed the door and then leaned back against it, breathing deep. Hayes had the exact same effect on me at seventeen as he'd had at twelve. I couldn't afford to lose my willpower, and a crush was exactly the kind of thing that could rob me of it. Not to mention the fact that all my complicated feelings toward Adam were still unresolved—maybe this sudden interest in someone new was just a means of avoiding the Adam factor. I told myself that this jaunt down to the beach with

Hayes was a fact-finding mission and nothing more. I knew next to nothing about the Resistance, besides the odd fact that Madam Wang was a part of it, and I needed to know much more. Plus, Hayes probably had information about what had happened with Wang after we escaped the Forbidden City.

I emerged fifteen minutes later, looking as put-together as I had in a while. There was a selection of sundresses hanging in the closet, as well as a bikini that I had no intention of wearing. The Resistance was definitely living a different lifestyle than we were used to on the compound, which made me wonder how closely they still adhered to VisionCrest doctrine.

When I stepped into the hall, Hayes smiled broadly for a change, showing off a row of straight white teeth. The two men from the boat ride hovered at the end of the hall, watching us.

"Do your bodyguards really need to come with us?" I asked, knowing full well it was me they were keeping an eye on.

"Yes. My popularity is a stifling inconvenience, but I hope you'll be willing to look past it," he said, winking.

"Charm will get you nowhere with me," I lied.

"Guess I'll have to skate by on good looks alone then," he said, the air between us practically crackling. "Here, I brought you a banana."

"Thanks," I said, taking it.

Hayes led us around the corner, through another hallway, and down a spiral staircase. The house was massive and mazelike.

"How many people live here?" I asked.

"About eighty, off and on. The Resistance has bases in various places around the world, but Vietnam is a convenient cover considering VisionCrest is *persona non grata* around these parts. My mother and I have been traveling back and forth between here and Britain for about a year now, pretending to visit my grandmother. When my father was abducted in Tokyo, we came here to stay."

"Your father was abducted in Tokyo, too?" I asked.

He nodded. "The whole reason we were there was because Madam Wang had tipped us off that your father's abduction was imminent. My father was the head of the Resistance. Wang killed him. Now everyone expects me to take his place, but I have no idea what the hell I'm supposed to do."

I didn't really know what to say to that. How do you react to the news that someone's father has been murdered and they're supposed to step into his unfillable shoes? Actually, it sounded a lot like my life right now.

"I think I can relate to that," I said.

He smiled at me, in a way that was so warm and genuine I wanted to melt into his arms. Instead, I trailed along after him.

Hayes led us past a series of rooms on the ground floor. Through a crack in one of the doors I could see a group of believers, dressed in white, kneeling on the wooden floor of an open-air studio, chanting. It was the meditation of the Inner Eye; I would know it anywhere.

"Why does Vietnam let you guys stay when you're so clearly practicing what they've expressly forbidden?" I asked.

"The enemy of my enemy is my friend, I guess." He shrugged.

"You consider VisionCrest your enemy?" I asked, alarmed.

"No, of course not. We want to preserve it. We're fighting against the people who've been angling to take VisionCrest over, like Sacristan Wang. As you know, they're into some very bad juju."

The house suddenly opened up onto the jungle, and beyond it I could see the ocean glittering on the horizon. Votives still lined the pathway we'd taken last night.

"You mean Isiris," I said.

Hayes paused and looked at me. A worry line creased his brow. It was the first time I'd seen him look anything less than completely at ease.

"Madam Wang said she speaks to you. She thinks Isiris is trying to inhabit you."

"That sounds crazy," I said. I didn't want to admit it was also true.

"Yep," he agreed. "It's pretty far out there. Come on, let's keep going."

We walked in silence for a bit, Madam Wang's words rattling around in my head and leaving me unsettled. "Inhabited" was exactly the way I felt sometimes—would it actually be possible for Isiris to push me out of my own life?

The midafternoon sun was beating down hard, but the white sand of the beach was beautiful and the jungle provided a slice of shade that was nice to walk along. The ebb and flow of the water lapping into shore soothed my frayed nerves. I needed to take advantage of this time alone with Hayes while he was in a talking mood. The sooner Adam and I could get out of here, the better for everyone.

"So what happened to Madam Wang? Is she okay?" I asked.

Hayes squinted into the distance. "You want to sit down?"

"Sure." I shrugged and took a seat. It felt good to burrow my feet into the sun-warmed sand.

"Wang is going to have her hung from the Gate of Heavenly Peace. Tomorrow."

"What?" I gasped. "No! We have to stop him."

"They've closed ranks. Anyone even suspected of consorting with Madam Wang has been detained, probably in that creepy underground lab he has going. The few people we have on the inside who haven't been caught up in his dragnet can't afford to blow their cover."

"So you're just going to let her die?" I asked.

"It's not up to me, Harlow," he said. "Right now my job is to protect you. That's what Madam Wang would want— she made the ultimate sacrifice for you. Because she believes you're the only one who can stop Isiris."

I decided to play dumb. It was better if Hayes believed I had no intention of even trying.

"I'm not sure where she got that idea." I wrapped my arms around my knees. "I haven't got the first clue how to stop Isiris. So what's the plan?"

"The plan is to keep you safe and hope that Isiris gives away her location."

"Why not initiate me into the further mysteries and make me the official Matriarch? That would give us a much stronger hand to play—having the entire church behind us. Leaving the position empty creates a power vacuum, and there's no telling who might jump in. Or is the first mystery the only one you care about?"

"I don't joke when it comes to the mysteries. I take my role as your second very seriously."

"With what you know about Isiris, how can you still take all this VisionCrest stuff seriously?" I asked.

"Whatever Isiris may be, she is the beginning and not the end. I believe there is a higher purpose for her existence, and for ours. I believe in whatever—or whoever—created her."

I wasn't sure if he was for real or not. He could be dead serious—a devout drinker of the VisionCrest Kool-Aid— and I wasn't sure how I felt about that anymore. Or he could be putting on an act. If the Resistance didn't want me to be installed as Matriarch, it might be because they wanted that power for themselves. Either way, I felt queasy. There really wasn't anyone I could trust.

"Has Isiris ever given you any clue of where to find her?" he asked.

"No," I lied.

Hayes turned his head. I could feel him watching me, causing that little flutter despite all the other stuff going on. I closed my eyes, trying to focus on the waves. The next thing

I knew, his hand was on my leg, his thumb running back and forth over the inner curve of my knee.

"Do you remember when I stayed at your house in Twin Falls, five years ago?" he asked.

Flutter. It occurred to me that he might be manipulating me, but the flutter happened all the same.

"Yes," I said.

"There was something I wanted to do then, but I was too afraid. Now I really want to do it. I'm not supposed to, because I'm your second. It crosses about eight kinds of boundaries."

Double flutter. I turned to look at him. "I'm not a big fan of boundary crossing," I said.

"Then may I please kiss you?" he asked.

If I found Isiris like I planned, I might never make it back. This might be my last first kiss with someone. I nodded.

"I'd really like to hear you say it," he murmured.

"You can kiss me," I whispered, feeling illicit.

He leaned in close, brushing my hair back off my shoulder. We watched each other, eyes open, until at last our lips met. My eyes closed. His lips pressed against mine, tender and warm, tasting salty like the ocean. He kissed me a little harder as a wave crashed, then shushed in the background. As his lips parted mine, his hand slid a little farther up the inside of my thigh. It was more than I imagined—it was perfection. We lay down on the sand and he hovered over me.

"You're good at that," he said.

"I can do better," I responded.

He gave me a languid smile and came back for more.

Our kiss went even deeper, his body pressing rhythmically against mine. There was a heat building inside of me unlike anything I'd experienced before.

"Am I interrupting?" Adam said, with unmistakable anger in his voice.

We rolled apart and I sat up abruptly, brushing the sand off my skirt. My cheeks burned with embarrassment. After everything he'd done to me, I couldn't believe I was feeling guilty. But I was.

Adam was in swim trunks, carrying a surfboard. With his tattoo-covered chest and his ripped muscles, it was impossible not to notice how attractive he was. I was in serious need of some therapy.

Hayes stood up slowly. He and Adam were practically chest to chest.

"Don't think I don't know what you're doing," Adam said, the muscles in his jaw clenching.

"Oh, yeah? What's that?" Hayes asked.

"Harlow's the head of VisionCrest. Are you going to tell me that you and your little band of rebels don't intend to use her for her power? That you're not working her over right now, pretending to like her so you can control her?"

Adam's words made bile rise in my throat. My entire body began to shake with adrenaline. I got to my feet.

"Unlike you, I don't consider her a prop to be used in my schemes," Hayes said calmly. "I happen to like her for who she is."

Adam's eyes darted to me, the hurt written all over his

face. He clearly assumed I'd told Hayes about his betrayal, but it was just a lucky guess. I knew, just by his look, that he'd found someone to get us out of here.

"You don't know anything about me!" Adam drew back like he was going to deck Hayes, and the bodyguards who'd been hovering at the periphery moved in.

"Stop it!" I screamed at the top of my lungs. Everyone froze. "How about this? I'm not interested in either one of you. I'm not anyone's to control, protect, or detain. I'm here because I choose to be, and when I decide what's next, you'll all listen and obey. I'm going back to the house now to check on Stubin and Dora, and I don't want either one of you coming with me."

I stomped across the sand, pushing past the bodyguards and returning the way we'd come. As far as I knew, Adam and Hayes just stood there, watching me leave.

———————

"Adam and I are going to initiate each other into the remaining mysteries," I lied, feeling like a traitor. "But the Resistance can't find out. They have their own designs on power over VisionCrest—just look at the way they're holding us here like prisoners."

Dora's eyes grew wide. "Where, and from whom? There isn't a VisionCrest temple anywhere in this entire country."

Asleep in her lap, Stubin lurched into a coughing fit, but he didn't wake up. We were in the infirmary; I'd tiptoed there hours after that little scene on the beach, when the house was quiet. I couldn't stand the thought of running into Hayes or Adam, much less being subjected to both of them at once.

"Adam has a contraband copy of the first nine mysteries, which he stole from his father," I explained, having prepared for this question. "It's important that we claim our official roles as Matriarch and Eparch before Sacristan Wang's splinter group—or the Resistance—can take it away from us. And believe me, they both want to take it away."

The old Dora would have called me on this whopper of a lie. Instead, my best friend was reduced to offering an indignant square of her shoulders. After what we'd been through, nothing seemed impossible anymore.

"You're not going away without me," she said, stroking Stubin's hair. "I won't let you leave me out of this, too."

The way her eyes wrinkled at the corners told me I'd hurt her deeply—maybe beyond repair. But I couldn't give her what she was asking.

"This isn't your fight," I said.

"Oh, but it's Adam's?"

I opted not to divulge the fact that Adam was the one who knew everything all along, but who'd withheld the information from both of us. We had to seem united or I'd never convince Dora to let me go it alone.

"Dora, Stubin needs you. You said it yourself—if he's put in a high-stress situation, it could kill him. And you can't leave him here with a bunch of strangers. When it's done, we'll go back to Twin Falls together," I said. "We'll rebuild."

"You're lying to me, even now," Dora said. "You don't believe in the Fellowship."

I looked down at my feet. I didn't know what to say. "Maybe I do now."

"Is the General really dead?" she asked, even though she already knew the answer.

"Yes," I said, swallowing hard.

She looked at me. "This has something to do with that voice you hear, doesn't it?"

"Yes," I admitted.

"You should have trusted me," she said.

It sounded painfully familiar. They were the same words I'd said to Adam, and she was completely right.

"I'm sorry," I said.

She looked off into the distance, her lips pressed into a thin line. I wasn't sure I would ever regain her trust.

"When are you leaving?" she asked.

"Not for a while," I lied. "But when I do, it won't be for long. I'll be back, and I'll be missing you and loving you the entire time."

She rolled her eyes. "You're such a cheesemonger."

I sighed, relief coursing through me. "Only for you, babycakes. Only for you."

I got up and padded toward the door.

"Harlow?" Dora called.

I stopped and turned toward her. "I love you, too."

I'd only been back in my room a few minutes when there was a soft rap at the door. I expected it to be Hayes, apologizing for earlier and making empty assurances about how I was under the Resistance's protection but not their prisoner.

Instead, it was Adam. He looked hastily left and right. "Can I come in?" he asked. He was nervous and clearly still pissed about the Hayes thing.

"Fine," I said tersely, making it crystal clear that I was mad, too. I opened the door wider and he slipped in. I closed it behind him.

"They for sure know you're here," I said. "There's been guards posted outside my room since we got here."

"There's one guard, and I've been watching him for the last hour. He just took a bio-break so we only have a minute."

"I'm sure they're watching your room, too," I said.

"I went out the window. I'm pretty accomplished at sneaking in and out of bedrooms, as I'm sure you've gathered." He was trying to wind me up, but I wasn't going to take the bait.

"So what did you find today?" I asked.

"Well, you making out with that scrawny beach grommet, for starters."

"It was just a kiss. It didn't mean anything."

Adam scoffed. "Right. Well, I also found someone who can meet us at the floating market in Hoi An, tomorrow morning before dawn. They'll have a speedboat waiting off the main dock. We'll boat south along the coast to somewhere near Nha Trang, and we'll bicycle into Cambodia from there."

"I'm sorry, did you just say 'bicycle into Cambodia'?"

"It's the only way to stay low profile. Sorry, Your Highness;

no private jets for you this time. It will only take a couple days."

"That was apparently quite a surf session you had."

"Yeah, well—let's just say I was highly motivated. And based on what I saw at the beach today, my instincts to get us the hell out of here were right. You know he's using you, right?"

"You're such a hypocrite," I said. "Just tell me how we're getting away from here."

Adam's look darkened. I could tell he wanted to say something but was holding back.

"Fine. We'll leave the same way we came—on pretty boy's schooner. The roof outside your window is about fifteen feet off the ground. Bodyguards patrol on foot in a circular path around the grounds. They pass by here every fifteen minutes, beginning at the top of each hour. At five a.m., one of them will pass beneath your window—wait until he's out of sight and then drop and make a break for the jungle. I'll meet you at the beach, with the boat."

"We really want to do this?" I whispered.

"We really don't have a choice," he answered.

A look passed between us. For a split second we were the Adam and Harlow we used to be. Then he gave a little shoulder shrug.

"I've gotta go. Does Dora know you're leaving?" He was moving toward the window.

"I told her we were going to begin the Rites of Initiation," I said.

His features softened. "When this is done, that's exactly what we're going to do."

I nodded.

"You're welcome," he said, one foot out the window, on the sloping roof of the house, and one foot inside.

"You're a jerk," I said.

"I know," he said, then leaned back into the room. His lips landed squarely on mine, his kiss powerful and insistent. It knocked the wind out of me, and not just because it was unexpected. He smiled a bit, seeing my reaction. "But I'm a jerk who cares about you."

I watched him crawl away into the dark, wondering if this plan had any chance of working and knowing that no matter what happened, somebody was going to get hurt.

As I was crawling into bed, I noticed the mirror out of the corner of my eye. I could see that the girl reflected back was moving, even though I wasn't. I didn't want to look, but I couldn't help it. A low, static buzz invaded my brain as I turned my head.

My mirror image was pacing back and forth, back and forth, dragging her finger across the glass. She looked pissed. Her head jerked up and she caught me staring.

Return to me. Return to me. Return to me.

I couldn't look away. She pounded both fists against the glass, repeatedly. It made the sound of a freight train coming through the room.

Return to me. Return to me. RETURN TO ME!

The mirror shattered, shards of glass flying everywhere.

I dove beneath the bedspread for cover, half-expecting her to climb through the broken glass and step into the room with me. I waited, shivering with fear under the blanket, listening for the sound of footsteps.

At last, I gathered the courage to peek out. There was nothing there. No broken mirror. No rogue reflection. Just me, staring out, wide-eyed with fear.

I needed this to be over before I completely lost my mind.

FLOATING MARKET

The Hoi An central market was in its pre-dawn hubbub. Adam and I had abandoned our schooner at the city's edge, then walked through the covered maze of market stalls toward the main dock. Brightly colored fruits and greens of all shapes and sizes were being portioned out in flat, round bowls as vendors set up for the day. But the real action was up ahead—the farther we walked into the depths of the market, the closer we got to the throng of slight old women gathered at the docks, buying and selling flora and fauna from boats laden with organic riches. This floating market was like the floor of the stock exchange, only with thatched hats instead of three-piece suits and squid instead of ticker tape. Even from a hundred feet out, I could see that there was exactly the same amount of ruthless negotiation.

When we'd left Bên Trong Mắt, Adam had thrust a thatched hat into my hands, and now I pulled it lower to shield my eyes. I was wearing a long, burnt-orange Ao Dai dress and blousy pants I'd found hanging in my closet, behind the sundresses. My VisionCrest uniform was wrapped up in a little parcel and shoved into a backpack—it felt like the only proof of identity I had left, even if it was a dangerous currency in this part of the world. I wanted to believe that we'd be coming back, but the fact that I couldn't bring myself to leave my uniform behind told me I didn't fully believe that was true.

Vendors and shoppers wore surgical masks over their faces. We did too, but for different a reason: we were trying to hide. Everyone else was whispering about a virus. It was all over the news—small outbreaks of something so virulent that it made the victims vomit blood, then collapse and seize, like a dying fish, in a pool of their own platelets. Thus far the spread had been contained to small pockets. Nobody was sure what was causing the outbreaks, but it killed quickly, with limited chance to spread. I suspected that wouldn't be the case for long. It was just the opening salvo in Isiris's purification war, and a message in a bottle for me: Go to her, or else. The world was a ticking time bomb.

I peeked up at Adam, next to me. He was wearing an outfit of loose linen, his hospital mask covering most of his face and his sloped hat obscuring the rest. Even so, he was clearly out of place. It would only be a matter of time before someone recognized us. Yet all we had to do was weave our way through the rest of these food stalls without being recognized—recognition could lead to anything from a curious mob to a detention by the local authorities. Either way, we would be screwed.

I looked over my shoulder, expecting at any moment to see the Resistance bodyguards weaving through the crowd.

Every time I saw someone with a cell phone my heart skipped a beat—all it would take was one savvy mole, and they would be on us before we could make it out.

We were just feet away from the docks now. The briny, fishy scent on the wind smelled like fear. Last night I'd had a nightmare in which Dora, and Adam, and I were alone in a rowboat. I watched Dora deteriorate before my eyes, melting over the sides. Then Adam climbed over the side of the boat to save her, only to be carried away on an endless tide. I was left alone, floating in the middle of nowhere. It didn't take Freud to interpret that one.

I focused back on the here and now—anything beyond that was too scary. An elevated tension hung in the air. This was our make-it-or-break-it moment. The first of many, I realized grimly.

We broke free from the labyrinth of stalls and fought our way onto the docks. The throngs of tiny Vietnamese women, cigarettes dangling from their lips, brokered their deals. They bartered and bickered with one another as their husbands slopped buckets of fresh fish off the boats and onto the cement docks. The sun was just peeking up over the ocean, illuminating the hustle and bustle of the town's commerce.

A three-toned whistle rang out through the air behind us.

My spine stiffened in recognition. It was the whistle Hayes had used when we first approached the Resistance compound by boat. Adam and I both turned, combing the crowd to see where it was coming from. Another whistle. Then another. It seemed to be coming from all angles at the same time.

Adam turned to look at me, his eyes wild. "Run."

Someone had recognized us—not surprising, since there was a bounty on my head the size of a small country's GDP. It wasn't just the Resistance but also Wang who was sure to have his spies hunting us. Neither one of these groups could afford to have me on the loose, threatening to start my own rebellion that might topple their own bids for supremacy.

I tried to run, but the crowd was too thick. Women aggressively threw elbows and pushed one another, making it next to impossible to navigate quickly. I took another look behind me, and this time I saw them.

There, just a hundred feet behind us, worming their way through the stalls toward us, was a pack of beefy men who looked like they'd just broken out of a maximum security prison. It didn't much matter which side they were playing for, Wang or Resistance. They clearly meant us harm.

"It's just up here," Adam yelled, as we crashed through disgruntled ladies who spit on the ground in our wake.

I burst into a full sprint, mumbling sorries as baskets full of vibrant vegetables spilled onto the slimy boards of the dock. Adam grabbed my hand and pulled me along, bobbing and weaving as he steered us to some unknown launch point. The locals were stirring and pointing, the first seeds of unrest beginning to grow as people started to notice the two people who didn't belong running full-speed along the docks. I could hear the pounding of boots behind us, so close now that I dared not turn around for fear of losing crucial seconds.

The crowd thinned as we shot out onto a rickety pier that was surrounded by lichen-choked water. I looked up ahead and saw a speedboat waiting, empty save for a man in a peaked hat and surgical mask. That had to be our guy.

We stopped at the edge.

"We have to jump," Adam instructed, pulling me toward him. "On the count of three, jump as far as you can."

"I don't think I can make it."

"You have to make it! Do it! One, two, *three!*"

I leaped from the pier and toppled onto the smooth white seats of the speedboat.

"Come on," I screamed at Adam, who was still standing at the edge. Two women had grabbed him by the arms and were pulling at him. The men were steps from him.

"Jump!" I screamed.

My eyes locked on his, and I saw something rise up inside him. He leaped, nearly clearing the opposite side of the boat.

"Go! Go!" I yelled at the driver as he fired up the engine. There was a rumble and then a jerk, and I rolled back against Adam. We huddled in a ball at the bottom of the boat.

Just like that, we were chopping our way across the waves, watching the men panting at the edge of the pier, radioing frantically to unknown cohorts. As the pier receded in the distance, I recognized Hayes, emerging from the crowd to stand with the men who'd been chasing us. Even though I was too far away to see it, I could feel the disappointment in his eyes. Maybe things could be different some day in the future, if he gave up on the idea of protecting me—which was the same as controlling me—and realized that I didn't need him or anyone else to watch over me. I was just as powerful as any boy. More, even.

Miraculously, we made it out into open water without

being pursued and began the eight-hour journey to a little beach village just north of Nha Trang, where we planned to begin our trek by bike. Adam and I sat in silence for the first two hours. My mind was racing through every angle of our escape and what still lay in front of us; the more I thought about it, the more uneasy I became.

"I'm not sure about this plan," I finally whispered to Adam, hoping the din of the engines disguised my words from our driver.

"Going by boat is the only way we can stay untraceable," Adam said. "The Resistance has the police in its pocket, and every single main road is going to have checkpoints and surveillance. They can't touch us out here—we disappear off the map, and they have no idea where to find us."

I tipped my head toward the driver, who didn't seem to be aware we were talking.

"Are you sure the people who helped you set this up aren't going to give you away?" I whispered in his ear.

Adam looked warily at the driver. "What are you suggesting? We have to have a guide or we'll never find our way."

"I'd be willing to bet that by now the Resistance has bribed someone to spill your plan, so unless we change our course, it's pretty much guaranteed they'll be waiting for us when we dock."

Adam rubbed his hand over his face. He was exhausted—both of us were. We couldn't afford to make sloppy decisions. Not when we were so close.

"What are you suggesting?" he asked.

"I'm suggesting that we have him make an unexpected

stop in the next place that looks reasonably inhabited and we run like hell to get away from him. We use the money we have to hitch a ride to where we need to go. Screw the bikes."

"Is this just your attempt to avoid exercise?" he asked, flashing me a devious smile.

"Partially." I grinned back.

"Well, then, I guess there's no point in arguing," he said.

It felt good to be back on civil terms. If we were going to make it through what lay ahead, we were going to have to work as a team.

HOLIDAY IN CAMBODIA

We stepped out of the decrepit Jeep belonging to our Cambodian guide as the long summer day slipped toward night. We'd come to the end of the road. According to the Jeep's GPS, we were about ten miles away from the latitude/longitude coordinates inked on Adam's wrist. Ten miles of densely packed jungle, which we now stood on the edge of.

The foliage was a bit of a relief, after several days traveling the barren, dusty side roads of the Cambodian countryside. Where Vietnam was built in shades of green, Cambodia was a spectrum of sun-beat browns. The dirt-smudged faces of the hungry, sweet children who chased after our car as it ambled through tiny village after tiny village, smiling and waving at the foreign sight of strangers, haunted me.

This was a place beyond the self-indulgence of religion. I told myself that someday, when all of this was over, I was going to come back here and use the money and power of VisionCrest to make something good in this world for these kids, instead of worrying so much about the next world.

The air was soporific, draping across my neck like a yoke. A wall of green, thirty feet high, surrounded us; there wasn't a hint of civilization except for the Jeep idling in the weeds. The air smelled like vegetative rot and the sky was bleeding from pink to purple. As if the odds weren't already stacked against us, Adam and I were going to be making this trek in the dark. I shuddered.

"Too bad I left that vintage Dead Kennedys T-shirt at home," I said weakly.

"'Holiday in Cambodia' used to be my favorite song," Adam said wryly. "I'm thinking it's time to re-evaluate my top-ten list."

The jeep fired up its engine. The driver rolled down his window and gave us a strange look. He clearly thought we were several cards short of a full deck, asking to be dropped off in this remote jungle without a ride out. And, since the clothes we'd left Vietnam in were in tatters, we were back in our VisionCrest uniforms. Luckily, we were so far off the grid that people here didn't have time to worry about some first-world religion—they were too busy trying to survive.

As the droning noise of the Jeep receded into the distance, a buzz of another kind began. I knew exactly what that meant. I looked at Adam.

"Isiris is close by."

We made slow, silent progress over the mucky ground. Water soaked through my Mary Janes, my feet sliding in my socks and the bright burn of blisters following my every step. I tried not to think about the heat, which was sucking moisture out of my every pore. Or about the leeches, which the driver said lurked in the thick tangle of leaves and vines that rose past my knees, tickling the exposed skin of my thighs in my ridiculous VisionCrest uniform.

Our chauffeur had gifted us a beat-up and potentially faulty compass, pointing us in the direction we supposedly needed to go. Adam had a little LED pocketlight that he pressed every once in a while to make sure we stayed on course. The driver had also given us a little rucksack with a few bottles of water in it, handing it to us apologetically, as if to say it was enough to get us there but not to bring us back.

We'd been trudging for hours without a break when I heard the scraping of leaves against Adam's clothes stop short. I bumped into him, unable to see in the dark.

"What is it?" I whispered.

"Shhh ... " he said, very softly.

I strained my ears. There was the stealthy but unmistakable swish of something moving through the foliage.

My heart hammered inside my chest.

The hush of parting foliage grew closer. I grabbed onto Adam's arm. There was nothing to do but stay still.

The thing exhaled softly. All movement ceased. I could almost feel whatever predator it was testing the air. Zeroing in on us. Adam's muscles tensed. I held my breath.

The thing began to slink closer, its approach nearly soundless, like silk scarves sliding over the underbrush. It was the sound of stalking.

Then a rumble of thunder rolled across the sky, dangerously close, drowning out all other sounds. My stomach clenched. The smell of ozone filled the air. A spectacular crack rang out ahead of us, and the entire jungle lit up with an electric-white glow.

Now I could see what was standing there. A black panther, frozen mid-stride less than ten feet in front of us. Its yellow eyes glowed, and then we were plunged back into darkness. It began a hollow growling, which sounded like a saw running back and forth over an aluminum can.

Purity.

The word whispered through the trees. Another burst of light split the air in two, and I saw that the panther was crouched as if to strike. The thunder crack was nearly simultaneous, practically lifting me off the ground. The heavens opened up and the downpour began.

Come to me.

"Not now," I hissed. Isiris had impeccable timing.

"What?" Adam yelled.

The panther let out a long, extended roar. If we ran, he would chase us; it wouldn't be a long pursuit.

"What should we do?" Adam asked.

From outer blindness, inner sight.

Isiris's voice in my head was more insistent. Maybe she was guiding me.

"Follow my lead," I said, taking his hand.

I took a step toward the panther, imagining where it stood and trying to go around it. The veil of rain obscured all sight and sound. I had to go entirely on instinct. Adam tugged at my arm as if to hold me back, but I simply held his hand tighter and pulled us forward.

We took five shaky steps, then ten, before something

bristled against my thigh. Fur, slick with rain. It was hard and immovable as stone, but it did not jump to attack.

I forged ahead, quickening my step. We moved on silently for five minutes through the rain. I held my breath, waiting to be pounced on or bitten at any moment. Another flash of lightning lit up the canopy a bit more dimly; the thunder was farther away now. The rain began to subside. But in that moment I saw the panther. He was prowling alongside us, only inches away, as if he were our escort. I suspected that might be exactly what he was—Isiris asserting her ownership over this space. Reminding me that I was in her territory now.

"I think he's gone," Adam said. "Guess he wasn't hungry." Apparently, he hadn't seen what I had.

"Yeah," I agreed.

I didn't let go of Adam's hand the rest of the night, knowing our silent sentinel was with us.

THE VIOLET HOUR

Most religions have a complex mythology that everyone assumes is simply an allegory and only the crazies take literally. An angel appeared or a bush caught on fire, and the mysteries of the universe were somehow revealed. Until the events of this trip, I'd thought the same was true for VisionCrest. I'd assumed that my father was only posturing, cultivating a mystique to package and sell his self-help mumbo jumbo when he claimed to have happened upon an ancient temple in the middle of the Cambodian jungle. But as the Violet Hour bathed the temple in shades of purple, I could see with my own eyes that the Fellowship wasn't built on allegory. It was absolutely real.

Honeycomb spires like tongues of flame twisted against the near-dawn sky. They were lit by a flickering glow, emanating from behind the hulking sprawl of the colonnade. Columns guarded the silence like sentinels. A hivelike hum from within the temple's depths radiated across the ground and tore its way through my chest. There was a pair of crumbling staircases, worn into non-existence until they blended into one another. To the casual observer, this would look like another lost temple of the Khmer empire melting into the Cambodian underbrush. I knew it for what it was: the gateway to Isiris's world.

Adam and I gave one another a sidelong glance that transmitted uncertainty and fear. There was nothing that could save us out here, except each other.

"You can trust me," he said, as if reading my mind.

"A promise is only words," I answered.

"Time passes differently in there," he said. "I thought I was gone days, but it was months."

We looked back at the temple. It was made of sandstone and its edges had been eroded by the passage of time, as if some alien civilization had heralded the All Seeing Eye millions of years ago. In the center, an enormous carved eye sat in an upside-down triangle, just like the VisionCrest logo. Bursting out on all sides were massive trees the size of office buildings. Exposed root systems spilled down like Medusa's tangled, ropy tendrils. It was as if the temple was an organic being, thrust out of the womb of the ancient forest.

Isiris's voice had been suspiciously silent since we first encountered the panther.

"It's the Violet Hour," I said. "Seems appropriate that we'd arrive now."

Adam's mouth was set in a grim line. "Maybe it's not a coincidence."

"There's our friend," I said as the panther slid out of the

jungle and rubbed up against the base of the eye. "He's been with us all night."

"You knew?" Adam said, surprised.

"Did you?" I asked.

He chuckled. "Yeah. I just didn't want to freak you out."

"I kind of started to get the feeling he was protecting us," I said.

Adam sighed as the reality of our situation settled back in. Nobody was going to protect us.

The sky got lighter by inches, and the temple seemed to fade into the greenery as if it might disappear with the sunrise. I remembered what my father had said about the temple seemingly materializing out of nowhere, just before dawn.

"It's time," I said.

We approached the structure, picking our way through treacherous brambles that raked across my skin. The temple loomed larger and larger as we approached, as if it was growing and expanding. Finally we were right in front of the eye. From this vantage point, I could see a patchwork of symbols etched across the stone. They were the same as Adam's tattoos.

His face had gone bone-white, and I knew he was thinking about his parents. Wondering what he would find on the other side.

Right at eye level, there was the imprint of a palm. I didn't know how, but I knew exactly what I had to do. I grabbed Adam's hand and then raised my other hand, placing it over the slimy stone. My palm print fit perfectly inside. I swore I could feel a hand pressing back from the other side.

"*Isiris fi ainek*," I said, not knowing where the words came from.

A feeling of complete contentment flooded me. Every care, every fear, every desire drained away from me. Something dark within me stirred, as if it had been sleeping all this time.

There was the sound of scraping stones, as if the rocks were hinging in on themselves and becoming something new, forming themselves around my words. I had a sense of becoming insubstantial, of falling through the stone itself. It smelled musty, like wet woolen socks left to rot in a basement. My sight became blurry, faded, like at the onset of a vision. Only this time it was real. The only point on my body that I could still feel was Adam's hand in mine. Wherever I was going, he was coming with me.

When things came back into focus, we were facing three arched doors. Adam and I looked first at each other and then behind us—there was just smooth stone there, no sign of an entryway. The room we were in was small and circular.

"Is this the same as last time?" I asked, letting go of his hand.

"I wasn't conscious when I was brought here, or when I was taken out. The only thing I ever saw was the room where I was held. Maybe it's some kind of test," he said.

Choose. Isiris's voice whistled around the perimeter of the tiny room.

"This is Isiris's way of showing us she has the upper hand. She wants us to choose," I said.

I examined the three doors and walked up to the one on the left. I put my hand on the brass knob, wondering how such a thing could even be inside this place. I turned and pulled it open.

There was a tremendous sucking sound. On the other side of the door was an expansive landscape of swirling funnel clouds, black as death. In the far distance, I could see what looked like enormous pyramids, like the ones in Egypt only dark as midnight. My body responded viscerally, fear hollowing out my insides. A crushing sadness crept up from my toes, turning my legs to lead.

"Close it!" Adam yelled over the suction sound.

His voice snapped me out of it and I pushed the door, the wind pulling it shut with a crack.

I bent over, breathing hard. "What ... was ... that?"

"The wrong choice," he said.

"It was like ... another world or something."

"Or something."

I stood up and pushed my hair back from my face. "Door number two?" I asked.

"This one's gotta be the one hiding the cash and prizes." Adam moved right up behind me and put his hand on my arm.

"Here goes nothing," I said.

The second door opened with an anemic creak. Before us stretched a long, dark hallway with doors lining both sides. Its depths dissolved into darkness, so it was impossible to tell what else it might contain. There was a chill radiating from within that made me feel even more afraid than the first door.

"This is it," I said.

"Should we open the last door, just to be sure this is the one we want?" Adam asked.

Harlow…

"No," I said.

"I'm really wishing we had some freakin' bread crumbs right about now," he said.

"No kidding," I answered.

I took a tentative step inside, Adam following behind. The hallway seemed to tighten around us; I wasn't entirely convinced it was only in my mind. A second after we crossed the threshold, the door slammed behind us, shutting us in and smothering us in blackness. The chill deepened.

Adam looked over his shoulder. "Harlow, the door isn't here anymore."

Somehow I wasn't surprised. It was like we'd crawled inside the recesses of a madman's dream, and in a way we had. This place was Isiris's in-between, and I had a feeling that it bent to her will.

"Put your hand on my shoulder," I said. After a moment, Adam's hand found me.

I walked slowly forward, trailing my hand along the walls on either side of us, which were undeniably getting closer. When I felt another door, I stopped.

"Let's open it," I said. Adam remained silent, as afraid as I was of what might be lurking within.

I pulled. It was a small room, dimly illuminated, with a dingy mattress on the concrete floor, covered by a thin gray blanket. There were eight tick-marks carved into the stone wall by the makeshift bed. Empty shackles hung from the wall; a deep brown bloodstain covered the floor. Adam's inhale was sharp.

"This is it. This is my room," he said, his voice lifting like it was some kind of positive sign.

"The room you were kept in? How do you know?" Of all the doors we could choose to open, it seemed impossible that this could be the same one.

"Those are my tick-marks. That means my mother is right around here," he said excitedly.

He fumbled along the wall of the hallway for the next door. I followed the sound of his eager footsteps. He pulled open the next door, and a salty tang filled the air. As I came up behind him, we were looking through the ruined depths of a blue-green ocean, the remnants of a great city of twisted metal on its sandy floor. It looked just like New York, as if the city existed in some parallel present where the world had been flooded. I could almost feel the water sliding against my skin. It cast a soft blue light into the hall. I reached up, curious to touch it. My hand bounced back, repelled by the unseen barrier.

"She's not here." Adam's voice cracked. "Isiris must have her somewhere else. We've got to hurry."

I just watched the buildings, unable to look away.

"Harlow, come on. We have to go."

Adam had to physically pull me back and close the door. He took my hand, moving us quickly down the hall as I shook off the fog that had come over me while watching the submerged cityscape. Something was piecing itself together in my mind, some idea of what the landscapes beyond the doors meant, but it wasn't completely clear yet.

We walked on, passing an endless stream of identical

doors in near-total darkness. Suddenly there was a wan light in the far-off distance. We both saw it at the same time.

Adam stopped short. "Do you see that?" he whispered.

"It's coming toward us," I said.

My heart clenched. This wasn't the proverbial light at the end of the tunnel. It was some *thing*, taking a more and more human-looking shape as it drew close to us, illuminating the doors on either side of itself as it skimmed over the floor without actually touching it.

"What should we do?" Adam asked.

I considered the doors to the left and right of us. Maybe one would lead to another hallway, but that wouldn't buy us much. It would only serve to make us more lost. The fleeting thought that we might be doomed to wander an endless labyrinth of hallways and doorways leading nowhere seized me; I pushed it away, forcing myself to focus on the present danger of whatever was heading straight toward us.

The thing was close enough now that I could make out its form. It looked like a woman, her limp posture like a wet rag suspended by a hook, except she was semi-transparent. The tops of her feet dragged across the floor as she skimmed toward us, the sunken shadows where her eyes should be not fixing on anything. She seemed to be looking right through us.

"Move out of the way." I tugged at Adam's shirt and we both squeezed against the wall as she passed by. As she passed, it felt as though I'd plunged into a frozen pond. We watched her light recede, the way we'd come, then wink out as blackness subsumed us once again.

I buried my face in Adam's chest. "Was that a wraith? The followers of Isiris you told me about?"

"Yes," he said, his voice raspy.

"Maybe we should follow it," I said. "Otherwise we might never find Isiris."

"If she's here, we'll find her." Adam hugged me tighter. My eyes stung with the threat of tears; it felt punishingly good to be inside his embrace.

He kissed the top of my head. "Come on, let's keep going."

I grabbed his hand, and this time I didn't intend on letting go.

Several hours later we finally came to the end of the hallway. There was a door directly in front of us. I closed my eyes and concentrated, willing Isiris's presence into my head. There was only silence.

"Ready?" Adam asked.

"I should go first," I said.

"Zero chance," he replied.

I knew that tone. There was no use trying to argue. An electric wave of foreboding shot down my arms to the tips of my fingers.

"Okay. Let's get it over with," I said.

He turned the knob. Sunlight flooded the hallway, and I shielded my eyes as I stepped into an immense round room. It was made of small stones, with a narrow ramp ribboning its way around the inside edge—up, up, up, as far as the eye could see, until the blinding glare of what looked like the sun blotted out the rest. It was like staring up from the bottom of a wishing well. For all I knew, it went on forever.

In the center of the floor, a series of black stones formed a symbol. Another replica of the All Seeing Eye.

"This is the place my father described to me—a cylinder that goes up as far as the eye can see, with doors everywhere. This is the room where Isiris gave me to the General," I said.

Glancing behind me, I saw that the door we'd come through was no longer there. "Our door is gone."

"I don't think it was ever really there to begin with," Adam said.

"What do you mean?"

"She's toying with us." Adam tilted his chin up to the false sun and closed his eyes. He looked defeated.

"What's wrong?" I asked. It was a stupid question—what wasn't wrong?

Adam let out a ragged breath. Nothing had ever sounded more hopeless to me.

"I thought I was going to walk in here and kill Isiris. Rescue my mother. Set us all free. I'm an idiot," he said.

Purity, Isiris's voice whispered in my ear. Adam didn't flinch. I squinted, looking up at the doors cascading down the stone walls, but no one was there.

"You're not an idiot," I said.

"Maybe we should go through one of these doors. See what's on the other side," he murmured.

It was an odd thing to say.

He opened his eyes and saw the narrow-eyed way I was looking at him. "Why are you looking at me like that?" he asked, putting his hands up.

Death.

I blinked at the floor and put my hands up to my temple as a skull-crushing migraine ripped through my head. There was a ring of fire behind my eyelids. My mind glowed red with VisionCrest's All Seeing Eye.

A scene came alive in my mind. It was Koenji—the Tokyo neighborhood with the nightclub where I'd first realized that I might still have a chance at being something more to Adam than a friend.

"Harlow?" Adam's voice sounded like it was underwater.

Everything was still, except for the periodic reflection of a yellow light against a storefront. It might have been a siren or the blinking neon of a livehouse. Either way, the eerie vision was missing something. It was devoid of human life.

My mind flickered to the next thing. China, the Great Wall. This time the vision was not empty. Bodies were everywhere—bloody. Dead and unmoving, strewn across the top of the world. Next came Beijing. The scene was mayhem. Bodies littered the edges of Tiananmen Square; blood ran in tributaries along the downward slope of its edges. The not-yet-dead were crawling and collapsing in intervals, clawing over one another in a desperate bid to flee the virus that was eating them from the inside out.

My mind spun in circles, flashing scenes I recognized from our tour. What was missing was any sign of anyone healthy, upright, fleeing, running, or not in the throes of dying.

Ashes. Ashes. They all fall down. The pain and suffering was too much to bear.

A shock of white blinded me. At first I thought it was the usual electrical storm in my brain, but then I realized it was something else: the vision passed just as every door in the cylinder flew open. A sound like beating wings filled the air above us.

Streaming through the doors, one after the next, were wraiths just like we'd seen in the hallway. They floated above us, filling the space like it was a pitcher. Then, all at once, it was like they noticed our presence. In a simultaneous motion, they looked down at us.

In front of me, Adam's face went white. But he wasn't looking at them. He was looking over my shoulder.

"Sacrifice," Isiris said.

This time her voice was real. And she was standing behind me.

ALL SOULS

I spun around and faced her. It was like looking into a mirror.

Isiris took a step toward me and raised her palms into the air, flashing symbols of the Inner Eye inked on each of them. She bent her pinky and ring fingers, her thumb and other fingers creating the symbol I recognized from the Rite. Another memory came crashing back, an older one: me, slipping through the shadows when no one was looking, past the curtain into the inner sanctum of the Twin Falls temple. Sneaking through one of the doors and wandering down the hallway. Seeing my father performing a ritual on one of the Ministry initiates. He made the same sign Isiris was making now, pressing his hand into the man's forehead.

It had all come full circle. Isiris was the fount of Vision-Crest, my father just her vessel.

The wraiths, now dropping toward us as if magnetically propelled, halted and then scattered. They slid down the outer walls, crumpling in on themselves, huddling like chastised children along the bottom perimeter of the cylindrical chamber. Isiris's arrival had frozen them like wound-down toys. They looked lost and afraid, and I realized now that whatever they were, they weren't a threat to me. But she was.

Isiris wore a long purple robe, and her hair was wound in elaborate knots and braids. A bracelet with charms that looked like human eyes wound up her forearm. She closed her palms, and Adam and I both dropped to one knee as if magnetically drawn into the floor. Her power coursed through me. Controlling me. It wasn't all bad; in a sick way, it felt kind of good. Like we were connected. It was the way I imagined other people felt about their biological parents. If she was what created me, I wondered what that made me. Was I even human?

"Harlow."

I lifted my head and met her eyes. A desperate part of me wanted to see kindness there. Instead, Isiris's gray-green glare drilled through me. She tilted her head.

"I thought I might feel something for you. But there is nothing," she said, the corners of her mouth turning down. Hearing her speak was surreal; the reflection that taunted me was standing right in front of me. Her words wounded me, despite the fact that the sight of her made my stomach turn.

Isiris then turned a palm face-up and flicked her hand. Adam and I both stood automatically, like puppets on her string. She glided toward us. Fear swept through me. But it was Adam she was now focused on. She stood before him and put her hand up to his face. Then she leaned in, raised up on her toes, and placed a tender kiss on his lips.

"I knew you wouldn't fail," she said to him.

He was completely still, not returning her overture. It was impossible for me to read his allegiance. Maybe his contrition had all been a ruse to get me into this place; if so, I was colossally stupid. Isiris looked at me and narrowed her eyes. There was nothing but coldness in their fathomless depths.

"Follow," she said. Her robes fanned out behind her like the great wing of some horrible purple dragon. I looked at Adam, wanting him to give me some sign of a reaction. The wraiths sped from their spots on the periphery and huddled en masse around the hem of her robes, crowding close as if searching for warmth.

Isiris marched up the ramp that wound into seemingly infinite space. Adam followed closely behind, and I brought up the rear. It occurred to me that I might resist, but I could feel in my very cells that it wouldn't work. Isiris could command me.

As we passed the still-open doorways that lined the ramp, Isiris dismissed the things huddled around her with a flick of the wrist, her hand making the same three-fingered symbol. They dispersed through the doorways, seeming to know who was meant to go where by some form of silent communication with Isiris.

I looked through the doorways as we passed. Each displayed a different tableau, every one of them remote and inhospitable-looking. A distant mountaintop. A snow-crushed tundra with what looked like the Eiffel Tower rising out of it. A desert stretching across an endless horizon, with a Stonehenge-like formation at its center. The wraiths were tossed one by one through these doorways as we wound our way farther and farther up.

I was so absorbed in the strange events unfolding in front of me that I hadn't noticed how quickly we'd ascended. Finally we were so far above the ground that I could barely make out the symbol of the Inner Eye on the chamber floor below. My head swam and I hugged the wall, unable to take another step. I happened to look down at my hand. It was floating over the space of an open door.

At first I panicked, worried I would accidentally fall through into an alien world. But there was a solid resistance there, and I realized something—the wraiths could leave, but I couldn't pass through even if I wanted to. I snatched my hand back as if burned.

Isiris spun around, as if sensing my wandering attention. Only one wraith was left, clinging pathetically to her skirts. Isiris smiled at me, the same wicked smile I'd seen reflected in mirrors I thought were playing tricks on me.

"Through each of these doors lies a world—parallel realities, alternate to your own," she said. "In the Violet Hour, souls who have died in one world pass through the temple and on to another world, with my help, of course. And now, with yours. What shall we do with this one?" She motioned to the thing huddled at her feet. It fidgeted, distressed.

I didn't respond. The information she'd just shared was overwhelming. Disembodied souls? Alternate realities?

"Well? Would you like to keep this soul for your collection? Another lost wretch with which to pass the time? Or will you send him on and be alone?" Isiris asked me.

"I have no clue what you're talking about." I clenched my fists.

"Act now, or its journey is ended," she said. "The Violet Hour is almost over."

The thing looked at me, its eyes hollow shadows. I thought of the specter that had passed us in the endless hall, aimlessly looking for a way out. I couldn't let that happen to this … this whatever-it-was in front of me.

The doors began to whoosh closed in unison. There was a door just behind me. Without thinking, I made the initiate sign with my hand. Looking at the wraith, I flicked my wrist toward the door, which led to a misty forest of evergreens. The wraith sped away from Isiris, barely slipping through the door before it closed.

I felt an overwhelming sense of both relief and horror. Why could it leave, but I could not?

Isiris clapped her hands together in delight, looking at Adam with her face beaming. "Perfect," she said reverently. "The moment I created Harlow was the moment I knew I was truly God."

She thought she was God. Even more frightening was the possibility that she was right. Adam looked at me with real fear in his eyes.

"What did you just do?" he asked.

"I don't know," I said, on the verge of tears.

"You just ferried your first soul. This is cause for celebration. Now come," Isiris commanded.

She breezed past me and opened the door I'd just sent the spirit through. Instead of revealing the forest, it led to the

273

ground floor of the chamber. The tinny sound of Victrola music filtered across it, along with the thunder of a thousand whispered voices. There were people there—not spirits or specters, but real flesh-and-bone people. Their movements were jerky and mechanical. Adam and I looked at each other—these were the zombie things he'd told me about.

Everything here was upside down, like we were trapped inside an Escher painting: impossible staircases leading to nowhere and doorways that opened onto themselves. There was no way we were ever leaving unless Isiris wanted us to. Somehow I doubted that was part of her plan.

We walked through the door, ending up right back where we'd started. Isiris raised her palms. In unison, the revelers stopped. Dead silence. And then they turned to us. I gasped.

None of them had eyes.

Isiris grabbed me and pulled me into the crowd. A thousand pairs of empty sockets followed me. A fist-sized lump of fear lodged in my chest. I thought of Mei Mei, her missing eyes a sick tribute to the cult of Isiris.

"The Guardian has returned to take her rightful place!" Isiris bellowed.

The Guardian? The hush over the crowd was heavy.

"They've been waiting to see you," she said. "Well, not to *see* you, exactly. Obviously."

"Where are their eyes?" Adam asked.

Isiris thrust me into the pathway formed by the crowd. As she pushed me toward the center of the eye, people were falling to their knees; some were even prostrating themselves, only to get trampled by their fellow revelers. They were sniffing the air as if trying to catch our scent. As they grabbed at us, crushing panic closed in on me. Adam stumbled along behind us.

"They won't touch." Isiris looked at me sidelong to gauge my reaction. "They know how to fear properly."

"What are they?" I asked.

"Lost souls—the ones I kept from passing through the doors. Once their cycle is interrupted, they become flesh. Although the flesh soon disintegrates and they are useless as dust. Luckily, there are always more. Even in the underworld, God must have her believers. Just as she must have her slaves." She looked meaningfully at me.

My toes and fingers went numb with dread. That meant me. I was going to be enslaved or, worse, sacrificed at the altar of Isiris. Either way, she would never let me go, and everyone in my world would be doomed to die of the horrible virus she'd unleashed. I had to find out what she wanted. There was a reason she'd created me, and a reason she'd brought me here. It was my only bargaining chip.

Isiris pushed me to the center of the eye. Thousands of her zombie-like followers were now on their knees, surrounding us. They had all gone terribly still.

"Give them a smile. They've waited so long for your arrival, and they owe such a debt of gratitude to you for liberating them. You owe them a little showing off, don't you think?"

"Liberating them?" Adam asked.

"From the oppression of the non-believers," she answered.

"They don't owe me anything," I said. Just the idea of it repelled me.

"Of course they do. They thank you for being my body

in the heathen world. The conduit through which I communicated my religion, however much your surrogate father corrupted it. For taking your rightful place and setting me free."

My heart beat faster. Taking my place and setting her free where?

"Rise!" Isiris commanded.

The eye began to rise from the floor, like an altar, and we rose with it. The artificial sun beat down on us, glancing off the heads of the crowd, which was now stirring. I felt almost like I was being burned at the stake; there was a spark of madness in the crowd that frightened me to the core. The view from up high was even more surreal. The flock was a bleating, shoving amoeba of color and movement. Upturned faces, with empty craters where eyes had once looked out upon some unknown world.

Isiris held up her palms and the drumbeat of the crowd was silent once more. She was controlling them with her mind, invading them the same way she'd invaded me. That was why she'd robbed them of their sight. The followers looked hungry, like they might devour me if I happened to slip and fall into their clutches. I felt the energy of expectation radiating off of them and flowing over me, unwanted.

"The Guardian is safely home." Isiris made a sweeping gesture with her arm. "She will take care of you when Adam and I pass into the world."

"What is she talking about?" I whispered to Adam, feeling a stab of panic. He wouldn't meet my eyes.

She walked over to Adam and slid her hands up his shirt,

pulling it up and over his head. "You have done well. You're mine and you will be rewarded, just as I promised."

She began to kiss her way across the tattoos on his chest. Adam looked at me. His look was inscrutable. I didn't know which version of Adam was the act and which version was real.

He took her hand, turned it palm up, and kissed it. "When will we be joined together?" he asked.

"It's almost time." She smiled. "I will take your eyes, and in the Violet Hour we will walk together into the one true world, and the doors will close forever."

Adam leaned in and kissed her, this time like he meant it.

He had been playing me all along.

REFLECTION

Isiris dispersed the crowd with another tidy flick of her wrist. I was reeling, sick with betrayal. The altar retracted, lowering us to the floor, and Isiris sent Adam off too, with another kiss— one that was more about ownership than tenderness. As a clutch of her eyeless followers led him through a doorway into another nameless hallway, Adam gave me one quick glance. I wondered if it was the last time I'd see him, and whether I even cared anymore.

Isiris led me in the opposite direction, through a series of doorways. We entered a near-replica of my bedroom in Twin Falls. This temple bent to her whim, an elaborate delusion of grandeur.

"Do you like it? I've been practicing at being you," she said. She sounded oddly insecure, like she needed my approval.

"You're not much of an actress," I said.

Her eyes darted to me, and for an instant I saw that my arrow had met its mark.

I felt a tug of power. This was her weakness—she wanted to be something she wasn't. She wanted to be me. It wasn't very godlike of her. A thread of doubt took root inside me.

The crack in Isiris's veneer vanished as fast as it had come. With the twitch of an eye, her glare turned cold. She sat down on my bed, pointing to the chair at the vanity. I studied her movements, trying to see a reflection of myself in them. At the same time, I hoped I wouldn't. I sat down in the chair and faced her.

There was a question burning a hole inside me, a question I was almost too afraid to ask. I had to know, but the answer might be too awful to bear.

"You said, before, that you created me. How?"

Her mouth pursed, like she was a petulant child who wouldn't share her toys. "That is something the Guardian doesn't deserve to know. Only God knows things like that."

"Stop calling me the Guardian."

"What else would I call you?"

"My name is Harlow."

"Not anymore. I'm Harlow."

She made the sign with her fingers. Her robes disappeared, replaced by a disheveled VisionCrest uniform. Her hair fell down her back. Now I really felt like I was looking in the mirror. I thought about the nightmare I'd had in Tokyo, where I'd come face-to-face with my mirror image. Just like then, I wondered if I was dreaming or awake. Somehow I'd fallen through the looking glass.

"Sorry about Adam," she said.

"No you're not."

She grinned. "I'd never been kissed before. But once he kissed me, I knew he was going to be with me for eternity. I would say that someday you'll know what I mean, but you won't."

I shrugged my shoulders, pretending that my heart wasn't clenching with every word she said. "To be honest, I could care less at this point. Adam's a jerk. You deserve each other."

Again, her face betrayed a moment of insecurity. "I made you. I've been inside your mind, watched the world through your eyes. I know that's not true."

I sat forward, sensing an opening. "Are you sure? Don't you think I can feel you when you're there? Maybe the things you think you know aren't real at all."

The corners of her lips turned up a bit. "I know how much you love Dora. It's going to be very satisfying to dismantle her. First, I'll start with her teeth. Crush them, molar by molar. Maybe cut out that tongue she loves to flap so much. I'll take her eyes last," she said.

My stomach roiled. I couldn't let Isiris leave the temple. Yet I didn't think she *could* leave, or else she would have already done it. But the way she was talking hinted that she had a way.

"If you can just walk out of here, then why haven't you already left?" I challenged.

"Things must be as they are meant to be. I am the heart of the resurrection tales in every version of mankind, in infinite worlds. Inscribed on the walls of this temple. I am Aphrodite.

I am Tanit. I am Ishtar and Osiris. I am Buddha. I am God. I will walk the earth I choose, when the time is right. I am infinite, and so are those who follow me. You are here to take my place as Guardian, and in doing so, you release me. My time is just beginning, and yours has ended."

"Not to overstate it," I said.

She looked blankly back at me.

"Basically, I'm like your understudy?" I asked sarcastically.

"I have been the Guardian, and now that honor passes to you. The yin and yang. It is time for me to enter my kingdom on earth, and you will stay here to shepherd lost souls."

The words sent my mind racing back to Madam Wang and the seemingly nonsensical declarations she made while examining my tea leaves: *I see the mirror image of your soul. In it lies your greatest source of power.*

My reflection contained my greatest source of power. It suddenly occurred to me that if I was a part of Isiris, maybe I could do all the things that she could do. Manipulate the temple. Invade her mind. Gain control.

A sliver of hope sliced its way through the hopelessness that gripped my heart.

"So, now that I'm here, you'll be able to leave," I stated. "So you can hang out and be God on earth."

"Now you understand," she answered. It sounded like BS to me, but it was clear she believed it.

"After you pluck out Adam's eyes, of course."

She nodded.

"So I'll be stuck here?" I asked.

"You will. The gate requires its Guardian."

I thought of the last Violet Hour, how my hand had met a barrier in the open doorways. Why had I been able to leave with my father when I was a baby, yet was unable to leave on my own now? By Isiris's logic, I should be able to pass through those barriers if she was still installed as Guardian. What was different? There had to be something more to it—a piece to the puzzle that was missing.

"Is blinding Adam part of the whole ritual of breaking yourself out of here?" I asked, thinking of how she'd taken one of my father's eyes before he carried me out of this place as a baby.

"No. But he must belong to me. When we walk into the world together, that is how it is meant to be."

"You can't force someone to belong to you," I said.

"You belong to me," she said. "I created you."

A wave of disgust rolled through me. "If you created me, what does that make me? I must be a god, too."

Isiris's nostrils flared. She clearly hadn't considered this question, and she only had room in her mind for one deity. I didn't really want to know the answer; whatever I was, however I came to be, I knew who I was inside. The rest didn't matter.

"It makes you mine. Come here," she commanded.

She held her hands out, palms up. I could feel her putting pressure on my mind, pressing for an entry. My body began to rise, but beneath that was an instinct to resist. Madam Wang's prediction rolled around in my mind: *in it lies your greatest source of power*. I might be more powerful than Isiris.

Isiris stared at me intently, boring into my mind. If I could feel her attempts to enter my consciousness, I might also be able to prevent them. Maybe even turn the tables. For now, though, it was important that she believed in her illusion of total control. Luckily, self-delusion was a towering strength of hers. I stood up and crossed the room.

Put your hands in mine, her voice said in my head.

I placed my hands over her palms. It was like placing yourself in the mouth of a Venus flytrap. Her skin was smooth and papery, unlike my own, which was cold and clammy. I assumed the next thing would be the onset of a vision. I held my breath in anticipation for a moment, but nothing happened. No squiggly worms. No film reel burning.

Isiris closed her eyes. It was like closing a circuit and flipping the electricity on full blast. The sheer force of her pulled my mind in circles, squiggly white worms now doing the rhumba around the edges of my vision. Instinctively, I pushed back. It felt like she was trying to drain me of my memories. I tried to grab onto some thought, some snippet, something I might shove through the hole in my mind that she'd created. Control the flow.

Suddenly it wasn't Isiris pulling, it was me pushing. I was doing something I'd never before done. Vivid scenes of my life funneled through me and into her—I gave her what I knew she craved most. Sitting on the General's lap. Laughing to the point of sickness with a gap-toothed Dora. Adam pressing me up against the carriage and kissing me with the heat of the sun on my face.

A menagerie of memories. A private collection, which she consumed as if starving. It was like giving an addict just a taste. Then I shut off the flow. I kept the most important things—the vulnerabilities, the secrets of trusted friends, the insights about Irisis's own weaknesses—hidden behind a locked door inside my mind.

It was a test. She would fall for it, and I would have hope; or she wouldn't, and I was doomed.

Silence.

Her grip on my hand grew tighter. "Thank you for letting me have your memories. You have no idea how much they will mean to me." There was a sinister undertone in her voice. "Now I know what's really important to you," she added.

A hard edge flashed in her smile. My stomach dropped like a stone. Maybe she'd seen more than I realized.

"Why did you have Sacristan Wang make the virus?" I asked.

She dropped my hand. "I'd entrusted the man you called your father with the most important thing in all existence."

"Me?"

"Of course not you," Isiris snapped. "You were just the conduit through which I could communicate. Your proximity to him made it easy for me to influence his actions. What I entrusted him with was the secrets of the Inner Truth, the keys to immortal life. This whole hidden world—which no one but me can begin to truly understand. But instead of doing as I'd instructed, he co-opted the Truth for his own material gain. He corrupted it and turned it into a vile, sickly reflection of its true self, and you did nothing to stop him." Her words were venomous.

I thought of my father taking me as part of a bargain for self-gain. I wondered at what point along the way he actually began to feel something for me. The sting of tears threatened and I had to bite them back.

"VisionCrest," I said.

"Yet sometimes I work in ways that are mysterious even to myself," Isiris continued. "At first, I couldn't see the genius hidden within my own plan. Even if it's imperfect, Vision-Crest has immense power. And even better, you are now its leader. Or I am, rather."

"So the virus is your means of consolidating power? Anyone who doesn't bend to your will gets exterminated—is that it?" I asked.

"And those that remain will worship me. A promise and a sacrifice. Purity exacts a price."

"I think I've heard that somewhere before," I said.

"Your friends are immune to the virus already. Low-level exposure will give anyone immunity. Adam's tattoos are not just a sign of our eternal love and fidelity; he's a walking inoculation. I had to make sure he was protected. You really can't trust people like Adam's father or Sacristan Wang," she said.

So Adam had been right. The tattoos made him an inoculated carrier. And that was probably the reason why Dora, Stubin, and I didn't get sick. We'd spent enough time in close proximity to him to build up resistance. But by that logic, it didn't make any sense that Mercy got sick. As much as it irked me to remember it, she'd spent more time in close quarters with him than any of us.

"What about Mercy? She wasn't immune," I said.

Isiris tilted her head. "A tweak to the formula, courtesy

of Wang. I understand that Mercy is having a hard time dying. Still, I did us both a favor, don't you agree?"

"No, I don't."

She shrugged. "The virus will be released on my command. It kills very fast, so it can be targeted."

It was evil beyond imagination.

"I saw a vision, earlier, of people in Japan and China—the places we've visited—dying. Was that real?" I asked.

"I just wanted you to see the possibility of what you helped create. You've played an important role. I thought you should enjoy a taste of the future of your world, even if you won't be there to enjoy it."

Fear stabbed me in the gut.

Isiris stood up. "I'm afraid it's time for us to go. Do you think Adam will like me in this uniform? It will be the last time he sees me, after all."

"You look beautiful," I said, stroking her ego.

Isiris's eyes lit up. "Of course, you'll be there to witness it. I insist."

"I'd like nothing better," I lied. I had to find a way out of this, and I was almost out of time.

SACRIFICE

The beat of footfalls at my back swallowed me in a sea of soft thunder. There was no way of knowing how many of Isiris's followers were with us as we descended the ramp, Isiris and Adam ahead and me in their wake. We circled our way down to the eye. The pseudo sun that normally lit up the cylindrical chamber was somehow extinguished, leaving us in near-total darkness except for the flickering of candles and the eerie radiance of Isiris's zombie followers.

Not one word was uttered the entire way. Adam had looked my way only briefly when he was handed over to Isiris, his mouth set in a line of grim determination. The tattoos rippled across his bare chest and his sapphire eyes looked black in the darkness. Whatever innocence remained in us, I feared it would be lost tonight.

Adam's eyes moved to the knife clenched in my fist. His jaw tightened—he knew exactly what it was for. Isiris had given it to me, with instructions that I would deliver it to her when it came time. In that moment, Adam's eyes revealed his true allegiance—and it wasn't to Isiris. I knew he was planning something drastic, a last-ditch attempt to save me from this disastrous situation by sacrificing himself. Just like me, Adam was playing Isiris's game in hopes of turning the tables in the final hour. I gave him a tight jerk of my head: *No*. He looked away.

Abruptly, the thrum halted. An ellipsis of expectation dangled in the air. Inside these walls was a truth about me that flowed much deeper than I'd realized. I was overcome with a thought that was both thrilling and terrifying: maybe Isiris was right. Maybe this *was* where I belonged. For some reason, the image of Dora popped into my mind, but she felt a million miles away. Our friendship seemed alien, part of a world that had ceased to make sense the moment my foot touched these ancient stones.

Isiris and Adam stepped into the center of the eye. Isiris turned and motioned for me to join them. The altar rose into the air once again. Below us, the roiling bodies of believers crawled over one another like maggots on dead flesh. The lit sconces threw shadows that crept across the ancient stone. The room was choked with swaying bodies, and completely impassable.

Above us, believers lined the ramp. They were more sedate than those on the floor, and wore a ceremonial white that must have signaled some kind of status. The common thread among all the followers was the dark, empty eye sockets and the way they moved in unison, as if some invisible thread bound them together.

The doors were all shut tight, but I knew the Violet Hour was close once again. At the moment when the doors flew wide to welcome passing souls, everything would be decided one way or another. I did not believe that Isiris was God, or even just *a* god, but she and the Violet Hour were mystical things that defied my ability to explain them. She had accused my father of perverting her religion, but the fundamental core within me coursed with the truth: Isiris, more than anyone, was perverting something ancient and powerful. It was a dangerous game.

As Isiris surveyed her followers approvingly, I reached out and took Adam's hand in mine for a moment, just to let him know he was not alone. Isiris raised her palms to the crowd and the dull roar of moans fell to perfect silence.

"With a promise and a sacrifice, eternity begins tonight," she declared. Adam tensed at the word sacrifice. I only hoped he held on—didn't try anything stupid before I could make my move.

"A ritual cleansing of blind sight ushers in an age of verity. The Inner Truth of the Inner Eye!"

The roar of the believers shook the stones.

"The Guardian stands before you, ready to restore the purity she helped destroy. She will make herself worthy of being your faithful servant. By offering her eyes as a blessing to our union, she redeems herself in the eyes of God."

Adam's gaze cut to me, panicked.

"What?" I said.

Isiris's lips curled into a satisfied smile. "Give the knife to Adam."

She raised her hand and made the signal. My hand moved as if of its own accord, as did Adam's. I dropped the knife into his waiting hand.

I looked back at Isiris, whose self-satisfied grin turned my veins to ice. She leveled her gray-green eyes at me. The crowd of believers had pressed against the base of the altar. We were trapped, and the situation was completely out of my control.

Get on your knees or he will drive that knife straight into his own heart.

I looked at Adam. His body was tensed as if for a fight. If I didn't do something soon, he was going to try to take action himself. I clenched my teeth and silently begged for him to hold on. I got down on my knees.

The knife's edge danced in the candles' glow. Adam's arm began to arc down, his muscles straining against the motion. I glanced at Isiris. Both her hands were busily working symbols, and her glare was intently focused on Adam. The tip of the blade was inches from my eye, and Adam's brow was furrowed in pain from the intensity of fighting her off. Any lingering doubts I'd had about him were erased completely.

I harnessed all the helplessness, rage, and despair inside of me. There was only one thing I knew that might give me a chance to beat Isiris at her own game. I concentrated on the aimless masses that surrounded us. Isiris's believers, robbed of their ability to see their own way forward, were vessels waiting to be filled with purpose and direction. While Isiris was distracted by her own selfish machinations, no one was paying attention to them.

Except me.

I sent a silent apology out to them. I did not want to become like Isiris, but right now, I had no choice. A ripple went through the crowd—a moment of indecision and restlessness. Then, action. Those nearest the base began to climb on top of each other, reaching up toward the altar. Isiris was so busy waiting for the knife to plunge into my eye that she didn't notice the tide turning.

It was working.

I pushed my way outward, commanding everything within the radius of my mind to advance on Isiris and take her down. For a moment, there was only anarchy, a jumble of confused limbs. But then there was a surge, as if every soul had shifted its course toward her.

Fight against her. Take her down.

I commanded the blind army as if it were the most natural thing I'd ever done. There was a connection reaching out from the center of my mind, spreading like a web in all directions. I could feel them moving inside the net I'd cast, all of us connected.

You have the power inside you.

Even Adam seemed to swivel ever so slightly toward Isiris. A swarm of stiff-limbed believers hauled themselves onto the altar, and the light of surprise dawned in Isiris's eyes. She blinked, glancing around like a bear emerging from hibernation.

She uses you for her own gain. There is no Inner Truth in what she's done to you. Take back control.

More believers were climbing over one another's shoulders, swarming out of the pit, up over the edge of the altar.

The realization of what was happening dawned on Isiris. I felt her control slipping completely away from her. Just as quickly she redoubled it, attempted to pull it back with a fury. Then she pounced on Adam like a jungle cat attacking its prey, her arm snaking around his neck from behind, her hand making the three-fingered symbol. She pulled him close as if he were her possession.

Fighting against her direction, Adam slowly turned the knife on himself. He pressed it against his chest, through the iris of the angry Inner Eye tattoo that covered his heart. My stomach clenched. I couldn't let Adam die.

"Harlow, forget about me. Don't let her use me as a distraction."

The blade dug into his smooth skin, drawing a thread of blood. I knew that in another second, Isiris would be overrun by her own creations—but not before Adam was stabbed through the heart.

"Call them off," Isiris ordered me.

I wanted to smash her perfect nose so far into her face that it would be permanently embedded in her skull. Things weren't supposed to happen like this.

Isiris's eyes locked onto mine as she tightened her hold around Adam's neck. His face contorted in pain. Her tongue emerged from between her parted lips and she ran it up his neck, from the hollow of his clavicle to just beneath his ear.

It was too much to bear. The net broke loose, and I lost the minds of the believers. I could feel them reeling away from me, and so could Isiris.

Adam plunged the knife into his own chest and blood sluiced out. His eyes rolled back in his head.

"Now his heart truly belongs to me!" Isiris screamed. Her eyes were wild.

Something inside me shattered. The banshee scream that came from deep within me filled the chamber and reached all the way to the infinite sky above. I dove toward Isiris. She recoiled, releasing Adam, who fell limp to the floor.

I landed on top of her. The look on her face morphed from fury to fear as I wrapped my hands around her neck. She was scrabbling for the knife, which had skittered just out of her reach. Believers flooded around us as Isiris tried to squirm out of my grasp. Through the chaos of limbs, I caught a glimpse of Adam, his eyes fluttering open and meeting mine. He mouthed something at me.

Kill her.

My fingers tightened around Isiris's throat and we were enveloped in the sea of believers, who were pushing and pulling against each other in a frenzy of misdirection. Isiris's face was red and her eyes began to bulge. She kicked her feet and tried to buck me off her, hitting me with her free hand while still trying to get ahold of the knife.

As the believers swarmed around us, liquid fear pumped through my veins. They could tear me to shreds if she managed to regain control. Then the light began to go out of Isiris's eyes. The twitch of her fingers toward the handle of the knife slowed. My stomach felt sour. What had I become? I'd turned into a monster, just like her.

The moment of self-doubt bloomed, and Isiris made one

last grab for the knife. I felt the power slide away from me. The tide of believers tore at us both, pulling us apart. A knot of them picked me up; I kicked and screamed. Isiris was trying to get to her feet, but believers were grabbing at her and pulling her in the opposite direction. It seemed they were under the control of no one. I'd lost sight of Adam completely.

The burly believer who had a grip on me raised me up in his arms, as if I were an offering to the others. He launched me off the altar, catapulting me up into the air. The last sensation I had was that of being weightless—existing outside of space and time. Then, blackness.

TRAPPED

The soft murmur of voices lifted me, layer by layer, out of my thousand-year slumber. They came sharply into focus against a background of thrashing drumbeats and urgent guitar chords.

"Bad Religion won't bring anyone out of a coma," Dora's voice said.

"How do you know?" Adam countered. "It's her favorite band."

"Because first of all, it's not 1986. And second of all, don't you think it's a little inappropriate, considering the whole crazy religious thing she barely survived?"

Adam sighed. "I'm running out of ideas. It's been three weeks."

The squeak of chair legs across linoleum caused my eyelids to flutter.

"Crisscross applesauce, did you see that?" Dora's voice moved closer.

"See what?" Adam's voice perked up.

A sliver of bright white light invaded my cranium.

"There! Her eyes moved!" Dora yelled. "Stubin! Stubin, get the doctor!"

A gentle hand rested on my shoulder.

"Harlow?" Adam's whisper was full of expectation.

I pried my eyes open a tiny bit farther, enough to see two blurry faces hovering over me—the outline of Dora's pointy glasses, Adam's hair adorably messy and pointing eighteen directions at once. He was wearing a hospital gown, and when he leaned over I could see that his chest was wrapped in gauze, three inches thick. But he looked generally okay. An overwhelming sense of relief came over me, as did the creeping tentacles of a murderous migraine. I tried to move my lips to speak, but it felt like I had a mouth full of glue.

"It's okay, baby. Don't try to say anything just yet," Adam said, smoothing his hand over my hair. Baby. I'd never heard anything so comforting in my entire life.

He leaned into my hair. "I love you, Harlow. I need you. Come back to me."

I faded back out of consciousness, floating away on a cloud of comfort.

———

The steady beep of the heart monitor called me back, this time with force. The room was dark, and it felt like a ballpeen hammer was being repeatedly pummeled into my skull. I turned my head a few inches, and Adam came into focus.

He was sleeping, his face smooshed against a beige armchair, a green hoodie pulled up over his head, dark lashes brushing against his cheeks.

Without even realizing I was doing it, I sat up. Fingers that felt foreign removed the oxygen tube from my nose. My scraggly fingernails scraped at the clear tape connecting the IV to a vein in the top of my hand, but it was like my skin was made of clay. The needle slipped out. It was practically an out-of-body experience, my limbs seeming to float through the air without my command.

I turned the palm of my hand over, noticing that the knife wound had healed so completely there was no sign of it. There was no sign of the initiate ring that should have been around my finger, either. My heart clenched at the thought that I might have lost the last thing my father ever gave me. It was strange; I must have been out a very long time.

My legs felt like they were disconnected from my body, yet I somehow managed to drop them over the side of the bed. The only place I wanted to be was curled up in Adam's lap, and there were only a few feet between us. I tried to call his name, but no sound came out. After who-knew-how-much time spent unconscious, it would probably take a little work to get my vocal chords back in working order. My legs took their first tentative steps, wobbling toward their goal. Just a few more steps and I'd be tilting into the warmth of Adam's arms. At least my body could feel my intent, even if my mind felt disconnected from it.

Out of the corner of my eye, I caught sight of a mirror

hanging on the wall. The image reflected back stopped me short. I was an absolute mess—there were dark half-moons under my eyes, my skin was chalky, and my hair hung limp and stringy. My hand moved to my face, gingerly pressing at my hollowed cheeks. It felt like I'd been shot full of Novocain—there was no sensation whatsoever.

But none of it mattered when Adam stirred and his eyes opened. He bolted upright and jumped to his feet, reaching out to steady me.

"Oh my god, Harlow! What are you doing? Are you okay?"

I nodded, a tear slipping down my cheek. That was funny—I hadn't even felt the emotion taking hold of me.

Adam pulled me close. I joyfully anticipated the laundry detergent smell of his hoodie mingling with his soapy boy smell. But there was nothing. Maybe my sense of smell was off—an after-effect of being out for so long? I rested my cheek against his shoulder, allowing myself to just feel his arms around me and take it all in.

"Are we in Twin Falls?" I whispered.

That was weird. I hadn't even been trying to say anything, much less that. The drugs in this place must be pretty mega.

"Yeah. The compound hospital. You're safe now," he said.

"I thought you were dead. That knife went right into your heart," I responded.

"It missed by an inch, actually. I was in the hospital for a few days after I carried you out, but I'm gonna be fine," he assured me. "We're just so lucky you found me in the chaos, and remembered how to get back out before you lost consciousness."

It was a miracle. I had absolutely no memory of leaving the temple—I must have been operating on pure instinct. It was more good fortune than someone could hope to have in an entire lifetime.

"I want to get to work as quickly as possible. The Fellowship needs its leader," my voice said.

My heartbeat quickened. That wasn't what I wanted to say.

"Hey, you need time to recover. The doctors think the coma was a reaction to extreme shock—I'm not going to let that happen again."

"What about the Ministry?" I asked.

Adam smiled, his dimple flashing. "Everybody understands, and they're completely behind you. VisionCrest will be here when you're ready."

You're right, I thought.

"No," my voice said. My head tilted up. "Not later. Now."

Something was very wrong. My eyes locked on the image of the girl in the mirror. A sly half smile lifted the corner of her lips.

"Okay. We'll figure something out, but you need to go slow," Adam said.

"What happened to Isiris?" my voice asked. My hand slid across Adam's shoulders, clearly visible in the mirror.

"You have nothing to worry about. It was complete chaos in there, but I caught a glimpse of her as we left. One of the horde threw her from the altar—she was completely knocked out by the fall," he said.

My last memory from the temple came rushing back. The moment before everything went black. Me, vaulting through the air, floating as if weightless, then smashing into unconsciousness. I suddenly knew what had happened.

It wasn't me that Adam had rescued from the temple.

"Isiris is trapped in her house of a thousand doors, exactly where she belongs. And she's never getting out," he murmured, leaning in closer.

I wanted to grab him, scream at him, tell him he had it all wrong.

"What about the Resistance?" my voice asked instead.

"They sent a delegation to bring Dora and Stubin home. They're here, ready to meet with you as soon as you're up for it."

"Oh, I'm up for it," my voice said. "I'm looking forward to extending my gratitude for all they did to subvert Isiris."

In the mirror, my pinky and ring finger curved down, making Isiris's three-fingered symbol.

Now there was no doubt.

I knew why I couldn't feel anything, control my limbs, or say what I wanted. It wasn't Harlow who had made it back from the temple. It was Isiris. Now I was the one trapped, while Isiris was loose upon the world. And everyone believed she was me—including the boy I loved.

I squeezed my eyes shut, willing the nightmare to end.

When I opened them again, everything was blotted out by the blinding glare of an artificial sun, somewhere far above me. A thousand doors flew open. The sound of beating wings filled the air.

It was the Violet Hour once again.

Acknowledgments

Darling reader. Thanks for coming to my acknowledgements party—you're the guest of honor! Let me show you around …

Behind that velvet rope is the VIP section. My incredibly supportive and uber-talented husband Reid is easy to spot—he's the one sporting a halo. Without him, none of this would be happening. Next to him is my bombshell mother, Marsha, who used to tell me as a teen that I'd become a writer while I rolled my eyes at her. I only hope to be half as beautiful as she is, inside and out. That's my dad, Lonnie—he's where I get my funny, and my ability to shove ten pounds of sugar into a five-pound bag. Next to them are my parents-in-law, JP and Roseann—they supplied the champagne that fueled many drafts of *The Violet Hour*. Never underestimate the power of a 1990 Krug.

See that group of incredibly literary-looking folk holding court by the ice sculpture? Right in the center is my inimitable, sassy, wish-upon-a-star agent Jennifer Laughran. Still can't believe she picked me; I'm so lucky that she did. Next to her is the Flux crew (dream team alert!): insightful, delightful story editor Brian Farrey-Latz, eagle-eyed production editor Sandy Sullivan, creeptastic cover designer Lisa Novak, and PR guru extraordinaire Mallory Hayes. Allow me to just say—what the Flux?

Who are the gorgeous creatures dipping strawberries into the chocolate fountain, you ask? Why, my critique partners present and past (YA, That's Why! represent): Ingrid Paulson, Martha White, Heidi Kling, Veronica Wolff, Mary Kole, and Alie Slavin—they made me and TVH so much more. Next to them, Jean from JeanBookNerd.com, who is a promotional wiz and absolute darling—her tireless efforts on behalf of TVH are something I could never repay. The little pixie she's talking to is Jessica Richey—my trusted beta reader.

Do you like the music? It's a mix of all the kickass bands that inspired TVH: Bad Religion, Minor Threat, Descendents, Dead Kennedys, Sex Pistols. Also Silversun Pickups, Warpaint, Metric, The xx, St. Vincent, The Hundred in the Hands, and The Naked and Famous.

Over by the bar, having the absolute most fun, are my lifelong friends—I am super grateful to all of them but most especially Michelle, Beth & Niemo, Sonia, Kris, and Jess & Cass. We'll probably be living in a retirement home in Boulder together one day, still throwing parties. The other pretty ladies are Kate (who took my fab author photos), Stephanie (who did my styling), and Kim (who insisted I read *Twilight* and started me on this whole crazy adventure in the first place). Oh, and did I mention my husband Reid? Yeah, I know I did. But he's the alpha and the omega.

The party's winding down now. There are so many people here I didn't get a chance to introduce you to, but there's always next time. Thank you so much for reading. I appreciate you. You will always be my guest of honor. XOX.

About the Author

Whitney A. Miller lives in San Francisco with her husband and a struggling houseplant. She's summited Mt. Kilimanjaro, ridden the Trans-Siberian rails, bicycled through Vietnam, done the splits on the Great Wall of China, and evaded the boat police in Venice. Still, her best international adventures take place on the page. Visit her online at WhitneyAMiller.com.